Also by Ivar Alastair Watson

Glimpses of Deep Spain

SCOTLAND
THE
BRAVE

A TRAGEDY

IVAR ALASTAIR WATSON

Matador
Unit 9 Priory Business Park
Kibworth Beauchamp
Leicester LE8 0RX, UK
Tel: (+44) 116 279 2299
Fax: (+44) 116 279 2277
Email: books@troubador.co.uk
Web: www.troubador.co.uk/matador

ISBN 978 1783065 240

British Library Cataloguing in Publication Data.
A catalogue record for this book is available from the British Library.

Typeset by Troubador Publishing Ltd, Leicester, UK
Printed and bound in the UK by TJ International, Padstow, Cornwall

Matador is an imprint of Troubador Publishing Ltd

In memory of Charlie Armstrong

PROLOGUE

What is one to do with one's life in modern European society? One who thinks what it's about? Most people haven't got time for that. That is the great problem of our era. Imagine asking a company director, an accountant, a dentist or a factory worker:

"And does your work fulfil the longings of your soul?"

The question is whether souls exist nowadays. This novel is concerned with the tragedy of individuals at odds with their society and the demise of the ship building industry on the river Clyde.

The fact that the liner Queen Mary 2 was built at a French shipyard was the nadir of the Scottish industry, and of a country that has lost its way. Would independence for Scotland lead to re-generation? That is the question.

Note: Some geographical 'inexactitude' is deliberate.

PART I

And the Angel of the Lord
said unto her, Thou art with
child, and Thou shalt call
his name Ishmael. And he will
be a wild man; his hand will
be against every man, and
every man's hand against him.
Genesis XVI 11, 12

Ishmael had been christened by his father, minister of the parish church in Lentilloch, where the spires of the lunatic asylum notoriously towered over those of the three moribund churches. He disliked the name, and for a time had insisted on his second name, Hamish. Until one day he saw it as an anagram: Ishmah. As though it was a curse.

It had been some sort of morbid joke by his father. Or so it was said. However that may be, Ishmael knew that he was apart; not as other men.

The young Ishmael, hero of the Black Watch in Korea, on returning to Britain found life pointless, withdrawing to a lighthouse. After much soul searching he determined to pit his strength against the challenges of the Scottish shipbuilding industry.

YOU WON'T DO

Ishmael got off the train at Helensburgh, making his way on foot along the shore towards Shandon village. It was a bright sunlit morning and his heart rose at the sea birds' cries and the lapping of the tidal water as his highland brogues crunched the sharp empty shells.

It was still early when he turned into the long drive to Shandon Lodge, flanked on either side by black-trunked beeches populated by legion crows. As he passed a doocot as big as a house on the right the Lodge at last came into view. A long rambling building on two floors of brownish-grey stone much stained by rain, with gothic windows and tall, angular chimneys. He glanced at his watch. It was five to nine as he pulled the long brass bell handle, which produced a dissonant clanking inside. It was two or three minutes before a sharp-faced man in leggings and a dirty waistcoat opened the door, inquiring laconically "Mr McCulloch? Follow me."

Ishmael was led down a long gloomy passage at the end of which the gardener, gamekeeper or whatever he was grudgingly opened a door indicating without a word that Ishmael was to enter.

It was a magnificent drawing-room with rather worn red sofas and chairs in profusion, portraits of crimson-faced Scots in highland dress on the walls and glass menageries with a variety of monstrous trophy fish besides small stuffed wild animals on top of heavy cupboards and sideboards. In spite of the dingy furniture and the pitch-pine panelling the spacious room was very bright, as half a dozen french windows faced south over the sea-loch, the sunlight gleaming on the silver surface of the water. Warming the room more than the damp smoking logs in the vast fire-place.

Ishmael had plenty of time to observe these details, finding himself still alone well after nine. Then a green baize-covered door beside a huge desk littered untidily with papers opened. But it wasn't the shipping magnate who came in. A lithe feminine figure of perhaps nineteen, with dark ringlets dangling on either side of a quaint pale face, tripped lightly towards Ishmael balancing a tea-cup and saucer in one hand.

Smiling brightly, she announced "This is an advance offering, Mr McCulloch. I'm afraid my father is late back from the hill but he should be here any minute."

Ishmael was amazed. Dazzled. As she looked at him with large dark brown eyes he felt a stab like lightning in his loins. But in his taciturn way he thanked her as she watched him in unobtrusive appraisal. And with a quick light step she was gone.

Ishmael was still abstracted when a heavy tread was heard and a pitch-pine door pushed brusquely open.

"McCulloch?" the huge figure queried, standing with his back to the fire-place and holding out his hand, so that Ishmael had to take several steps forward to grasp the horny object proffered.

"Shandon," he said gruffly. "What can I do for you?"

Lord Shandon was a great brute of a man with a fiery face fringed by tufts of greying ginger hair. He had big thick ears and a large red strawberry of a nose with seeds in it. He stood with arms akimbo and legs apart in plus fours, lovat green hose and mucky brown leather shoes, fixing Ishmael with a steely stare from small but sharp blue eyes.

"Want to work in the ship-building business? Must be mad! No future in it! There won't be any great ship-builders on the Clyde in ten years. Sam McLeish and company are seeing to that. Lithgows, Connells, Barclay Curle, Stephens, Scotts, they're all going bust. McLeish and his communist pals" he snorted in his great booming voice, "keep the men on strike while we're all being undercut by the Japs and the Germans. Who won the bloody war? It's the same with the British motor industry. Red Robbo and his pals are wrecking that while the Japs and the Germans sweep the world market. And the bloody government gives in to the unions every time. Beer and sandwiches in 10 Downing Street!"

Shandon strode over to the desk and rummaged through the papers. "Ah, here we are! Ishmael McCulloch, education Glasgow Academy. Pah! Couldn't your father have sent you to Fettes, or Loretto or Gordonstoun?"

"My father was killed at Dunkirk."

"Oh well, that explains it" grunted Shandon.

"And Glasgow Academy's as good a school as any," Ishmael interjected.

Shandon looked up from Ishmael's application with a cold gleam in his eye, fixing Ishmael with his stare as though to intimidate him. Glancing momentarily down again he read aloud

"Cunlith's management trainee. Left on completion of training."

"Why?"

"Because I found the relations between the workers and Management poisonous at that shipbuilder."

Shandon glared at Ishmael incredulously.

"You wouldn't be a communist, would you?" he barked. Then looking down the letter he came across

"Served as 2nd Lieutenant in Black Watch, Korea. Awarded Military Cross."

"Damnation! Why the bloody hell didn't you say so?"

"Say what?" Ishmael queried.

"Say you were an officer and a gentleman, you bloody fool! And didn't you have to say 'Sir' to your superiors?"

"Yes, we had to use that form according to military rank. But in civvy street it's a matter of respect." Ishmael answered with a clearly sardonic inflection.

"Of what?" Shandon roared, apoplectic. "You won't do," he shouted, the strawberry turning purple. "Let's not waste any more time. I don't stand impertinence or malingerers in my yard, whatever the Sam McLeishes may say or do. Good morning, young man! And good luck to you!"

"And good luck to you! You'll need it!"

ENCHANTRESS

Ishmael slammed the door as he stalked out of the room, allowing himself a wry smirk once out of sight. But suddenly a figure came running towards him in the dim passage.

"What has happened? Oh Heavens! What did my father do? What has he done now," begged the wraith-like apparition as she tripped towards him like a bird. "I heard the shouting" she said half-tearfully and half as though suppressing laughter.

They walked out together towards the sea loch, and stopped on the shore facing one another, the water lapping restlessly. Ishmael was awe-struck by her looks: that quaint face with shining, deep brown eyes framed by those enchanting ringlets. She smiled tremulously, her upper teeth jutting slightly forward, giving her an enchantingly innocent look as she scrutinised that scowling, craggy face with a thick black scar on the left jaw line scarcely hidden by a bristling black beard, black as his short hair and smouldering eyes.

'He's stocky and tough-looking but sensitive for all that' she thought.

"My name's Catriona" she laughed nervously. "I hope it's not too much for you. But they all call me Sheila. It's my second name. I know your name's Ishmael. My father told me to receive you if he was late, as my mother's in hospital. You mustn't think badly of him. He's desperately worried about her, and the workers in the yard have driven him to distraction. It's as though they want to destroy the Scottish shipbuilding industry."

There was a long silence.

"What are you going to do?" Sheila suddenly asked, as though imploring him to do something.

"I'm going up north" Ishmael answered absently, "partly to get away and be by myself for some time, and partly because they're looking for a manager at the Loch Mhor estate in Wester Ross."

Sheila's face fell. "But there's no future in that. And what will you do with yourself in that wilderness? Wester Ross! That's a godforsaken part of the world, even if the hills and lochs are beautiful. You'll go mad with loneliness. It'll kill you!"

She said 'it will' because her intuition told her that he would take the job and he would stay there. There was something forbiddingly lonely about him, a look that defied communion with other human beings.

"Well" she said with a note of resolute finality, "if you're back in Glasgow some time, you know our phone number. I'm usually at home in the evenings and at weekends."

"And in the mornings and afternoons?" Ishmael asked, looking closely at her.

"Well, you see, I'm a medical student at the Uni."

"So you're going to be a doctor?"

"Can't you believe it? Don't I look as though I could do that? I've never finished anything" she added disconcertingly, and ominously.

They parted on that foreboding note, both aware of a deep and mysterious attraction that was to torture them.

WARNING

When the dilapidated West Highland train reached Achnasheen that June morning the sky was so black that it was almost dark, a howling wind whipping the chimney smoke of the sparse crouching hovels eastward. There was no sign of the Loch Mhor estate Land-Rover nor of any human being, so Ishmael called Shiel, his young border collie, and they turned out of the torrential rain into the bar of the Achnasheen Hotel.

"True to its name: 'Stormy Place'," Ishmael greeted the barman as he ordered a pint of McEwans ale, shivering slightly in the draught.

"Do you speak the Gaelic, then?" inquired the swarthy figure in the dark shadowy bar.

"No. A few place names and odd words. What happened to the Indian Jew they say had this hotel?"

"That's my father, sir. But you, are you the new manager for the

Loch Mhor estate? He was expected off the Kyle Of Lochalsh train today."

"I've applied for the job. Why?"

"I wouldn't be taking it if I was you" the barman answered in that Indian sing-song that has echoes of the Welsh.

"And why not?"

"The last manager left suddenly. They say he was terrified."

"Terrified of what?"

At that moment the harsh sound of a klaxon reverberated through the bar.

"That'll be the driver from the estate come to pick you up."

Ishmael drank up the bitter dregs of his pint and calling his collie went out.

"Good luck, sir!" called the Indian voice.

JOURNEYING TO THE END OF THE WORLD

Shiel jumped into the back of the Land-Rover and Ishmael seated himself beside the driver who seemed half-witted, sniggering and smiling in an imbecile way.

As the Land-Rover rumbled past the ghostly Loch Achcroisg and then Glen Docherty, with occasional glimpses of the beauty of Loch Mhor in the sporadic shafts of sunlight penetrating the turbulent black and yellow clouds, the whole journey lived up to Ishmael's romantic notions of the highlands. The wild desolation of the country from Loch Luichart, the sense of crossing an immense wilderness as though journeying to the end of the world; the atmosphere of tragic loneliness appealed to him strongly. The menacing sky, the eerie wind and incessant torrential rain touched something in his soul that paradoxically gave him a feeling of uplift. That sense of apartness from society and closeness to the elemental powers.

After five or six miles westward from the bottom of the glen the driver suddenly turned off the road down a darkly wooded track to a derelict pier at the loch side. The driver let out a high-pitched squeal, leaping out and vaulting over the gunwale of a big sea-going launch moored to that perilous jetty, pointing to a huge white hunting lodge on the far side of Loch Mhor. Ishmael and Shiel jumped in while the half-wit grappled with the crank handle of a heavy Kelvin motor. It kicked back with a force that could have broken his wrist, which the imbecile found a great joke. But after a couple of vigorous turns the engine fired and the launch chugged past a small island with a ruined castle and across the choppy white waves, lurching and rolling in the heavy swell created by the wind.

Having landed they clambered up through sopping bracken to a bothy at the side of the resplendent lodge. Ishmael knocked at the half-rotten wooden door marked ESTATE OFFICE, which shuddered on its hinges as he pushed it open in response to the harsh cry of 'Come in.'

A figure was seated at a bare wooden table but with difficulty got up and tottered forward to shake hands. A tall, thin man with a stoop, he had a hard face with small watery eyes.

"Gordon Mckay, Factor of the estate," he announced in a reedy voice. He then put his scrawny hand out to pat Shiel, who snapped and growled. At which the half-wit shrieked with laughter.

"He'd better no be worryin' the sheep" the factor rasped.

"He's trained" Ishmael retorted, ordering Shiel to lie down.

Glancing above the factor's chair Ishmael observed a wall clock marking the correct time but going resolutely backwards, anti-clockwise. The factor slumped down again in his rickety chair with obvious relief. Gordon McKay was what you would call a smart Alec, in spite of his decrepit appearance. He let off a volley of catch questions, which Ishmael parried nonchalantly. This began to ruffle and irritate McKay until he asked

"If ye saw an otter, now, racing upstream, what would he be doing?"

"Going after salmon" Ishmael replied. "Or maybe looking for a mate" he added, just to give the factor an answer he could contradict.

"Wrong" countered the factor triumphantly. "Wrong and right. He would be going after the salmon, though, just like the poachers are doing. They're coming aat night aand taking our young fish. Selling them cheap. Doing the rounds of the hotels from here to Inverness. No questions asked if they're cheap enough. Thaat's what you've to put an end to. Is thaat quite clear?" He pointed a gnarled finger at Ishmael.

It was quite clear to Ishmael that he was to get the job. Manager of the Loch Mhor Estate, one of the best in all Scotland.

The factor took him in a brand new Land-Rover marked Loch Mhor Estate (Ishmael later learned that the idiot was the Factor's son) to the manager's cottage that was to be his home. It was some miles farther west, on the north side of the loch, and four miles from the nearest dwelling at the small village of Kinloch. There was a very battered old Land-Rover standing beside the cottage, with two bullet holes in the driver's door.

"Thaat'll be your personal transport. What's left of it. Here's the key aand the key of the house. You'll find a day's provisions inside, which will be charged to your account. And here's the duty roster of them as will be working under you, ghillies, game-keeper and shepherd. They'll be instructed to call at the Manager's cottage tomorrow evening at eight o'clock sharp. Except for the shepherd. He'll be out on the hill but you caan find him when he goes for his dinner at Succoth Farm about midday. Aand laast but not least, here's a contract you've to sign and deliver to me aat the Estate Office aat ten in the morning, when we'll be doing a tour of inspection of the estate. Is thaat quite clear?"

"There's one thing I want to know now" Ishmael enquired, "what was the trouble with the previous manager?"

But the factor did not answer; he drove off slowly westward in the relentless rain.

A NEW LIFE, A NEW HOME

Ishmael went into the lochside cottage. The two rooms downstairs had been knocked into one, making at least a spacious living room with an enormous fire-place. Going up the very narrow steep staircase he found two cramped bedrooms with dormer windows huddled under the slate roof. There was a steady bleep-bloop from a leak in the right-hand one, so Ishmael threw his gladstone bag onto the pile of blankets in the other. A narrow bathroom over the kitchen and an outside lavatory completed the accommodation.

Going to collect wood for the fire from the shed at the back of the house he came upon dozens of empty whisky bottles drawn up in accusatory rows. It did look as though the previous manager had left in a hurry. Some smelly old socks were hanging in the porch and a pair of well-worn boots stood in front of the fire-place. There were two newish pipes whose stems had been bitten through on the mantel-shelf beside a pint mug of beer that had dried up and was now covered in green mould.

It was about half-past one in the morning, when the light was fading. Suddenly Shiel growled. Ishmael silenced him and listened. There was a shuffling sound outside that isolated cottage, like the muffled steps of several men. Ishmael threw open the door. But all was quiet. Absolutely silent. Yet those steps were not phantasmagorical.

Ishmael turned back into the cottage, poured a large dram of Glen Morangie into a heavy glass and sat down in a high-backed chair by the smouldering fire, Shiel stretched out at his feet.

'How could Sheila come here, to this wretched cottage, she a millionaire's daughter? 'A God-forsaken part of the world' she had called it. And yet it was just what he wanted. Isolation, magnificent mountainous country, where he would have minimum contact with other human beings. And everyone knew that the highlanders were a very fine people, hospitable, honest, brave, even if somewhat simple.'

'How could Sheila ever put up with the kind of life he was heading for? Not that he had any intentions regarding her. His experiences with women had not been encouraging. The series of 'affairs' he had had all ended broken. Yet in spite of his glowering aspect, his ugliness even, women threw themselves at him. But no, this place was no place for Sheila.'

And yet, there was Sheila's image floating before him.

MADNESS, MADNESS MAY IT BE

Sheila had thought of nothing but Ishmael since he marched off towards Glasgow that beautiful June morning. Even though her mother was still seriously ill in hospital. She felt terrified that she would never see him again. She looked out over Loch Shandon that evening without taking in the glint of the moon on the shimmering water. She saw only the semblance of loneliness that for a moment had betrayed Ishmael's inscrutability.

Suddenly she decided to get in touch with him. She flitted over to her little escritoire and impulsively wrote a fateful note.

Ishmael. If I should never see you again I should die a little death. Shall I come to Loch Mhor or will you come to Glasgow?

It's not me that writes this to you but some strange force that impels me, that has taken possession of me. Sheila.

She addressed the envelope to The Manager, Loch Mhor Estate, Wester Ross, and rushed downstairs to leave it on the hall table for the mail van in the morning. She raced down, fearing that she might otherwise quaver in her resolve, and then slipped into her bed. Several times in the night she was minded to run down and retrieve the letter. It wasn't until she heard the driver's cheery 'good morning' and the slamming of the door as the mail van drove off that she got out of her bed and did a little dance round her bedroom.

"Madness! Madness may it be!" she sang softly.

THE HOODIES PECKED THE EYES OUT OF THE ONE, AND THE ENTRAILS OUT OF THE OTHER

Having done the rounds of the vast estate with the snappish factor in torrential rain that morning and afternoon, on returning to his cottage Ishmael piled the big sitting-room fire high with logs and put out two bottles of Glen Morangie and heavy glasses besides beer tankards and half a dozen tins of McEwan's ale for chasers in expectation of the visit by the game-keeper and the three ghillies at "eight o'clock sharp" as stipulated by the factor. Ishmael looked forward to getting to know those highlanders to work under him.

Well after eight there was a loud bang on the door as the three ghillies came sheepishly bumbling into the jolly atmosphere of the long room with a blazing fire.

The first to enter was Archie Gillespie, a thirty-five year old with rotten teeth, a straggly beard and curly ginger hair that was already half gone. He shook hands without looking Ishmael in the eye and slapped a white paper packet on the table.

He was followed by 'wee' Jimmy Cameron who said affably "It's a welcome you are, Mister Maanager" but then shot a sidelong glance and a grin at Archie who winked at him in return.

The third, who had waited in the background, was a huge man with a shuffling, shambling manner, and came forward wheezing "Angus McLeod" as he held out a big hairy paw to Ishmael. He was clearly half drunk, although he tried to ingratiate himself with remarks on the weather. He began fumbling with an arm in a deep pocket of his bulky coat and fished out a half bottle of whisky, opening the top and wiping it with his massive hand as he offered a swig to all. 'Big' Angus as they called him accompanied this with incomprehensible phrases and staccato gasps with a little smile that flickered on his unnaturally red lips protruding from a tangled mass of a brown spade beard pierced by a continuously winking right eye.

Like Archie he was half bald, though he couldn't be more than forty.

Just then the door slowly opened and there was a tremendous ha – ha – harrumph of a sneeze as a tall, gaunt and gangling figure whose deerstalker cascaded torrents of rain into the room, edged nervously forward stuttering "It's not wanting to bother you I am sir," turning desperate eyes round the room until they lighted on Ishmael, "but I've got an urgent problem with the sheep. Uh – hu – huh … harrumph … if you could spare a – a – minute, sir, and uh – uh – uh harrumph … and come to the byre. There's two sheep half dead and …"

The byre was four miles down the road at Succoth Farm, so telling the ghillies to help themselves to whisky and chasers Ishmael pulled on his poncho, called his collie and shaking hands with the sneezing shepherd propelled him into the Land-Rover parked outside in the downpour.

"I've got to get the sheep off the hill for a couple of nights, sir, Mr Managersir" stammered the shepherd, having at last suppressed his sneezes as the Land-Rover rumbled through walls of water. "The sheep's fleeces are sodden and two of them cowped over this evening and couldn't get on their legs. The hoodies pecked the eyes out of the one and the entrails out of the other one" turning his eyes on Ishmael as if to plead with him. "I've got the two in the byre and the vet's on his way, sir, but the rest of them are still on the hill, sir, in this downpour."

"Ishmael's the name."

The bewildered shepherd became silent until the Land-Rover came grinding and shuddering to a halt at the byre door at Succoth Farm. The vet was already waiting outside in an ancient Austin.

They all jumped out and once in the byre the vet, crouching under a wide fedora and talking through a massive moustache, said "It's lucky I got here. I've four old cars and this was the only one that would start. That's a beautiful collie you've got, it's yours isn't it Mr …?"

"Ishmael's the name" answered Ishmael, shaking hands. "Yes, he's a wonderful colllie, from Glen Shiel. I got him for £10, but he's worth £10,000 and I wouldn't sell him for that or any price."

By the light of the shepherd's lantern the vet injected painless euthanasia liquid into the wretched creature with the bloated, bleeding entrails, and crouching still turned his eyes up to the shepherd: "Send the blinded one to the butcher in the morning."

Whereupon the three turned into the sitting-room of Succoth Farm, cluttered as it was with battered furniture, Sheena, the shepherd's bedraggled wife darting out of a bedroom upbraiding her husband for not warning her of the visit, rushing about collecting things for tea while the sopping trio warmed their bones with the shepherd's whisky more than by the moribund peat fire.

I AM THE BOSS OF THE SHEEP

"The factor told me" said the old shepherd loudly, 'Never haave we haad the sheep off the hill in June, aand never will we. Is thaat quite clear? I am the boss of the sheep.' The shepherd exploded with a guffaw, repeating over and over 'I am the boss of the sheep.' The old man doubled up with hoarse laughter, until Sheena reappeared with tea and scones, shrilly scolding her husband. "Mind what you're saying, John, or the factor'll haave us out aas he's threatened."

"Hud yer wheesht, woman" the shepherd retorted, "away ye go to the kitchen now."

"Get all the sheep into the byre right away, John" countermanded Ishmael, clapping him on the back, which started the old man coughing and guffawing again "I am the boss of the sheep."

"As a matter of fact," laughed Ishmael, "I am the boss of the sheep, it's in my contract, so get them into the byre without delay. Christ!" he added standing up, "I'll have to get back and see what those ghillies are up to. Be seeing you, Ewan," he called out to the vet as he clambered into his Land-Rover.

BAPTISM BY FIRE

When Ishmael got back to his cottage there was a strong aroma of roast meat in the air. Opening the door he saw that the two whisky bottles were empty and the six beer cans were littering the floor. All three ghillies were now drunk, Archie lunging forward with a tankard of frothing liquid.

"We've kept this last of the beer for you, Mister maanager" he spluttered, leering sideways at wee Jimmy and big Angus, who were laughing their heads off, as Sandy proffered the tankard to Ishmael. Looking at it closely under the light Ishmael could now see that it was an unspeakable cocktail of human filth. Grabbing Archie by the collar he pulled a blazing brand out of the fire and thrust it below Archie's straggly beard singeing it. When Ishmael released his hold the terrified ghillie ran round and round the long table, Ishmael intercepting him as he tried to reach the door, a little flame flickering in his whiskers.

"If it's so good, what's in this tankard I'll let you drink it" said Ishmael between clenched teeth as he pushed the mug towards Archie, still menacing him with the burning brand.

"Come on now, drink it down or I'll singe you again."

Under that threat, Archie picked up the tankard and as nonchalantly as he could drained it to the dregs, slurping a gobbet of white slime that remained on his lip. The other two ghillies cringed in a corner as Archie boasted with an air of satisfaction "I've many a time drunk worse for bets in the Inverness lock-up."

"What's this stench of roast meat?" Ishmael demanded.

"Well, it's like this, ye see" said the cowed Archie, "Aas I was passing the kitchen window of the Kinloch hotel on my way here six lovely steaks comes flying out, so we roasted them at the fire. There was two for you, mister manager but as you was sae long comin' we haad two each ourselfs. We always used to share them wi' the maanager as was here before. He didnae dare refuse."

"You'll come with me to the hotel owner tomorrow morning, you ruddy thief."

"Ye neednae bother, mister maanager, it was the owner's wifie that chucked them out in that white paacket I left on the table. She and I get on really good, particularly when hubby's nae aboot."

At this big Angus and wee Jimmy recovered their nerve and let go a horrible gurgle of laughter. But Ishmael had heard enough. Catching Archie again by the collar of his bright orange boiler suit he frog-marched him to the door and threw him out with such force that he stumbled and fell into the thick oozing mud outside. The other two ghillies, ordered to get out, didn't need to be told twice, and sidled unsteadily out. "And be at the bothy at seven tomorrow morning" Ishmael ordered; after this baptism of fire they obeyed his orders with hatred and rancour.

As he was closing the door Ishmael heard the sullen curse of Archie as they staggered off into the twilight. "I'll get thaat baastard, see if I don't."

I'LL BE TELLING HIM
YOUR LORDSHIP CALLED

Ishmael opened the windows to clear the stench of the ghillies, cleaned up the mess they had left and got out his last bottle of whisky and a couple of clean heavy tumblers, which he left on the mantel-shelf.

"Why won't the game-keeper have come?" he asked himself. The rain had relented so he decided to walk the four miles to the Kinloch Inn at the west end of the loch and call at the game-keeper's house on the way.

The trees at the side of the track would still be dripping, which meant putting on his poncho and his old Black Watch khaki balmoral but it was a relief to get out in the beautiful June summer light and the walk was invigorating. He threw sticks for Shiel both into the loch and off the track, which the collie rushed to retrieve and drop eagerly at his master's feet for a repetition, bounding joyfully into water or uphill.

It wasn't long before they reached the outskirts of Kinloch where Ishmael turned off the track to the game-keeper's ramshackle house, with the usual dormer windows upstairs and a small porch beneath the alders. As he lifted the latch of the wooden gate he could see a body in the porch with a towel round her head staring out at him. She opened the porch door.

"Mrs McCrone?"

"Yes, thaat's me, right enough" the middle-aged woman replied with a giggle, seeming to be uneasy. "Would it be me or my husband you're wanting to see? I think you are the new maanager of the estate, aam I right now?"

"Quite right. Ishmael McCulloch, Mrs Mc Crone."

"Oh well, the name's Jessie, but I'm afraid Mr McCrone's out on the hill, Ishmael" she said; and then let out a prolonged deep belch rising from her well-developed midriff. Ishmael took a step back. She already appeared slightly insane, what with the turban round her head and the fixed expression on her white, drawn face. When Ishmael asked her to tell the keeper to call at the manager's cottage she followed this up with two double farts.

"Aand what would you be wanting to see him about?" she enquired, one eye raised interrogatively, the other fluttering downward.

"Business, madam."

"OO, well, then, I'll be telling him your Lordship called" she retorted, affecting a wobbly curtsy and a bubblyjock's squawk.

Ian McCrone was concealed in an upstairs bedroom with the sash window ajar, listening to and observing the meeting of his demented wife with Ishmael through two correlated mirrors.

WE'D BETTER SKEDADDLE

As Ishmael got back on the track a lone heron passed wing-a-wing over the dark water heading for Torridon. It was now a fine evening and he soon passed the Kinloch Inn. In view of the beautiful sunset at the end of the loch he decided to follow on to the confluence of the loch and river. As he approached the river mouth he could make out five or even six figures manipulating a net from one bank of the river to the other. Two or three cigarettes glowed in the half-light. Ishmael followed along the north bank of the river towards the bridge until he found what he expected. A grey Austin Sherpa hidden under the trees. He took out his knife and quickly punctured the four tyres, taking care to pierce them in the sidewall, so rendering them useless. Opening the unlocked door he found the keys in the ignition. He threw them the fifteen yards that landed them in the river with a small splash.

"There's one rising yonder at the bend" was the hoarse whisper that carried over the babble of the river.

Ishmael then opened the bonnet, cut the plug leads and extracted the rotor arm, lobbing it too into the water. It fell silently. Looking into the back of the van he found about twenty glistening salmon. He slashed them all from head to tail, before taking cover.

He could see the half dozen figures stumbling with the heavy net to the van, cursing as they tripped over stones. When they reached the van there was an explosion of oaths.

"Ya bloody eediot!" he could just hear. And then "I tellt ya tae guard the buggerin' vaan. Ye'll pay for this, ye baastard ye." The curses grew even more numerous as the full extent of the damage was discovered. Then, "We'd better skedaddle. Away an' get the Land-Rover" was the last tense whisper Ishmael heard. Ishmael made a sign to Shiel, who had been lying low all this time and now followed him back towards the Kinloch Inn, keeping in the shadows of the alders until they crossed the bridge and reached the bar door. Although it was long after hours he wasn't surprised to find glimmers of light and sounds from within in spite of the door being locked and the windows shuttered. A rat-tat with the knocker and the door was gingerly opened and a face, a cheerful woman's face, said "Come in, luv."

There was a huddle of not very savoury-looking men at the bar who glanced round when he and Shiel came in and then turned their backs.

"Better weather now," he said to the pretty barmaid.

"Yeah, ain't it" she answered in an English whine. "River's quite near flooding. Coo! Just as well there's a bridge now."

"Why d'you say that?"

"Because I might be a widow," she laughed coarsely. "Two owners of the inn got drowned fording the river at Anancaun years ago. That's right, ain't it, hubby" she called to the morose man serving at the far end of the bar half bald but with an outsize moustache flecked with black and grey.

"That's right" he muttered in a strong Edinburgh accent. "What was it, Tam? A pint of Younger's?" before serving one of the group huddled by him. "It was at Anancaun."

"D'you know what Anancaun means?" she asked. "Gaelic, ain't it?" Answered by a chorus of "Ford of the heads" from the men being served by her husband before Ishmael could respond.

"Is he the owner, then?" Ishmael asked.

"Yep, he is that" the barmaid answered "though I don't know for 'ow much longer" she tittered. "There's no trade to speak of 'ere, except out of hours stuff."

"Could I see your menu?" Ishmael asked.

"Yeah, of course, but the kitchen's closed tonight, I'm afraid, ducky. 'Ere you are, though."

I'd just like to have a look for another time," said Ishmael, "and would you give me a pint of McEwans please? And a couple of those cheese and onion baps."

"Yep. Ah thought you was never goin' to ask," she tittered again, hitching up her skirt and showing a bit of leg as she reached up for a pint mug.

As he sank his pint the colour of the dark foaming river, Ishmael saw what he had expected on the menu:

Freshly caught local salmon

Grouse and venison in season

"And out of season" he muttered to himself.

"You're the new manager of the Loch Mhor estate, ain't you?" the landlady asked with a knowing look.

The group of men at the far end of the bar turned their heads.

"That's right. Did you know the previous manager?"

"Did we know 'im? You bet we did, ducky! In 'ere morning, afternoon and night 'e was. But 'e didn't 'alf 'ave to leave in a 'urry, 'e did!"

Once again the heads turned momentarily.

"Why was that? What happened to him?"

"I guess 'e got wind that 'e wasn't wanted round 'ere."

"And why was that?"

"Oo! Ah couldn't tell ya, ducky! 'E jus' scarpered like. They couldn't get anyone to take the job. Until you came, that is."

The conversation at the far end of the bar abruptly stopped.

Ishmael called his dog and set off towards his cottage in the eerie light of that June night along the track winding under the alders by the loch. It wasn't more than three minutes before the poachers, four locals and two Glaswegians burst noisily into the Kinloch Inn bar. Two minutes later the phone rang in McCrone's house. "Break every bone in his body."

When Ishmael had covered about a quarter of a mile along the track to his cottage it was still dark and gloomy under the trees. Suddenly a figure sprang silently from the shadows, knocking him to the ground and sprawling on top of him.

Ishmael got the spectre in an arm lock round the neck, exerting greater and greater pressure until he felt the gasping figure's pulse slow, Shiel growling menacingly the while. When he knew he was about to lose consciousness he released his hold. But he remained alert for any revival of belligerence. There was none, so he rolled the figure over, sat on his chest and demanded

"What's this then? State your name quick and explain." The

25

figure gasped and coughed, and then said in a weak voice

"Ye've near killed me. Ye've very near killed me."

"Name," barked Ishmael.

"I'm the keeper of the Loch Mhor estate" the creature moaned. "I was acting lookout … I mean I was keeping a look out for them poachers … an' I suppose you're one as doesn't know a friend when he sees one."

"Name!" Ishmael repeated menacingly.

"McCrone. Ian McCrone."

Ishmael laughed as he got off the prostrate body. He had a very good idea, from what the keeper had told him, what he was and what he had been up to. Acting as lookout for the local poachers. But he helped him to his feet and told him to follow him to the manager's cottage. When the keeper got up, Ishmael saw by the advanced dawn light that he was a giant of a man. Even bigger that 'big' Angus.

"There they are" Ishmael said as he shepherded his unwilling companion into the house.

"There are who?" the keeper asked nervously.

Ishmael laughed drily. "I had that bottle and those two glasses waiting for your visit. Didn't your wife tell you?"

"Well, no, thaat she didn't, for I didn't go home after … since the morning," he replied as he sank into a proffered chair.

Not only was he enormous, but he had a huge bald dome of a forehead that seemed a foot high, with a red, mottled birth mark that spread right across like a map of Australia, crowning a stupid but cunning face. Red nosed, blue eyed, he was wearing a camouflage jerkin and trousers, and colossal brownish boots enclosing unbelievably outsize feet. He greedily slurped his whisky, watching Ishmael over the rim of the glass with mean little eyes.

'Stoat's eyes,' Ishmael thought.

McCrone kept feeling his neck with a great ham fist and eyeing Ishmael incredulously. He kept silent, apart from the slurping sounds of his drinking. Ishmael knew well what he was thinking. 'How could a man of his size have reduced him to begging for mercy. And how much, or what, did he know?'

Ishmael half-filled the heavy glass, and after gargling a draught McCrone spoke at last.

"An' what for were ye on the traack at thaat time o' night, mister, eh…"

"Ishmael McCulloch, manager of the Loch Mhor Estate."

Ishmael helped him out. "And what for were you on the track at that time of night, Mr McCrone?"

"Well, it doesn't need incomers to be questioning me like thaat, after near killin' me on my own lawful business." McCrone sneered with an ugly look. Ishmael realised that McCrone was one of those who became aggressive after a dram or two. He had intended to prize information out of him, maybe get him to divulge, in drink, what had been going on. But he could see that McCrone was a nasty as well as a cunning customer and thought for a moment of the distraught wife. He decided to get rid of him.

"Call at my house at 8.0 in the morning," Ishmael said peremptorily, getting up from his chair and opening the door.

"Finish your whisky and we'll talk over business in the morning."

"Christ! It's mornin' a'ready" said McCrone ill-humouredly. He walked out without saying anything, giving Ishmael an ugly glare as he left.

McCrone turned up precisely at 8.0 and bumped into Ishmael outside his door, just back from supervising the ghillies. The gamekeeper was a different man, both to look at and to deal with. His dome was embellished by a pork pie hat, which made him look comical. His attitude was cringing and apologetic.

"I'm very sorry, Mr McCulloch, I fear I was a bit het up last night…"

He was going to go on, but Ishmael cut him short.

"Get up on the hill and shoot as many of the hoodies as you can. You'll know they've been attacking the sheep, so the sooner you deal with that, the better." He then gave him orders about grouse and deer, but said nothing regarding salmon. He would wait and see. For he was as sure as one could be that Mc Crone had been lookout for the poachers. Or for a rival gang.

HIGHLAND FEUDS

Ishmael didn't trouble to get in touch with the police. Their reaction would be to send a constable on a bicycle from Gairloch. Which would involve a great deal of wasted time. He knew what their reaction would be in Inverness.

They were busy fighting crime and a few salmon purloined did not warrant officers' time. Many parts of the highlands in those days were much like the old wild west. The very sparse population was spread out over immense distances and what with single-track roads and poor communications, communities tended to sort out problems themselves. It was regarded, besides, as unmanly to involve the police in local disputes. And so such criminal offences as there were tended to go unsolved officially. Feuds and grudges were settled by individuals, often by underhand methods. Besides which, many of the criminal offences were the work of outsiders, here today, gone tomorrow or earlier. Criminal gangs from Glasgow made periodic visits involving cattle rustling and deer massacres. There had even been visits by the Irish with huge furniture vans. They would drive round the highlands, selecting remote hunting lodges and even mansions which were unoccupied, many of the lairds being absentee landlords living in London, so that it was relatively simple to denude their dwellings of furniture and other valuables and sell the loot at auction in the south.

In the early afternoon a red Royal Mail Land-Rover stopped at Ishmael's cottage.

"Good afternoon to you, Mr McCulloch, and welcome to the highlands" said a friendly female voice in a mist of whisky fumes emanating from the vehicle's open window as she handed out an envelope. "I hope you'll be keeping well. Thaat's a lovely collie you haave."

"Thanks, Jeannie" said Ishmael tersely "the same to you."

When Jeannie had driven off Ishmael went into the cottage and opened the envelope.

"Mercy! It's from Sheila," he muttered. "What extraordinary writing, enormous spidery script all over the page, with her name printed at the top and all: Catriona S. McCorquodale."

'It's not me that writes to you but some strange force that impels me, has taken possession of me.'

Ishmael stood up and sank a dram. "Devil take it! I won't let her come here; she'd be horrified by this place, this hovel of a house."

He wrote her a note pulled from a ring-file.

Sheila, I'll come to Glasgow at the end of the month, on 30th. It'll have to be in the evening. Go to the Central Station hotel at 6.0 p.m.

Slainte,

Ishmael.

The following evening Ishmael left for Succoth Farm, that rambling old stone house built round a courtyard. A little girl of six or seven opened the door and quickly hid behind it. "Mum, there's a maan come to… I don't know what he's come for but he's got a doggie with him."

At that the shepherd's wife, very harassed-looking and wiping her hands on her apron, came rushing to the doorway.

"Oh, Mr McCulloch, do please come in. We've got terrible trouble. The factor's told John he's to leave at the end of the month. He came here in a rage this afternoon when he found out the sheep had been in the byre at night…"

She was interrupted by the gaunt, gangling figure of the shepherd, who also looked distraught as he asked Ishmael to sit down on a battered old sofa.

"We're very pleased you haave brought your collie, Mr McCulloch. He's a very fine dog and we'll be honoured to look after him while you're in Glasgow, sir, Mr McCulloch sir."

At that moment three teenage girls came shyly into the room, making much of Shiel.

"Five of them we haave" laughed Sheena apologetically," aand we have two grown-up sons, but they've not been home for I don't know how long. We're thaat anxious to see them, what wi' John not being well aand our trouble wi' the faactor. One's tied to his work in Glasgow aand the other's abroad. Fine upstanding men they are, though I say it myself. I'm writing to them to tell them about our troubles…"

"Your tongue's running away with you" the shepherd interrupted.

"What's this about the factor?" Ishmael demanded.

"'I'm the boss of the sheep' he shouted at me again" laughed the shepherd. 'Aand they should never have been in the byre in June, as I told you before,' he says."

"That was only part of the trouble" Sheena interrupted again. "The faactor says he's had complaints from the ghillies about John. John's epileptic, you see, aand the ghillies an' all say they won't work wi' him. They say he's got evil spirits aand when they saw him fall down once in the heather foaming at the mouth they raan for their lives. Big, strong men, afeart they were. But they're no afeart o' being under the influence o' drink, they're not."

"Thaat's enough, Sheena" John insisted. "Away and get tea. Ye said ye haad the kettle near boiling. We'll not be bothering the gentleman wi' our troubles." When she left, John took over.

"Yes, the faactor's told me we've to leave at the end of the month. I don't know where we'll go. We've been halfway round the highlands and the lowlands aand the borders too, but it's always the same. The men won't work wi' an epileptic."

"Yes, thaat's it" the wife said returning from the kitchen, breathlessly handing Ishmael a cup of tea and nervously fiddling with milk and sugar. "Our furniture's all broken up wi' loading and unloading it on and off lorries. When John takes baad I've to put a spoon over his tongue so he doesna' bite it off, ye see. But after a couple of days he's aas fit to work aas any maan."

"Why didn't you let me know about this before?" asked Ishmael tersely.

Husband and wife both began to answer at the same time, the girls staring fixedly at Ishmael throughout the tangled narration.

Abruptly Ishmael stood up to leave. "You'll not be moving. It's my responsibility as Manager, I can assure you. I'm going to see the factor immediately. If there's any difficulty I'll phone you tonight, but there won't be. And thank you all for so kindly looking after Shiel. Please don't let him out of the courtyard," he added, fondling his dog who was looking at him interrogatively.

★

"What the devil d'you mean by countermanding my order thaat the sheep must not spend the night in the byre? I am boss of the sheep, as you should very well know," asserted the Factor.

"You are not the boss of a single sheep. Let's clarify the question of responsibilities without further delay. Here is my contract" Ishmael said, laying it on the table sideways so that both he and the factor could read it simultaneously. "And keep a civil tongue in your head" he added with a ferocious glare.

"Let us focus on page three" said Ishmael. "There you can see the clear division and limitation of responsibilities:

'The Manager is responsible for all livestock, deer, fish, game birds, cattle and sheep.

It is the Manager's duty to employ gamekeeper, shepherd and ghillies and to supervise their work, and if necessary to dismiss each or any of these employees for failure to fulfil adequately their tasks.

The drawing up of contracts, besides administrative matters such as payment of salaries, accommodation, national insurance falls to the Factor.'

In case of doubt regarding interpretation of any clause of this contract final arbiter shall be Major Tooth, of Tooth's Gin, Laird of the Loch Mhor Estate, Wester Ross, Telephone number Henley on Thames 2151.

"It doesn't say anything about your being boss of the sheep" said Ishmael with his customary sardonic intonation.

To his surprise, the factor laughed drily, saying "Wrong aand right. Live stock are specified but you will realise thaat the sheep on which the shepherd's argument was based and which he referred to were moribund, that is to say on the point of death. In which case, therefore, they could not be classified as livestock, could they?"

Ishmael stared at the factor in amazement. "So you are the boss of dead sheep, is that it?"

"Just a minor misinterpretation" answered the factor emolliently.

"As for dismissing those workers under my jurisdiction" said Ishmael, truculently, "would you like me to get in touch with the laird?"

An expression of alarm crossed the factor's face. After all the trouble over the previous manager, the factor dreaded confronting the waspish Major Tooth.

"Listen, Mr McCulloch, as I have already apprised you it is clear that there has been a minor misinterpretation of your contract. We'll leave it at thaat. And by the way, congratulations on your dealing with the poachers at the west end of Loch Mhor."

"How did you know about that?"

"After twenty-five years as factor of Loch Mhor estate there is nothing I don't know."

Ishmael glanced at the wall clock marching resolutely backwards and left.

★

As soon as he got back to his cottage Ishmael telephoned Succoth Farm. "Just to make sure you're not left in suspense, John, I can assure you, having spoken to the factor, that you will not be dismissed, and I look forward to seeing you when I get back."

"From the depths of my soul, I thank you Mr McCulloch, sir, indeed I do, aye. Indeed I do. I was afeart when I heard the phone ringing we'd to leave."

Next morning Ishmael jumped onto the Wester Bus to Inverness and caught the train to Glasgow.

That night his Land-Rover parked outside his cottage exploded in a ball of fire.

★

When he arrived at Glasgow, walking down from Buchanan Street station to the Central Hotel, Ishmael wondered if Sheila would be there, and where it was going to lead. He didn't know her at all apart from that fleeting meeting on the shore at Shandon and the mysterious note she had sent. And yet he felt he had known her more than any other woman or any other person in his life. He asked himself why knowledge of a being should depend on time. Could one not know the essence of another in a fleeting moment? Might that not be infinitely more important than the grind of the years? He recalled that lightning strike at his loins. He felt deeply, he knew in his bones that …

And there she was. Hovering anxiously in the lobby, she rushed over as soon as she saw him and stood trembling before him with an interrogatory sparkle in her eyes.

"I was afraid you weren't coming," she said tremulously. "Not that you wouldn't come, but that something might happen."

"Why? Am I late?" Ishmael smiled faintly, taken aback by this encounter.

"No, you're early" Sheila said solemnly.

"Let's have a dram" answered Ishmael. "The bar's on the left."

Sheila had an apricot juice, while Ishmael knocked back a Glen Morangie. And quickly ordered another. Sheila watched him sink the second with her little nervous smile.

"How are things at Loch Mhor?" she asked.

Other customers in the plush bar, elegantly dressed in suits and cocktail dresses also regarded Ishmael with some curiosity. An incongruous couple people's faces insisted. She with her well cut, dark brown skirt and jacket and neither make-up or any ornament, though she held under her arm a large and very expensive brown leather handbag; yet he, with his glowering aspect, wore an open-necked khaki shirt under a well-worn tweed jacket. He had deposited a battered Gladstone bag on a chair and kept one hand on it while, as it were, marking time with his highland brogues on the deep pile carpet.

"How are things going at Loch Mhor?" she asked again, noting that he had withdrawn, scowling with disdain at the conventional burghers.

"We got a poachers' van, vandalised it. Otherwise things are more or less all right, thank Providence."

"Why do you say 'thank Providence'?"

"Because I wouldn't be saying 'Thank God."

"Why is that?"

"Ask him."

Sheila looked at Ishmael closely and not a little perplexed. Then she burst out laughing. "Do you think he'd answer?"

"Has he ever answered?"

"I think he might," Sheila said distantly. And after a pause, "What do you do in your spare time up there in the north?"

"I haven't had any spare time to speak of yet, but I'll take my collie, Shiel, for walks in the hills."

"Is that because of the poachers?"

"Aye, it is."

"Are there a lot of them?"

"There seem to be."

"Couldn't I come and help you? Then we could fight in the mountains."

Ishmael scrutinised her eager, innocent face, and couldn't suppress a faint smile. "I don't think that place would be right for you. Look, why don't we go out for a walk and get away from this dump with its artificial light and people? It's a breezy June evening."

"Nothing artificial there!" one of the burghers at an adjacent table ejaculated in a booming voice. "Straight from the cowshed!" Which caused his dinner-jacketed companions to laugh boisterously.

"Allow me" said Ishmael, getting up and taking a step to the burgher's table. "You don't look as though you've got the strength to lift that cocktail fork."

So saying, Ishmael picked up the little saucer of salmon mousse and pushed it into the burgher's face. The burgher half got up, but thought better of it, lowering himself down again on his chair, spluttering

"Would you believe it! In the Malmaison! Waiter! Waiter!"

"That's right, dear, it's not worth it. Don't you get mixed up in anything, Herbert. Here's a serviette. Give it a good wipe," urged a grey-polled crone in a crimson silk dress. Turning her raddled face to Ishmael she squawked

"You're just a Glasgow keely!"

One or two of the burghers at the adjacent tables sniggered.

A waiter loitered indecisively and disappeared; while the barman grinned.

Ishmael stood still, looking then askance at them all as he and Sheila slowly left.

They turned out of Gordon Street, Sheila putting her hand lightly through Ishmael's arm as they walked along St. Vincent Street, cutting through Sauchiehall Street towards the University. Ishmael dumped his Gladstone bag in the Kelvingrove Hotel, a clean haunt of commercial travellers, and then, as he came out Sheila said "Follow me, Ishmael, I'm going to lead you on my own private tour."

Ishmael nodded, and so it was that they came by Templeton's carpet factory.

"Don't you think all factories should be like that?" Sheila asked as they stood in front of the replica of the Doge's palace in Venice.

"I think the best thing to do with factories would be to put all of them underground" Ishmael replied tersely.

"No" said Sheila, "if we're going to have factories, why shouldn't they be like that? If our age has no inspiration, why not take it from the exotic or from the past? Why not neo-Gothic, sky-aspiring like Beckford's Fonthill?"

"As for Fonthill, it fell down. But aren't Glasgow's new high-rise blocks of flats sky-aspiring?" said Ishmael drily. "Aren't New York's skyscrapers?"

"Of course not. They're all money-aspiring. Get the most you can out of the smallest ground rent."

"And what d'you think of a city like Bath?"

"Again, it is a triumph of the past over the present, and why not? We can't do better."

"It's a museum, dead, lifeless. You couldn't live in it. A tourist and geriatric museum. A mausoleum. You'd be better in one of Glasgow's old tenements."

"Well, what about Rennie Macintosh or Greek Thomson? I suppose you'll object to the Greek. Anyway, why do you think architects have lost inspiration?"

"Because this is an age of decadence, even more than the decline of Rome. There's no genuine impulse, other than money. And the life of the senses. It's a meaningless hedonistic dance of corpses to machine music. We've cut ourselves off from the mainsprings of life, from reality. Everybody knows it, and no one does anything about it."

As they walked on, Sheila asked, "Do you read anything?"

"Conrad," he paused, "Somerset Maugham's eastern tales."

"What are you reading now?"

"'Victory.' Conrad's exploration of the possibility of living a life independent of society."

"And is that possible?"

"Well in that novel, society comes to the man who has rejected it."

"And what about you? Why do you want to be alone?"

"I can't think of anything better. Now, what are you reading?"

"Alice in Wonderland."

"Is that the kind of book you like?"

"Oh yes, and I love Peter Pan's Never Never Land. And Edward Lear's nonsense rhymes. I dream about the land of Cockayne and Tennyson's The Lotos Eaters. Do you know 'Kilmeny'? That's my favourite."

"No, I don't, though I've heard of it. James Hogg, isn't it?"

They were now approaching the Necropolis, and Ishmael said suddenly

"Going back to what you were saying about neo-classical, neo-Gothic and the exotic, imagine a city full of Templetons, Parthenons, and all, it would be a city of the dead."

"Well, and why not? What's all this about being up to date? Just what does that mean? Isn't the Necropolis, this city of the dead, the most marvellous, evocative and touching tribute to humanity?"

"It's true there's no money to be made out of it, except by the undertakers, but I wouldn't like to be buried here."

"Then where would you like to be buried? I wouldn't like to be buried at all, nor cremated, unless I could get to the Land of Cockayne."

"On a small uninhabited island off the West Coast of Scotland."

"Come to think of it, so would I. With the wild birds' cry and the sound of the sea. And a flat tombstone that no adventurous tourist could damage, without any inscription. And that nobody would remember."

"These books you like" said Ishmael meditatively, "are they maybe escapist?"

"Yes, and no. Kilmeny certainly isn't escapist, unless you think spiritual yearning is."

"Do you like fairy tales?"

"Yes, I do. I love Grimm and Hans Andersen. But The Little Match Girl, for instance, is critical of a society that leaves a child to starve."

"Sheila," said Ishmael, "your family is very rich. Do you as a family concern yourselves for the unhappy poor?"

Sheila gave him a disconcerted glance.

"I think in a way we do. My father is what you would call paternal, but if he didn't build and finance ships, which often make a loss, what would those working men do?"

"And you personally?"

"I feel like a hyena when I go round the wards of the hospital, and I hope, or had hoped" she said with a momentary but uneasy qualm "to go and work with Schweitzer in Africa."

"Romanticism. Would you be doing it to save lepers or to save your own soul?"

"At least I've got a soul, you bloody bugger" exploded Sheila to Ishmael's amazement. "You cynical, dried up old reprobate." And having said that, she threw herself against his shoulder, crying and laughing at the same time. Ishmael put an arm round her, and wondered.

"Here he is!" Sheila cried joyfully, "my airman," when they reached an impressive pseudo-Gothic mausoleum behind a patch of grass.

"What do you mean "Your airman?"

"You see, I often come here. Look at the inscription."

The inscription, which had been added as a post-script to what was evidently a family tomb, read

Pilot Officer Ian Johnstone
Born 8 March 1922. Died 11 December 1941
Shot down in flames defending Clydeside in his Spitfire
Per Ardua Ad Astra

Ishmael looked, and suddenly felt a strong revulsion towards this child with her whimsical fancies. A revulsion that soon joined in war with that irrational, inexplicable attraction he had been compelled by since they stood on the shingle at Loch Shandon. Brusquely he broke off from her arm locked gently with his.

"Let's get out of this place and back to the living. When does your bus leave?"

"At 9.0, from opposite the Uni."

They walked in silence, crossing the hot, dusty streets in what seemed an interminable tramp through the hubbub of traffic and passing crowds intent on amusement in picture houses, theatres, discos, bingo halls, restaurants, pubs and whore houses. 'So much for the living' thought Ishmael grimly. The whole evening had suddenly gone wrong. Ishmael was glowering and Sheila, sensing his mood, kept giving anxious glances at his hard-set face. When they reached the bus terminal by the university it was 8.20. The bus was waiting with open doors but with nobody, neither driver, conductor or passengers.

"Come on, we'll go for a walk in the park until it leaves" said Ishmael abruptly.

"I can perfectly well wait here by myself, why don't you just go now?"

"We'll go for a walk in the park" Ishmael insisted irritably, walking off. Sheila threw her big leather bag down on one of the side seats at the entrance to the bus and followed him.

The atmosphere in the Kelvingrove Park that windy evening was uplifting and Ishmael's hackles gradually subsided in communion with the trembling aspens, the multitudinous birds, the fresh smell of grass and the sound of rippling water in the lochans, and above all the quietness. He had been wondering why he had come at all and was aching to get away.

Sheila knew this intuitively, but her spirit hated and rejected it. Though she knew it was a passing reaction. Yet she knew he must not go back to Loch Mhor in that state. But she hadn't counted on her own impulsiveness. There was no rational plan, no scheme. They were walking towards a huge spreading cedar. When they were beneath its windy shadow Sheila lightly touched Ishmael's arm, so that they stopped, facing one another. Looking boldly into those black eyes she asked

"Are you going to ask me to marry you?"

Ishmael started. "A commitment. None of your modern free-booting" he muttered as though to himself. And then, to Sheila

"Perhaps, some time in the future."

"In the future? What's the difference between now and the future?"

"Have you been reading my mind?" expostulated the astonished Ishmael. "That was exactly what I was thinking just before we met this evening. One may know instantly the essence of a person – but not of all people. A fleeting moment may reveal the truth, which the sluggard years never could."

"Yes, I might discover trivial details about you: that you don't wear slippers in the house, you like your eggs soft-boiled."

"What do these things matter?" Sheila passionately affirmed, catching at Ishmael's sleeve. "You know I'm a scatterbrain. I'll never finish anything. What more will you discover in the future?"

Ishmael threw his arms round Sheila's waist, hoisted her off the ground and whirled round and round with her legs splaying out as they spun. She hugged his shoulders tightly until, breathlessly they looked into each other's eyes. Sheila kissed his neck, his face, his eyes, and Ishmael held her like a vice. And as they looked up at the great cedar there was a flash of lightning before the tremendous crash of thunder.

"Oh Ishmael" cried Sheila, "this moment … of eternity."

"Quick, we must get moving. Nowhere more dangerous than under a tree. Let's run for it."

The top of the cedar was smouldering and blackened from the lightning strike. Huge hailstones cascaded violently round them as they ran, exhilarated, for the exit and the bus.

"Get under my jacket" Ishmael yelled in the din of the repeated thunderclaps. "Where's your bag, Sheila?" he panted as they reached the park gates.

"I left it on the seat by the door."

"Was there much money in it?"

"About £400 I think."

"Are you crazy? You must be. It'll be stolen."

"No, no it won't, I'm sure. Nobody would take it. And what does it matter?" Sheila gasped as the storm temporarily abated and sunlight reappeared in shafts through the scurrying clouds.

When they got to the bus it was packed and there the bag was just where she had left it on the only empty seat. Sheila jumped on, and the bus started off.

"Write to me" she called out from the doorway. "Give me your answer. I mean your question" she laughed. And so did the passengers as Ishmael stood bedraggled and stone-faced on the pavement.

NO MAN IS AN ISLAND

Ishmael walked back down Sauchiehall Street and turned into The Highlandman's Umbrella in Argyle Street. 'No Women Admitted' said a big sign on the door. A wry smile flickered on Ishmael's face as he shoved his way through the throng and across the saw-dusted floor. The pub was packed and he was lucky to find a space in the corner by the bar itself. 'Spitting Prohibited' was scrawled on the wall above the highland malts and blendeds. In spite of the prohibitions, Ishmael felt a sense of relief and community in the smoky atmosphere of cloth caps and tattooed arms. He got the barman to put up a double dram of Glen Morangie and a pint chaser of McEwan's ale. Just as he lifted the pint mug an elbow jogged his arm and a good part of the beer spilt.

"Sorry" said a cheerful old face under a greasy cloth cap.

"Hey Jimmy, another pint of ... McEwan's was it?"

"Never mind" Ishmael responded, "it's nothing. Knocked the dust off it. "Don't bother" he said to the barman.

"Got caught in the storm?" asked the tall, thin man in a battered glengarry with streamers standing next to cloth cap, looking up and down over Ishmael's drenched shirt and jacket.

"That's right." He had hoped to be left alone to think over his encounter with Sheila.

"Oot the army recently?" Glengarry persisted, eyeing Ishmael's army issue highland brogues as well as his khaki shirt.

"Aye, about a year ago. I'm only in Glasgow for the day. Back to the north tomorrow," he answered, hoping that would close the matter.

"An' what d'you do there? I caan hear frae yer aaccent you're frae here aboots," said cloth cap.

"Manager of the Loch Mhor Estate. Just started."

"Oh Christ!" said cloth cap. "This is Sandy Logan, our local Scottish Nationalist Member of Parliament" indicating glengarry "and I'm Jimmy Anderson."

"Pleased to meet you" Ishmael answered, just managing to suppress a grimace. "I'm Ishmael McCulloch," nodding to each in turn.

"Jimmy's retired" said S.N.P., "used to work at Shandons."

"What was that like?" Ishmael asked sharply.

"It was all right," answered cloth cap. "We built the greatest ocean liners in the wurrld, in them days. Queen Mary and Queen Elizabeth. But it's all gone tae buggery the noo."

"How?"

"Because naebody wants ta dae a job o' work. Driven old Shandon off his rocker they haave. Used tae know us all by our first names. He haad the yard like a big family. But they're all wasters now."

"An' why would ye be workin' up in Wester Ross? English laird, isn't it?" SNP asked facetiously.

"Yes, you're right. But I'm my own boss, more or less. Laird doesn't know anything about hill and river work and hardly ever comes up from Henley-on-Thames it is. Or so the factor says. Leaves us to get on with it. Anyway, the estate makes a loss, and he pays for it. Major Tooth he is, of Tooth's gin."

"Aye," persisted cloth cap, "but what makes ye want tae live there an' do thaat job? There canna be much pay in it."

SNP had bought a round of drinks. Ishmael sank his dram before answering.

"I like to be alone. Independent. Next to wildlife and close to nature."

"Nature's a cruel an' cold compaanion."

"And human beings?"

"There's some an' there's others. But there's others."

"Well, put it this way. However good, I want to be independent of them."

"Ye cannae dae thaat," said cloth cap, with a worn smile.

"Why not? I'm doing it, in so far as is possible."

"No man is an island" said cloth cap.

"Who the divil said thaat?" asked SNP.

"Listen, Sandy, you're a Member of Parliament, an educated maan" said cloth cap, winking at Ishmael. "Listen now:

42

'No man is an island, entire of itself:
Every man is a piece of the continent, a
Part of the Main; if a clod be washed away
By the sea, Europe is the less …'
I cannae mind the next bit … but yes:
'Any man's death diminishes me, because
I am involved in mankind; and therefore
Never send to know for whom the bell tolls;
It tolls for thee.'

"Come on then, who wrote thaat?"

"It's Gray's Elegy" said SNP, "I ken by yon bell tolling."

Hamish and cloth cap looked at one another and burst out laughing.

"Who was it then?" SNP asked defensively.

Cloth cap raised his eyebrows interrogatively, looking at Ishmael.

"John Donne" Ishmael answered laconically.

"Think o' it" said cloth cap, "even a hermit that lives on grass aand berries, one day he gets the toothache real terrible, or his appendix bursts, what then?"

"Guy painful" said SNP "an' he'll be scunnered when it comes tae grub."

"He dies" Ishmael answered "in the second case, even if he goes mad in the first. But we can choose to die or go mad. Of course you're right, up to a point. But I did say independence in so far as possible all the same. What I mean ideally is absolute independence of spirit. It's true, in minor ways, I've to depend on my pay and other workers. And maybe a woman."

"A wumman!" guffawed SNP derisively. "Aye, they're fine an' bonny when they're young lassies. But they'll taak awa' all yer friends. A merrit wumman willna staand a maan hayin' close friends."

"Well, I haven't got any friends" Ishmael laughed. "And I don't want them, anyway."

"Are we no friends in here the night?" asked SNP.

"Yes, certainly we are" Ishmael answered. "I was only joking," he added with slightly heightened colour.

"So you are an Ishmaelite!" said cloth cap, with a wicked grin.

"No. I am against no one. Though in my job at Loch Mhor it might be said that in effect I am. But my idea of independence is that no one interferes with me, and I interfere with no one. Why should my feelings be dictated by the mass? Why should others have power over me?"

SNP had been impatiently trying to get a word in. "What the hell is an Ishmaelite?" he queried.

"A maan who's against everyone, and who everyone's against" said cloth cap.

Ishmael downed a dram before adding

"No, it's just that the idea of universal communion with other human beings is horrible. What about church congregations all bleating together? Or human masses marching together into the future? I don't want to belong, or to be what's called a useful member of society. So far as I'm concerned, society can go its way, and I'll go mine. But if anyone interferes with me, Scotland's motto's my motto."

"What's thaat, for goodness sake?"

"Nemo me impune lacessit," answered cloth cap.

"Oh Jesus! Is thaat Gaelic?"

Cloth cap and Ishmael couldn't help laughing, but they didn't want to upset SNP.

"It's Latin" said cloth cap, "and it means 'whoever harms me will be repaid.' You might say 'Vengeance is mine'.."

"Or 'wha'll daur meddle wi' me'," said SNP triumphantly.

"So you don't want to become one with the universal?" said cloth cap grinning. "You're goin' ta be awfy lonely."

"I don't want to be a minion in heaven; or in hell, for that matter," rejoined Ishmael.

"Almost everything you've said is negative" said cloth cap, smiling. "I don't want this, an' I don't want thaat. Ye say ye don't want tae be a minion in heaven, but I've a suspicion ye'd no mind bein' the boss o' heaven. That right?"

They all laughed, SNP tipping his head back so far that the streamers of his glengarry dangled into an indignant fellow drinker's beer.

"What's wrang wi' thaat," spluttered SNP. "He's right enough.

Like auld Scotland he wants independence and tae be boss in his ain country. But he'll be friends wi' them as disna interfere wi' him.

We could even be friends wi' the English if they'd show us respect. 'The Queen of England' they say, an' refer to Great Britain as England. Unless it's English fitba' hooligans; then they call them British. And what's sae maadening is that they dinna notice. Call themselves civilised but they're right insensitive. Ye wouldna say 'I'm goin' tae the Scottish Embassy,' would ye? But one day we'll haave thaat."

SNP did a hilarious mimicry of English accents. The good old la-di-dah. Forgetting perhaps that Yorkshiremen and Lancastrians also wince at the southern assumption of superiority. Superioritah.

SNP was obviously relieved to have let off this diatribe, but there was clearly more to follow.

"Ye did right, Mr McCulloch …"

"Hey, would you cut out this 'Mr McCulloch' stuff. The name's Ishmael."

"Well, Ishmael, ye did right tae get tae the hielans. Thaat's where yer true Scot is, not like them namby pamby Edinburgh folk. The Hielans is the real Scotland. Idealists they are, as opposed tae us canny Lowlanders."

"Away ye go" laughed cloth cap. "Idealists my arse. They're the most treacherous, good-for–nothing brutes ye ever saw. Whit aboot Glencoe? Whit aboot the clans as haad jined Butcher Cumberland at Culloden?"

"Whit for did ye say 'good for nothin'?" demanded SNP.

"Because all a hielander is good for is tugging his forelock. The whole o' the hielans is bed an' breakfast hovels, an' them as work on estates are employees o' the English, most o' them. Sorry, Ishmael, it's got tae be said. The hielanders are a race o' ghillies, waitin' tae tug their forelocks tae foreign millionaire grouse shooters, stag stalkers an' fishermen. Apart from thaat, they niver did a day's work in their life, sittin' all winter starin' comatose intae the peat fire. An' spongin' off the social security for their pay. Aye, an' in summer, stealin' game, as ye'll know, Ishmael. Celts, they are, and a lazy good-for-nothing lot."

"Hey, hey, wait yer hurry noo" said SNP, ordering another round out of the side of his mouth. "Thaat's nae true. Not the half o' it. Think o' the hielan' games an' the Edinburgh tattoo that make a fortune outa tourists. There's nae forelock tuggin' there."

"Maybe not," grinned cloth cap, revealing stubby yellow teeth, "but that's just typical o' the hielander. Comic opera, it is. Scotland's become a big stage for comic opera. Dressin' up in all thaat fancy dress thaat came in wi' Queen Victoria as was in love wi' her ghillie. They were her tame pets, like the Queen's Own Cameron Highlanders wi' the bully-beef tartan. All them bearskins an' spats an' horse-hair sporrans wi' half a dozen tassels, like the Argyll and Sutherland highlanders dress theirselves up in were niver highland dress. All the auld highlanders haad was a plaid an' a leather pooch. They wouldna' be runnin' aboot the hills in all thaat fantaastic rig-out. An' even the middle class an' lowlanders, has taken it up the noo, wearin' white socks wi' all that fancy dress for weddins. White socks! Whit hielander ever wore white socks? Caan ye believe it?"

"How d'ye ken thaat?" objected SNP.

"D'ye think the auld hielander haad the money tae pay for all that ridiculous rig-out? Would a hielander pay? Just think o' the name o' this pub. As ye ken, The Highlander's Umbrella is what they call the railway bridge over south Argyle Street. Ye'd never see thon payin' oot for bearskin bonnets. A stingy lot o' misers thaat's got the Scots the name o' bein' mean. An' I've seen it mysel. I was at the Hielan Games at Strathpeffer and there was one of yer hielanders sittin' on a hillock ootside the ground watching it all for nothin' through a telescope! It's God's truth I'm tellin' ye. I couldn'a hardly believe it."

They all laughed so boisterously that even their neighbours glanced at them in the general hubbub while Ishmael took the opportunity to order another round of double-double drams and chasers.

"But the real simple highland dress and the bagpipes are our link with our past" Ishmael retorted. "Our ancestors wore that dress and heard those pipe skirls. We don't want to be like the Americans that have no past of their own and destroy anything more than fifty years old."

"Thaat's it" said SNP, "the wearrin o' hielan' dress keeps the auld

Scotch fightin' spirit goin'. Whit was it? Nemo me impune lacessit" he said, beaming with pleasure at remembering the motto.

"Fightin' spirit!" rejoined cloth cap. "In auld Scotland there was thaat. But where's the country that would hae let the English taak the oil aff the Scottish coasts, an' charge us higher prices for petrol than London? Caan ye imagine the Irish, or even the Welsh, lettin' thae English taak their oil? Scotland could hae been the Kuwait o' Europe. An' the English hae the cheek tae say they're subsidisin' Scotland. Dinna talk tae me aboot fightin' spirit. The Scots let the English walk all over them, as they haave done since Culloden. The English even outlawed the wearin' o' hielan dress an' the Gaelic language after Culloden. Killed the language, they did. An' thaat's the reason why the modern revival of hielan dress has turned intae fancy dress. It's no naatural."

"We could have been independent" Ishmael interrupted, but the idealistic Scots, those who wanted that, never mustered the votes."

"Right you are" said SNP, "and I'll tell ye why, if ye'll excuse me, Mr McCulloch – sorry, Ishmael. It's because the Scottish middle class is all anglicised. Send their sons tae English public schools, as if Scotland wasnae the source o' the eighteenth century enlightenment. And haad, and haas, a far better educational system than England ever haad. All anglicised they are, the Scottish middle an' upper class, wi' twee aacents. They cannae pronounce their r's or ch's. I ken a Glesga lawyer whose name's Buchanan an' he calls isself Bewkennen. Aye, an' they look like leggy lassies, they young anglicised middle class in kilts, an' speak posh English, they do, ashamed o' their ain language.

"Yes" responded Ishmael, "some of what you've said about the middle class is true. But you've got to remember that it's that middle class that built the great shipyards on the Clyde, and the steel industry, all the heavy industry in fact that we're now losing, and that's not all their fault. And you know as well as I do that it was the middle class who provided the officers in the world war."

"And how then do you account for the faact thaat the Highland Division surrendered at St. Valery?" asked cloth cap.

"I'll tell ye why" snorted SNP, "because it was the time o' Dunkirk an' the Scots were ordered tae hold up the German advance while the English scuttle on tae the boats tae Dover. The Hielan Division was surrounded. What option haad they? It was like the Germans at Stalingrad. There was no way oot. An' I'll tell ye another thing. It wasnae the highland sojers that surrendered; it was their anglicised officers. It was some English-lookin' general in a big staff officer's hat that surrendered tae Rommel."

"I'm sorry tae rub this in Ishmael, but over an' over again it's the upper classes as betrayed Scotland. Just taak the hielan clearances."

"Aye" said cloth cap "an' the hielanders let the sheep come in tae displace them, an' the hielans has been full o' sheep ever since. The hielanders were like a lot o' sheep theirselves the way they surrendered tae the lairds an' ran awa' tae Canada an' America an' New Zealand an' Australia. Could they not haave stood their ground an' united against the lairds?"

"Christ, maan, they did fight, but what could they do when the lairds brought the army against them?" protested SNP. "Of course they weren't united because they were all divided by the clan system wi' a laird at the head of each of them. Each clan, I mean. That's been the curse o' Scotland, the patriarchal system. The hielanders were treated like the serfs in Russia, always wi' an upper-class anglicised Scot tae betray them. The hielan regiments even were patriarchal: the Cameron Highlanders were the serfs o' auld Cameron o' Erracht, and the Gordon Highlanders were the vassals o' The Cock o' the North, none less than the Duke o' Gordon. More or less private armies, they were. An' you Jimmy, sayin' you were all like a happy faamily in Shandons yard just goes tae show the Clyde shipbuilders were a lot o' patriarchs, all perfect English-speakin' Tories in shite-caatchers."

"Well, some o' them maybe" said cloth cap, "but when he was a young maan Shandon wasnae like thaat, an' he never went tae ony English school. So far as I ken he went to Fettes. It was like workin' wi' a friend, an' he didnae put on airs."

"Then he was a patriarch in sheep's clothing" burst out SNP, an' whit aboot the trouble at Shandons noo? It's anarchy. How's thaat then?"

"Listen" said Ishmael through clenched teeth, "whatever you say

I believe the true highlander's a good, simple-living man, as brave as any in the world. I agree that there has been, maybe still is, what you call forelock-tugging, and you can blame the old clan organisation for that. Nevertheless it bred an amazing camaraderie. It wasn't all bad, and remember the highlander was a religious man. The church ministers told him it was God's will that the sheep should come in and displace him, so the lairds could make a fortune out of wool, seeing as small holdings with half-a-dozen starved cattle were no longer viable. You can't blame the simple highlander for that. They were tricked, duped, conned. The highland smallholder was faced with the so-called spiritual pressure of the church ministers, as Sandy said, and the lairds' bayonets. I can't agree with you, Jimmy, that the highlanders were supine. They were already starving when lairds, army and church united against them. They fought till they were decimated, starving. What else could they do but emigrate?"

"Well, Ishmael," said cloth cap, helping himself to the round Ishmael had bought, and eyeing him over the glass as he sank the chaser, "dinna be stayin' in them hielands. Ye willnae find them people as is there like what maybe the auld hielanders were. Ye're idealising them like our friend Sandy here. It may be thaat the best o' them did emigrate an' left us wi' a lot o' forelock tuggers, layabouts an' rascals. Funny isn't it, how the only small businesses that prosper, or nearly all of them, in the destitute hielan' villages are run by the English. Onyway," he said turning to the rotund barman, "gie us another round o' double Glen Morangies an' three chasers o' McEwans." The drams were pounced on and dry throats slaked by the chasers.

Cloth cap drank pensively and then said,

"Are we no goin' roond in circles the noo?"

"Thaat's dead right, an' it's you Jimmy as is goin' roon an' roon wi' yer prejudices against the hielanders, roon an' roon," whooped SNP, slightly tipsy and nearly falling over as he did an imitation highland fling, the streamers of his glengarry flying as he whirled round.

"Last orders …" boomed the stentorian voice of the publican, a great rubicund fellow with a broken nose. The congregation didn't miss the invitation. A crowd of maybe a dozen Glaswegians at the far side of the bar took the last orders as a signal for a song. No sooner had they got started than the whole company took it up. Inevitably it was

I belang tae Glesga
Dear old Glesga toon,
There's something the matter wi' Glesga
For it's going roon and roon.
I'm only a common old working chap
As anyone here can see,
But when I get a couple o' drinks on a Seterday
Glesga belangs tae me.

'Cloth cap' and 'SNP' joined in with gusto, and so did Ishmael, though he was not, after all, a Glaswegian or even a common old working chap.

BURNT OFFERING

It was after one o'clock in the morning when Ishmael clambered up to his 4th floor room in the hotel. He extracted two miniature whiskies from the little fridge bar and sat on an armchair by the window, reflecting on the evening in the Highlandman's Umbrella and his encounter with Sheila.

His reverie was interrupted by the screaming of a child from the adjacent tenement. Much irritated, Ishmael tugged open the rickety casement and saw a howling infant dandled from the arms of a young woman leaning out of the window where flames appeared to lick the curtains blown in the draught. It was obvious that the woman could not long sustain the weight of the child she was hopelessly trying to shield from the encroaching fire.

Ishmael vaulted through that rickety casement and edged along the foot-wide parapet towards the mother and child. He held onto a drainpipe, which broke free from its stanchion and clattered down past the four floors, crashing into the railinged basement. Undaunted, Ishmael leapt the gap dividing the tenements and grabbed the bairn from the woman's trembling hands. She screamed hysterically but with the child clinging to his neck, its hot breath in his ear, he turned back to his hotel room. When he got to the window, he deposited the protesting infant inside and made his way rapidly back to the now burning window frame of the neighbouring building.

The woman was leaning as far out as she could, the curtains now burnt away and merely smouldering.

"Ah canna gang alang thaat ledge wi ye. Ah'll faw doon tae they railings" she called desperately from the now smoke-filled room. The distraught woman lunged forward and threw her long arms round Ishmael's neck, pushing him perilously towards the edge of the parapet.

"Ah cannae, ah cannae" she screamed. "Save ma bairn, never

mind me, ah cannae." And she broke into a terrible hacking cough.

Without a word Ishmael struck the hysterical woman a sharp slap, breaking her deadly clutch, and hauled her over the smoking window ledge, heaving her over his shoulder in a fireman's lift. Almost skidding off the parapet as she clawed at his legs, Ishmael staggered along, the woman coughing terribly as though her lungs were a furnace. Grappling at last with the rickety frame of his own bedroom window he heaved her over the bottom of the casement, letting the woman tumble onto the floor before vaulting in after her.

Ishmael quickly laid her gently on top of one of the twin beds, her hacking cough now setting in motion a terrible anthracitous rumbling in her lungs.

"It's nae the smoke, it's the cancer o' the lungs ah hae" she mumbled. "Gie us ma bairn, gie us him, mister."

But the child was sound asleep on the other bed so Ishmael went into the bathroom to wash off the sooty marks on his face, neck and hands, glaring at his ghastly countenance in the mirror.

When he emerged, the woman in her late twenties was stretched out naked on his bed. Her body was terribly emaciated, her legs and arms as thin as sticks. But most striking was her torso bristling with goose flesh and her ventral line was very slightly swollen, as though she was pregnant. She was tall and slender, her small breasts clinging to that skeletal body. A burnt offering.

Ishmael laid over her the robe she had left by her side and ordered her to put it on. She did not speak. There was a nobility in that clean cut face which was at once contorted by that awful cough. But she obeyed and painfully moved into the bathroom.

When she emerged in that loose dress, blue behind and bright orange in front, she looked queenly; but still she did not speak.

Suddenly a figure jumped in through the open window, holding out a handbag and grinning under the visor of his helmet.

"Madam left this on the table" he laughed. "A fair fright she's given us, washing them claes in the bathroom an' dryin' them on yon electric fire. That's all it was, bed-claes an' curtains on fire!" And splashing through the puddles of his dripping fire gear, he winked at Ishmael as he heaved himself out of the window.

Still the woman remained silent when a nurse and a medical

orderly knocked and entered the room. They conducted mother and child downstairs to a waiting ambulance, leaving Ishmael with an overwhelming sense of pity at her desolate beauty. He wondered what could be the story of that tragic figure and how he could save her. He was on the point of following downstairs when an inner voice said "And what could you do, Sir Galahad?"

Next day Ishmael felt relief. The old train was arriving at Inverness. It was a bright day, seagulls scudding and wheeling over the platform and sitting on chimney pots with their 'Tia, tia.' It was good to be back in the north at this diminutive so-called city. Just a country town with lawns growing down into the river Ness. Translucent brown water inhabited by salmon and otters, herring gulls diving between rows of small houses on the banks.

REPRIEVED

Shandon's wife was making an unexpected and rapid recovery. The doctors said what they had feared was a malignant tumour in her womb was in fact benignant, if any tumour can be called that. But they decided she must have a hysterectomy to be on the safe side.

Shandon shed tears privately when he got the news, and Sheila skipped about like a young lamb. They visited Ella at the Western Infirmary an hour after the consultant, an old university friend of Shandon's, telephoned the wonderful news. They were driven in Shandon's Austin Sheerline by Tam, the handyman, as Shandon didn't trust himself to drive in his highly emotional state. He turned to the window several times on the way, ostentatiously pulling out his handkerchief with a flourish in an attempt to disguise his wiping of his eyes, snorting as though he had some obstruction in his nose or his throat. Sheila knew perfectly well that he was scarcely in control of his feelings and made a point of keeping up a jolly monologue about the wind, the waves on the sea loch and ultimately about the filthy state of the buildings of Glasgow as they approached the infirmary.

Ella was sitting in an armchair in her private room and jumped up with alacrity when Shandon and Sheila entered, embracing first her husband, who responded with his bear hug, her small head on his breast, so diminutive was she and so huge was Shandon. Sheila swept her mother off her feet in a swirl round the room and they all burst out laughing.

"You old rascal" chirped Ella, "what d'you mean by being so worried!" her bird-like face, with a short nose turned down like a little beak dividing two brilliant black eyes, broke out in mischievous smiles. She looked like a Jewess, which she was not. She owed her dark complexion to her Celtic forbears who had lived for generations immemorial on North Uist, in the Outer Hebrides.

"I told you it would be nothing serious! But now you'll have to wait on me hand and foot when I get home after my little operation. The two of you!" she exulted.

And so the operation was carried out perfectly successfully, and within a week Ella was sitting up in her boudoir, like all bedrooms in the Lodge overlooking Loch Shandon. She was as good as her word, and had husband and daughter at her beck and call, all doors being left open, she tinkling a small silver bell unremittingly as each caprice took hold of her. Demanding to be read to now, have her needlework brought next and insisting on being kept up to date with all the gossip during her absence; and of course that of the moment.

She got Sheila to sing to her, and Shandon to narrate his trials at the shipyard. But Shandon was so explosive, things going from bad to worse that Ella desisted. She gave no inkling of it, but she was deeply worried about her husband. Shandon had had a mild stroke on account of the tribulations he had had to undergo from the mutinous workers, led by a so-called communist agitator and the toadying shop stewards.

One day, soon after Ella's return, as Sheila was sitting abstracted in a little chair by Ella's bed, her mother asked sharply, "What is it, Sheila?"

THE SECRET'S OUT

Sheila did not like to say anything about Ishmael. She had, and had had for a year or two, an unofficial engagement to a man a little older than herself. It wasn't really an engagement so much as an understanding particularly by friends and relations and colleagues in Shandon's yard, who assumed, as people will, that because Sheila 'went out' with no other man they must be 'more than friends.' His name was John Robson, a round-faced, jolly fellow, very pleasant and habitually smiling behind small wire-framed glasses. John was twenty-three and was the accountant at Shandons. Sheila and he had been friends since childhood and John had come to accept the general consensus that Sheila and he were to all intents engaged. Even though they weren't.

John was a very cautious young man who wore tweed suits, absolutely correct in his behaviour and his opinions, and was always indulgent to Sheila. Shandon looked on their relationship with benevolence, even if he did feel somewhat disappointed that Sheila had not accepted one of the many suitors from the sons of the great shipping families of the Clyde. But there was no doubt that John was a decent, honourable, trustworthy man, even if he would never set the world on fire. And that was a lot. Maybe more than the fortunes of the great shipping families.

Ella, on the other hand, thought the whole thing ridiculous. But knowing her daughter's somewhat capricious nature she never even by hint or suggestion intimated that she found John, for all his goodness, an incorrigible bore. But now she sensed that something was up, and even hoped …

When Sheila did not answer, continuing to gaze with a preoccupied air over the restless water of the inlet, she repeated her question.

"What is it, Sheila, my dear? Is it something you can tell me, something you want to tell me?" she asked, arching her little bird-like face over the edge of the bed, those sparkling black eyes fixed intently on her daughter.

When Sheila remained obstinately silent, Ella ventured, with some qualms,

"It's a man, isn't it?"

To her amazement Sheila, normally so cheerful and carefree, began to cry. And then, through her tears, she began to laugh nervously.

"I don't know what's the matter with me. But there's no hiding anything from you, is there, mamma," she said, looking at her solemnly from behind those ringlets.

And so she told her mother about Ishmael.

"Merciful heavens!" laughed Ella when Sheila had told all – all there was to tell – "But he sounds the most extraordinary character. I can't see any reason why you shouldn't get to know him better. Couldn't you bring him here some time?"

"That's just it" said Sheila tremulously, and then burst out laughing. "He's been here."

"Been here?"

"Yes, mamma, he was interviewed here for a job while you were in hospital. You know dadda's desperate to get a new manager. Well, Ishmael came and dadda got in a rage and called him a communist. It wasn't till he discovered he had been an officer in the Black Watch in Korea and won an M.C. that his attitude changed, but by then Ishmael was incensed and they parted with more or less a shouting match."

"I can just imagine it! Only too well. He's his own worst enemy. He's just a little boy, really, inside that great bull of a body. If he can't get his way he explodes. No wonder he can't get on with the workmen. They don't understand him. Don't realise he is kindness itself beneath that terrifying exterior."

At that moment Shandon came striding into the bedroom, saying he had to go down to the yard immediately. There was trouble.

OVER MY DEAD BODY

Shandon marched onto the launching platform in the lee of the great new ship nearing completion. More than six hundred men in cloth caps and boilers suits were jostling below, and he was greeted with jeers and catcalls.

"You've got yer shite-caatchers on" came a bellow from a sour-faced hand with a grey, deeply lined face.

"But they willnae caatch the shite that comes oot o' his mooth" yelled another from the back of the crowd. Which produced a great wave of ribald laughter that reverberated round the yard.

Shandon stood with his huge legs in plus fours astride the podium, his face so crimson it might have set on fire the tufts of greying ginger hair that bordered his head, the strawberry nose now puce.

"You're like schoolboys" he shouted hoarsely. "We're not here to bandy insults, but to bargain. We've got to reach agreement or this ship will never leave the stocks."

"You're dead right it won't" called out a handsome young shop steward from the front. "Unless you reinstate wee Wullie Deuchars as was laid off for alleged malingering when he wasnae doin' onything o' the sort, that ship'll never leave. An' I'll tell ye another thing. That foreman as laid wee Wullie off is isself got tae be laid aff. Permanent like."

This was greeted with a great shout of approval by the mass of workers, glaring up at Shandon as though they would kill him.

"Now look here" Shandon bellowed back in his great bull rage, "that Willie Deuchars was caught leaving the yard at half-past ten on Tuesday. When the gate-man asked for his pass he said "Bugger off you nosey nark."

Shandon was interrupted by a great howl of derisive cheers. "I've got a sick note" Deuchars said. That's what he said. But the gate-man followed him, and where do you think Willie Deuchars went?

He didn't go fifty yards outside the gates. Straight into The Highland Fling."

There was a renewed surge of laughter, until Shandon shouted "And he'll not be coming back to this yard. Over my dead body."

"Aye, it will be over yer dead body, ya bastard" came an enraged scream from the middle of the mob.

The shop steward appealed for calm, and almost pleaded

"Mr Shandon" (they never called him Lord, and he preferred that) "wee Wullie is fifty-two, he's got a wife tae keep an' bairns forbye. He's got a mortgage he's still tae pay off on his hoose. If ye turn him inta the street he'll never get another job. He cannae live on unemployment money. It'll be the end o' him."

"I never change my mind" Shandon shouted, terribly hoarse now. "If Deuchars had gone to the doctor, even without a pass ..."

But he was interrupted by a great angry roar from the men.

"Ane oot, all oot!
Ane oot, all oot!
We'll hae the foreman oot!"

And they marched through the gates and out of the yard, still intoning the refrain

"Ane oot, all oot!
Ane oot, all oot!"

HE'S GOT SOMETHING TO TELL YOU

As soon as Ishmael returned from Glasgow, having got off the shaky old Wester Bus at Kinloch, he strode along by the river beneath the alders, oyster catchers chattering over the shingle at the shallows of the river bends. When he approached the old courtyard of Succoth Farm the door burst open and Shiel raced down the track and over the gate with a flying leap into his master's arms, his forelegs fastened round Ishmael's thighs as he joyously licked his face.

"He's been pining for you ever since you left" called out the shepherd's wife, running down the path wiping her hands on her apron.

"Wouldn't eat a thing. Thank God you're baack, Mr McCulloch. John took baad on the hill yesterday. The keeper and Archie saw him lying frothing at the mouth. Would you believe it, Mr McCulloch, they didn't stop to help him but ran off to report to the factor. Mercifully they couldn't find him afore I got to John myself. Between us we got him hoisted up, hanging over my shoulder he was, and a fair weight he is though he's so skinny."

"How is he now?"

"Och well, he's coming on. He'll be wanting to see you, Mr McCulloch. He's been waiting and waiting. Says he's got something to tell you; but he mustn't get excited. Oh, excuse me, Mr McCulloch, the faactor left a message. You've to phone him urgently. Please use our phone."

The burnt out wreck of Ishmael's Land-Rover had been removed on the factor's orders. He was anxious to conceal the outrage from the laird. "Ye'll haave my own old Land-Rover, the one my son's got. It'll be delivered today."

"I hardly know what I'm doing" said the harassed shepherd's wife. "I've been so worried about John and your collie. Will you be coming in to see John, If I'm not keeping you baack?"

Shiel would not let Ishmael out of his sight and followed him in to John's big sitting-room where the shepherd sat propped up by cushions on a battered old green sofa.

"Don't you get up, Mr Anderson, please" said Ishmael. "How are you then?"

"Och, it's nothing more than the usual, Mr McCulloch. I'll be right for work the morra. Aand how did you get on in Glasgow, Mr McCulloch? Oh, thaat's a graand dog you have, Mr McCulloch. I wouldna mind haaving him for a sheepdog. He'd outclass my three, thaat he would. Och aye, he would thaat an' all. Jess is pregnant, ye know" he added, pointing at the collie bitch lying in front of the peat fire.

"I'm very glad you're all right, John. Get down, Shiel!" Ishmael demanded, nevertheless caressing the collie's white ruff. "Yes, you're right, John. He's such an intelligent dog, I half expect him to speak any time. His parents were both working dogs. I got him after scouring half Scotland. In Glen Shiel it was."

"Ahm, Mr McCulloch, there's something I've got to say to ye," said the old shepherd uneasily, shuffling on the sofa, clasping and unclasping his gnarled hands, as his wife disappeared to the kitchen. As soon as she had gone he fumbled to get a small tin out of an inside pocket. Taking a pinch of snuff, with a glance at the door leading to the kitchen, he sneezed and began:

"I've been thinking it all over, Mr McCulloch, sir." He was interrupted here by a fit of coughing, but recovering he stammered

"It was on the hill by Slioch when the fit came on me. I was lying on my baack, I think it was between spasms, I was aware of two shadowy figures looming over me. "It's thaat bugger of a shepherd" said the one, Archie the ghillie I'm sure it was. "Will I kick his heed in?"

"No, dinna do thaat" the keeper said very sharply, "we've enough trouble wi' thaat bastard o' a maanager thaat's come baack an's in wi' the bleeding shepherd."

"Pardon the language, Mr McCulloch, sir, but I swear thaat's what he said."

Again the shepherd broke off to glance at Ishmael as though he didn't know whether to go on.

"It's him we've got tae get" the keeper went on, I'm quite sure thaat's what he said, Mr McCulloch, sir, it was him, though I wasna in a great state ta ken who it was, wi' me contorting on the ground below them.

"Aye, I ken what ya mean" answered Archie "I ken mysel' how we caan get him where it'll most hurt the baastard. Thaat …o' his" – I couldna make out exactly what he was saying – "thaat'll real skunner him. Aan we'll no hae ony trouble wi' the polis. It's easy done. There'll be no risk tae ourselves, ye see."

"Aat thaat moment I felt a terrible spasm coming over me, Mr McCulloch, aand I let out a s cream thaat I couldna stifle. Then all I remember is Archie shouting, I'm sure it was him, "Let's get the hell outa here. He's got the evil spirits this old bugger haas. Let's awa' an' get the faactor tae see him an' tell him we willna work wi' a maan as is in wi' the divil.""

"Then a darkness overcame me, Mr McCulloch, aand the next I remember was Jessie planting a kiss on my forehead. Aand little by little between us, me leaning terribly on her, she managed to hoist me half up. Aand we staagered baack to the farm, Mr McCulloch sir." The shepherd paused to take a pinch of snuff.

"Aand I couldn't help noticing, when my wife was supporting me down the glen, me with my head hanging down, thaat there were verra deep recent traacks of a Land-Rover going up the glen and coming down again how deep the tracks were. So deep were the traacks it must haave been carrying a heavy load down."

"Well, there isn't anything very strange about that, is there?" Ishmael interrupted. "There are three other Land-Rovers on the estate, apart from mine, the factor's and the keeper's."

"Well, I'll tell ye what, Mr McCulloch, they were the traacks of pretty new tyres. As you'll know, Mr McCulloch, apart from the faactor's, all the estate Land-Rovers haave worn out tyres. But you couldn't mistake them. They left a deep zig-zag on the traack, aand they wandered all over the place, as if the driver haadn't got control of the vehicle."

"Yes," said Ishmael, "that would be strange."

"Yes, I'm agreeing with you there, Mr McCulloch. I think it might be an' all, Mr McCulloch, thaat's just what I've been thinking. But there's another thing thaat was stranger still. I made out what were definitely the hoof marks of a pony, coming down, Mr McCulloch."

Ishmael caught his breath. "Right then, I can guess what that means," he said, getting up to leave. "I'll go up tonight."

"Will ye no haave a bit o' high tea wi' us" Mr McCulloch, Sheena'll get it ready in no time. Sheena!" he called hoarsely. And when his wife came running anxiously in, fearing the shepherd had taken on again, she dashed at him furiously expostulating "John! Have you been taking thaat snuff again? You know it brings on the fits!"

And she ran through his pockets, though she couldn't find the little tin concealed under his shirt. But she found his empty flask.

"Dinna fash yerself, wumman" roared the shepherd unable to suppress a colossal sneeze as he stuttered "Away ye go to-to-to harrumph, to-to-to harrumph – the kitchen now aand get the high tea ready!"

But Ishmael had already opened the door, telling the shepherd to rest quietly for another day and not to worry about anything.

As Ishmael marched up the incline to his cottage he stopped short. The windows on the ground floor had been smashed. He hastily unlocked the door, and looking briefly round, found that nothing had been stolen.

But then, amongst the broken glass on the floor of the sitting-room, he found a piece of dirty paper wrapped round a stone. On it was scrawled in an illiterate hand

WATCH OOT. WE'LL HAE YE OOT.

★

SHIEL DOG

When Ishmael woke after a turbulent night there was a furious barking outside. Leaning out of the dormer window he could see Shiel was scanning the sky and then rushing backwards and forwards barking with all his soul and power; then he stopped, convulsed with internal sounds like suppressed sobs. Leaning further out Ishmael saw that the object of his obsessive attention was the vapour trail of a gleaming silver plane high and silent in the stratosphere. Again Shiel raced backwards and forwards, throwing up spurts of earth, grass and small stones, barking like a creature possessed, until the vapour trail dissolved into the heavens.

From that time Shiel repeated these manoeuvres whenever he glimpsed a silent vapour trail, ever mounting guard as though in expectation of a visitation from another world.

WHAT ABOUT GOD?

Not long after her Glasgow encounter with Ishmael Sheila was due to attend a twenty-first birthday party at Dalry Castle, home of Viscount Dalry, who was owner of Dalry Distilleries, one of the most famous malt whisky distillers in West Dunbartonshire. The Viscount dabbled in politics, and as Conservative Member of the House of Lords he was tipped to become Foreign Minister.

That would suit him very well, as he had a palatial pied-à-terre, as he called it, in Belgrave Square in London, where he normally resided and much preferred to the backwoods of Glasgow. He belonged to several clubs in St. James's, where he enjoyed convivial lunches and conspiratorial meetings with various very important personages. Besides his fairly amateur interest in politics he was able to indulge his passion for gambling and horse-racing, and his wife being four hundred miles away in the north, he frequently invited a youngish lady friend to Wheeler's or the Savoy Grill before going on to a show and, at a discreet hour, slipping into the pied-à-terre.

Lady Dalry was a blonde beauty of twenty-nine but a straightforward woman typical of the Scottish upper class who did not pay too much attention to her personal appearance and habitually wore tweed skirts and jumpers with low-heeled sensible shoes. She had married the Viscount pregnant at nineteen, just in time to escape any scandal. There was a miscarriage.

Lady Dalry liked to go for long rambles with her black Labrador and in the evenings she would read the books in her husband's library, which otherwise remained unread. But although a certain sadness could be detected in her looks sometimes, on the whole she was fairly content with the arrangement that their marriage had turned into.

She had an aversion to London, which fitted in very well with the Viscount's modus vivendi.

Lady Dalry had organised the party for her stepson, the Hon. Crispin Dalry, and invited some four hundred guests, the sons and daughters of the best society of Scotland, though she personally didn't give a fig for any of them.

The party was nothing if not lavish. There were fourteen uniformed footmen, besides serving maids in black dresses and white lace caps. A modern band had been engaged and a sumptuous buffet laid out on long tables in the gilded hall where dancing was to take place. Bottles of Bollinger stood in serried ranks in silver buckets at the entrance to the hall behind countless rows of glasses of the finest cut crystal. The hall was brilliantly lit by colossal chandeliers, which showed off the sheen of the highly polished wooden floor, which had been laid over the original stone. And although it was early July, huge logs, tree trunks, smouldered in the baronial fireplace.

By the time Sheila arrived the party was in full swing, myriad smart young men in dinner jackets, what might be called 'debs' delights,' chattering with expensively dressed and bejewelled 'young things.' Silks, satins, diamonds, emeralds, amethysts glittered resplendent by the light of the chandeliers, as a sea of near identical oval faces framed by long blond hair made scintillating chit-chat from small, pretty mouths. Some of it a bit bitchy; but not all of it.

As Sheila diffidently approached her hostess bearing a pair of silver cuff links for the eligible and honourable Crispin the band struck up a vulgar modern dance tune that was tuneless, and the hordes of eager aristocrats surged onto the dance floor to perform the twist.

Lady Dalry shook hands with Sheila, who wore a simple dark green satin dress, her ringlets setting off the pallor of her daintily quaint face. Neither she nor Lady Dalry wore jewellery or make-up, perhaps the only two in the throng. Lady Dalry, who like Sheila as she liked practically none of the elegant guests, gave her a little kiss on the left cheek, saying Crispin would be delighted with the beautiful silver cuff links etched with his initials.

"No one else has thought of anything so original" she smiled, strikingly good-looking in her black velvet outfit, which accorded well with her blond hair drawn back in a chignon.

"Let me introduce you to Julian Colquhon" she said, putting her arm round Sheila's waist and gently propelling the trembling girl towards a towering dark-haired figure taking a glass of Bollinger from a flunkey.

"Eeo, so glad to meet you" he gushed, as Lady Dalry made her escape, "I say, this bash is awfully, awfully good, don't you think? Simply splendid! What about a turn at the twist?"

Sheila silently observed the contortions of the dancers, waggling their pelvises and flailing their arms about with no apparent awareness of their partners. The so-called dance was like a sea of writhing snakes intent exclusively on their own individual jollification.

"No, thank you" Sheila answered diffidently, "I'm afraid I find it degrading."

"Eeo, come, come" said Julian "That's going a little too far, don't you know." Still hopeful, he gulped his champagne, ready for the fray.

"If you don't mind" said Sheila, "I'd rather just talk to you for a while."

Julian was only too glad to oblige. After all, Sheila wasn't at all bad-looking, and she was the only child of Lord and Lady Shandon. Quite a catch! Knowing that the most interesting topic of conversation for a young man is himself, Sheila asked Julian what he was doing at the moment.

"Oxford, you know, up at 'The House'."

"'The House'? What's that?"

"Oh, my goodness gwacious! Thought evwybody knew! Chwist Church."

"So you're going into the church?"

"Eeo, good lord, no. Not me! I'm going into politics, you know. That's why I've stayed on in Oxford an extwa year, to be Pwesident of the Union. Vital stepping stone to political pweferment, you see."

"Oh. How can you get funds to spend a year at Oxford for non-academic reasons?"

"Fortunately Daddy's fowked out the fees! Haw! Haw! Haw! Just in case you didn't know, Chwist Church is one of the most sophisticated and pwestigious colleges. Absolutely essential to get a good start! If the twuth be known, they had to get me a special tutor to get thwough the exams. I'm not fond of books, haw! haw!"

"And what are you planning to do in politics?"

"Become Pwime Ministah! Haw! Haw! I'm pewfectly sewious. I say, d'you smoke?"

"No, I don't."

"Well, look heah, this is my last fag, so I'll just wite my plan on the inside of the empty packet. First step, get into the Scots Guards fow a couple of years. Should be splendid fun, only cewemonial duties, no danger of active service and absolutely indispensable for contacts with the awistocwacy. Then, with a little, what shall I say, flattewy, get a position as pwivate secwetawy to a pwominent ministah. I've already got that worked out: the foweign ministah will need a new PPS after the next election. Which the Towies are bound to win. So I'm bulling up on foweign policy besides bulling up on the pwospective ministah. Haw! Haw! Cewtain to be Viscount Dalry. He's going to wenounce his title to get into the House of Commons. I'm getting myself invited to the gweat gwouse shoots in August, up by Loch Mhor. Got to keep noticed, don't you see. Fwom there on it's a dead cert I'll be a junior ministah, then a Cabinet ministah if I play my cards wight. And after that, with a little intwigue and a few pwomises to my fwiends who want ministwies, I should be home and dwy. Evewy action planned to pwomote my caweer, d'you see. Haw! Haw! Julian shook his gorgeous black mane and peered closely at Sheila with his myopic eyes. He seemed to be weighing up some further possible adjunct to his political career. But by this time Sheila was surrounded by a gaggle of eager admirers, bespectacled, snotty-nosed, acned, short, fat, tall, body-odorous, handsome, hideous but all assured that they were just the thing, bound to be irresistible to this innocent, seemingly timid young girl with great expectations.

She found herself led onto the dance floor now by a young man who was certainly handsome, with slightly high colour and gently waved hair. He had a most ingratiating manner and it took Sheila quite an effort of will power to reject his blandishments to join him in the jig-jig contortionist game. As she looked at him, self-confident and smiling, Sheila made a decision that brought a little smile to her eyes and lips. Which assured Giles that he was onto a winner. But what Sheila had decided was that if she was to be bored to distraction all evening she might as well find out what these young men were like, as they seemed so ready to confide their intimate ambitions to an apparently naïve but sympathetic young girl.

So Sheila put her hand on his arm and steered him to a plush sofa, where he sat grinning at her expectantly.

"Have you been to an English public school?" she began cautiously.

"Oh, yes, rather" Giles responded blithely, "I was at Winchester. They made us work hard, but it's paying off now."

"Paying off?" queried Sheila, wondering where this was leading.

"Well, you see, I managed to get into Keble College at Oxford to read divinity. Great competition these days. Keble isn't exactly one of the prestigious colleges, but it suited my aims to a T." Giles obligingly let out a "Tee, hee," as though to make his point.

"And what are your aims?"

"Um, er, I hope to get my gaiters."

"Your what?"

"Actually, I'm set on becoming a bishop," said Giles without any self-consciousness. He thought this would be a clincher with an eligible girl like Sheila. In fact, he already envisaged her as the bishop's wife. Not too pretty, so no worries about rivals or adultery and that sort of thing. And, not to put too fine a point on it, well-heeled. Her diffidence suggested submissiveness. Ideal match, he as beginning to think.

"And what have gaiters got to do with it?"

"Well, you know bishops wear gaiters" giggled Giles.

She could just see him in the pulpit pompously preaching and at garden parties making himself immensely affable.

"Are you a Pisci, then?"

"That's it. That's just where Winchester and Keble come in. Winchester's well known for its earnest, hard working scholars, and with Keble's high church Anglican leanings I should be well set for a bishopric with the Episcopalians. Got a first in Divinity at Keble" he modestly confided.

'That should nail her' he thought. But he was surprised to see her lip involuntarily curl and a shadow of contempt pass across her pale face.

"And what about God?" Sheila asked.

"God? Um, I can't say I actually believe in God. So difficult what with the advance of science and all that. I rather agree with the Archbishop of Canterbury who said, 'For God's sake, what is religion good for, but to reform the manners and disposition of men, to restrain human nature from Violence and Cruelty, from Falsehood and Treachery, from Sedition and Rebellion.' Tillotson it was, in a sermon to the House of Commons. Seventeenth century, as you may know. Quite essential for society to have some cement in this materialist age. It's that or anarchy, isn't it? What with all these strikes and so on" added Giles, looking into Sheila's eyes in the hope of approval. "I mean, we must have something to live for and by, if you see what I mean" he stammered, sensing now the cold disapproval of a girl he had taken for a walkover. Poor Giles had thought the gaiters were his trump card.

Sheila got up and Giles was saved his embarrassment by a simpering creature in a lounge suit and suede bootees who unceremoniously took Sheila by the arm, and propelled her to the buffet table. On the way a friend of Sheila's by the name of Sarah breathed in her ear

"Get away from him. He does crack. They're all veah tiresome, don't you think!"

The Hon. Hugh McNab sported an Oxford Bullingdon club tie, perhaps to show his indifference to the attire requested on the invitation card. He explained to Sheila, as he devoured a lobster, that after a club dinner the chaps used to beat up the rooms of the college swots "smashed some Pre-Raphaelite picture of one little weed as well as his family photographs and threw several of them into the pond."

"Splendid fun, it was! What with Bullingdon dinners, hunting and debs' parties in London, didn't find much time for study. Got a fourth in history. Had some trouble with dates. Put down the battle of Hastings as 966 in my finals. Picked me up in the viva, heugh! heugh! Confused it with the telephone number of the Bullingdon."

"And what are you going to do now?"

"Me! Going to get a job as a schoolmaster. Tried Eton and Harrow, but they said they took firsts only. But I've netted a super post as games master at Blenkington-Hilders. By the way, have you seen my E-type?"

"Your what?"

"My new Jag, you know. Daddy gave it me for my twenty-first. Come on, to the gardens and I'll show you."

They walked out through a cobbled courtyard into a paddock with MGB's Triumph TR3's and 4´s, Sunbeam Alpines and a phalanx of daddys' cars lent to diddums for the occasion: Austin Atlantics and Princesses, Rovers, Jaguars and Humber Super Snipes. And there, gleaming in scarlet, was the Hon. Hugh's present: a long, slinky Jaguar E-type convertible with the hood down.

"Can do 150 miles an hour chuckled Hugh. "What about a spin, eh? I say, I like your dress most awfully."

"Perhaps another time" said Sheila, guessing the Hon. Hugh's motives. "I'm afraid I'm not feeling very well."

Which was true. And she fled indoors, followed by an exasperated young aristocrat, to say goodbye to her sympathetic hostess, who ordered the Castle chauffeur to drive Sheila home in the Rolls Royce convertible.

As the Rolls drove sedately homewards, the wind blowing through her ringlets Sheila couldn't help comparing these young men she had met at Dalry Castle with her old friend John Robson: so reliable, so decent, so unassuming. And, inevitably, with Ishmael. They all seemed to have everything worked out, their futures programmed with mechanical precision. As if life could work out like that. And in every case it was a question of egoism. Ruthless, relentless but ultimately trivial ambition. Except for the clown who was to be a schoolmaster: a child who had not grown up and never would be anything but an overgrown schoolboy. Sheila was uncomfortably aware that because of her father's fortune she was an object of interest to these avid careerists.

John had of course had great success as her father's accountant and youngest director. Ishmael on the other hand, seemed to have no worldly ambition whatsoever. He was unique, as a young man, it occurred to her, who wanted only to be free of other people: to be an 'island.'

And yet she had seen the consequences. That dreadful look of isolation she had caught unaware. It was a challenge to her. While she despised the worldly concerns of the Scottish aristocracy at Dalry Castle, paradoxically that wilful loneliness that she descried in Ishmael drew her to him.

What would come of it? And what would come of the ambitions of Julian, Giles and the Hon. Hugh McNab? And, come to think of it, of Lady Dalry's own stepson, whom she had glimpsed only at a distance: the playboy, chemy aficionado and the ultimate deb's delight. In the end he came up to her, cursorily mentioning the cuff links and telling her in a cloud of gin fumes

"I'm in advertising, you know. Teaching people to want things. That's the great creed of our times. Our philosophy, d'you get it? Heugh! Heugh!" as he went off to collect another gin fizz.

Did they never think of any further reality? To ask the question was to invite a derisive answer. And yet, what exactly was Sheila looking for?

Sheila wanted from the depths of her tormented soul to sacrifice herself. Yet she was uneasily aware that it would inevitably be a grand romantic gesture, that as a young and rich aristocrat she was to renounce her wealth and background; that there would be glamour in the figure of the handsome youthful lady doctor toiling among the horrors of African poverty and disease to palliate the suffering. But she painfully recalled Ishmael's jibe: 'would you be going to Schweitzer's leper colony to save your own soul?'

With the apparition of Ishmael she had been quite ruthless in renouncing her unstated bethothral to John Robson as she crumpled into an ashtray his letter tentatively suggesting a date for their marriage. But that ruthlessness betrayed a certain instability with the transfer of her devotion – she had idealised her affection for the prosperous John – an instability foreboding the gradual abandonment of the African heroism and its substitution by dedication to Ishmael – "we could fight in the mountains" – and the inevitable lapse of her medical studies. Sheila was hypersensitive to these oscillations ("I have never finished anything") and hated herself for them. Yet how could she reconcile the kaleidoscopic constituents of her soul?

As the Rolls Royce pulled into Shandon Lodge, Sheila found herself in tears. "I am so afraid of what will happen" she said out loud.

SHAME

When he had found the threatening message amongst the shattered glass on his return from Glasgow, Ishmael determined to call right away at the Kinloch Inn, the centre of local gossip and intrigue. He patted his pocket to make sure his .38 pistol was packed and calling Shiel set off westward in the late evening light. At the bend in the track where he knew there was an echo from the rock face he whistled a perfect imitation of a curlew's call, which always brought Shiel racing towards him to jump up with his paws on Ishmael's shoulders in an embrace. As they were passing the gamekeeper's house the demented but delightful wife made strange signs to him. Ishmael responded with a friendly wave but didn't stop. The keeper's two score cows were lowing restively in their paddock and Ishmael saw that the bull, a wide-horned monster, was apart in a small enclosure, stamping and bellowing plaintively.

"Stupid bugger" muttered Ishmael, "he's driving it to distraction. Should have kept it out of sight and earshot of the cows."

Heading on rapidly to avoid the maddening midges he heard a blundering in the undergrowth as the great shambling ghillie, Angus McLeod, and wee Jimmy Cameron emerged.

"Hullo, Mr McCulloch. We're just coming down from the Kinloch Inn. Had a bit of business to do in the hotel, ye see" Jimmy said with a wink at 'big' Angus. The owner's away in Dingwall the day, ye see."

"Will ye no be haavin' a wee draam, Mr Ishmael?" said the shambler, fishing out the familiar half bottle from a deep pocket and as usual wiping the neck with his filthy hand. Ishmael declined but asked

"Did you see the state of the keeper's cows and bull as you passed? Why will he be keeping them apart at this time of year? The cows'll not be getting the attention they want."

The two ghillies exchanged knowing leers, and then burst out laughing.

"Is it so funny?" demanded Ishmael.

"Well, ye see, they'll be getting it all right, even if the bull's tied up" sniggered Jimmy.

"How's that?"

"Well. it's like this, ye see, Ian is very fond of the coos. It's a good thing he's so tall."

There were renewed guffaws.

"I don't believe a word of it" retorted Ishmael, "it's impossible."

"Mr Ishmael, he's been seen wi' sheep on the hill, and coos in his ain place. It's the truth I'm tellin' ye" affirmed Angus McLeod. "Thaat's why his wifie's away wi' the birds."

"That's it" added Jimmy, "tells her she's an old cow and he knows where there's younger ones."

Ishmael contemptuously dismissed the ghillies, wondering at the deathly silence of Loch Mhor.

WE'LL ALL DIE ALONE

When he reached the Kinloch Inn conversation stopped as he marched in, passing through a throng of sidelong glances. Everyone could hear his order for a scotch egg and a pint of ale; it wasn't till then that the hubbub began again. Shiel kept close to his master.

"Hullo there" said a voice at his side, "I believe you're the new manager of the Loch Mhor estate. I'm the local G.P." his neighbour said with a friendly smile, holding out his hand. "Stevenson's the name."

"Pleased to meet you" answered Ishmael, gripping the slender outstretched hand of a big, rubicund man with thick glasses and a jolly manner.

"What about a dram?" said the doctor, "I see you've got a lonely-looking chaser."

"Why not? Thank you."

"That's a splendid collie you have. Had him long?"

"Since he was a puppy. Do you live here? Hereabouts, I mean."

"Yes, I do. This is my local. Or should I say one of my locals." He laughed slightly tipsily "How about another?"

"It's on me this time. Glenmorangie, was it?"

"Like to see my car?" the doctor asked when they had downed a double-double of the miserable government measure. "It's an antique."

They pushed their way out through the sullen drinkers.

"Jesus! That's an Alvis Speed Twenty, isn't it? It's a beauty! I saved my pay in the army to buy a Railton convertible. It's amazing how cheap they are: too big for most people and uneconomical, but as I couldn't find the work I wanted I had to spend those savings to keep the wolf from the door."

"You're not telling me! You gave up a Railton! My God man, I'd even consider swapping this monster for a Railton. Can't get the spares for the Alvis."

And then, in a low voice, as they walked round the car, "You'd better watch it, old chap! They're after your blood here since you beat up the poachers' van and destroyed their catch. It was all round Kinloch that very evening. The poachers called at the inn just after you'd left. And blew up your estate Land-Rover not realizing you'd gone to Glasgow. They'll be incensed. Haven't you got a shotgun?"

"I have that." Ishmael patted his pocket. "And I always carry my old army .38."

"Ha! ha! ha!" guffawed the doctor. "You can't hit a door at ten yards with those. I was M.O. with the - - - - - - regiment in Hong Kong and they gave me one. A bloody joke they are, though the bullet's big enough to take a man's head off. If you can hit it, ha! ha!"

"Well, I regularly do target practice with mine, and I can hit a tin of peas at 10 yards" laughed Ishmael. "If you've still got yours we can have a competition some time."

"Grand! But I turned mine in on demob. Maybe we could take turns with yours."

"Medical officer you said you were, with the - - - - - - in Hong Kong. You didn't by any chance visit the Willow Inn, did you?"

"Didn't we just!" laughed the M.O. "Strictly health inspection visits, you know" he said, winking at Ishmael. "Had to make sure the lassies were F.F.I., Free From Infection, remember?"

"Don't tell me you signed the prophylactic book as Micky Mouse, did you?"

"No, it was always Donald Duck. Micky Mouse was the padre's nom de guerre. We often went together. He had to minister to the whoories' spiritual needs, ha! ha! ha! 'Body and Soul' they called us in the regiment."

Ishmael related how he had followed them up the stairs and seen their signatures in the official army book. Failure to sign on such visits meant a court martial if infection broke out.

"And how did you sign?" the doctor demanded. And when Ishmael replied 'Captain Hook' he exploded with laughter.

"Well, hell, it's a small world, isn't it? Ha! ha! ha! that calls for another dram. But let's get the hell out of here. D'you know the hotel at Badachro? Jump in."

And off they roared in the magnificent Alvis, Shiel crouching on the narrow back seat. "D'you know, old boy" shouted the doctor above the slipstream, "we're both in danger of persecution here. The Free Church elders are trying to get me for being drunk on duty. Ha! ha! ha!

"You know" said the doctor when they were settled at a table in a window alcove of the Badachro Hotel overlooking the bay, "I'd watch the keeper of the estate if I were you. A very nasty piece of work. Driven his wife crackers."

"I've heard reasons why" said Ishmael grimly.

"And you've heard right! I shouldn't betray a confidence of a patient, but since you've heard already I can assure you that's it. Cow pox! Ha! ha! ha! Come to mention it, I wouldn't be surprised if he started on the bull, the filthy bugger, ha! ha! ha! And by the way, he's a peeping Tom, you know. There's a couple of old lesbians at Kinlochewe. He's been up there many a night. They say he wants to see what they do in the bedroom, ha! ha! ha! Can you imagine it!"

Ishmael told the doctor about the broken windows.

"It'll be him" the doctor retorted, "you can bet your life it's him. He's been saying you tried to strangle him. Threw you off like a fly, he says. Glasgow keely he called you. T.N.F.N. But watch him! And Archie Gillespie. They're as thick as thieves.

Just then a middle-aged woman came into the small hotel bar, asking for a double room for the night.

"Yes madam, we have one free for tonight. Last one."

"Eeo how simply splendid! I say, do you do an English bweakfast?"

"We do a full Scottish breakfast, madam."

"Eeo mahvellous! Yes, do book us in. I say, heah's Kwistofer! Kwis, they do do an English bweakfast dahling. We are English, you know" she said turning back to the barman.

"Yes, I know madam. Room 34. Here's the key. First left at the top of the stairs."

"Eeo, thenks awfullah."

"Bloody bitch" muttered the doctor. They're all the same. Bloody ignorant. The only people that can be 'twee'."

After a thoughtful pause the doctor turned to Ishmael.

"What brings you to the highlands, old boy?"

"Run out of challenges. No more poles to discover or mountains to conquer. Everest's a rubbish heap now, they say. I want to know if I can live alone and find some meaning to life."

"We'll all die alone" retorted the jovial doctor, "so let's live it up, put some spirit into life" he added ordering the barman to refill their glasses with double whiskies.

As the Alvis purred into Kinloch the doctor invited Ishmael to join him for a night-cap.

"My good wife'll be in bed. I've got her well trained."

"You're pretty macho, aren't you" laughed Ishmael.

"If you criticise a bitch that's what they call you these days. Pussy cats all, they want us to be. With dish-mops and shopping bags. A man's man's a rarity now. But thank God there are still some."

"Another time, doctor. It's been grand to talk to someone who isn't a turnip head as most of them are up here."

"Rotten turnips too, ha! ha! ha! Never do with haggis! Can I run you down to your house?"

"Thanks, doctor, but I'll walk it. Good for Shiel."

MURDEROUS INTENT

Ishmael set off with his collie on the north side of Loch Mhor in good spirits. His encounter with the doctor had been cheering after the miserable homecoming. He would have to go down the glen tomorrow and follow the track up towards Lochan Shuna to see what had been going on there. The shepherd's report was ominous. But he pushed that out of his mind and thought instead about the jolly evening with Stevenson. He was so absent-minded that he did not notice that Shiel was running nervously ahead. The track through the beeches, alders and black poplars was a procession of blind bends and ups and downs by the dark water. There was still light as he approached the keeper's house, not yet visible through the dense undergrowth and low-hanging branches.

Quite suddenly, as he negotiated a sharp bend, he was faced at some twenty yards by that colossal bull straddling the track, its great head lowered, vapour pouring from its nostrils. Those horns were menacingly pointed at him. Momentarily, he thought of taking refuge in a tree. No time. With a bellow the great brute charged straight at him. Without shifting his ground Ishmael called to Shiel "Get him, boy! Get him!" And the valiant collie sprang at the head of the disconcerted monster, which turned aside and then fled back along the track. Ishmael recalled the magnificent collie, turned, and there between the branches was a dimly discernible face. It was the keeper.

"Keep your bloody bull off the public track, you damned fool" shouted Ishmael. "Or I'll hold you in a headlock till your heart stops."

But the figure silently withdrew into the thicket.

He had seen Ishmael head for the Kinloch Inn with his collie and waited for his return.

WE'LL REMEMBER YOU

Ishmael spent a cold night watch on the high track to Lochan Shuna. He began to shiver in the chill wind when he bivouacked for the night, getting some comfort from a draw or two from his whisky flask. But when the wind temporarily dropped the midges were diabolical.

He had left Shiel in his cottage for safety, dreading to embroil him in any cross-fire with the deer poachers. Shiel's saving his life from the charge of that bull had made him even more precious to his master, if that was possible. The bond between man and dog was deeper than that of best friends.

The canny old shepherd had been right: Ishmael had distinguished clearly the deep zigzag tyre imprints on the long track up the mountain side, and even stranger, the hoof marks of a pony going down, but not going up. It was amazing that the shepherd had been able to observe and recall these accurate details in the aftermath of a severe epileptic fit, staggering with the support of Sheena's shoulder.

After some five hours with no movement or sound on the hill, apart from the wind and the normal grazing of the deer, he decided to go back to his cottage. He turned east towards the downward track. But then, his reason overcome by instinct, he determined to investigate even farther westward towards Lochan Shuna. After making his way cautiously for about five hundred yards on the precipitous narrow path in the eerie pre-dawn light he heard a voice cursing. Edging forward stealthily he was just able to make out the form of a Land-Rover cowped over on one side. It was stuck in a bog.

Ishmael concealed himself behind a massive rock and watched. There were two men grunting and swearing in angry subdued voices as they tried to extricate the Land-Rover. They were shoving heavy boulders underneath, attempting to get the vehicle upright. After much heaving and pushing they managed to get it semi-level. Then they collected big stones to make a causeway, coming close to the rock Ishmael was behind. It must have taken some two hours before the Land-Rover, wheels spinning, made some progress in jerks backwards. But it would only move so far, slipping back again, the front wheels still embedded in bog.

The two men then ran round to the back of the Land-Rover and began pulling a cumbrous shape out of it.

"Curse them!" Ishmael muttered. "It's a doe they must have shot."

The poachers staggered forward under the weight and dropped it into the boggy water behind the front wheels, easing the carcass in until it was embedded under both wheels. The smaller of the two then jumped into the driving seat and revved up, while the big man waded into the bog over his knees and pushed with all his might. He was big, heavy brute, and slowly, very slowly, between heaving and the pull of the motor the Land-Rover creaked over the doe's body and landed on the causeway. When they had got it out, they both sat on the bonnet, the big man gasping, the other taking a bottle out which both drank from.

"Thaank the devil for thaat" stage-whispered the big brute.

"You caan say that an' all" the diminutive thief answered, grabbing the bottle from the big man and gulping the little whisky left.

"Highlanders!" Ishmael's throat tickled from the chill air after all those hours. Involuntarily he coughed once before stifling it. There was a low cry from the driver.

"Archie, is thaat you? Did ye get the crowbar?"

There was silence, except for a gust of wind.

"It'll be a deer" said the big man. "I've heard two or three coughing the night."

The two poachers retrieved the mangled doe from the bog and slung her into the back of the Land-Rover. Ishmael could make out the unmistakable form of a Bren gun stowed in the back also, along one of the side-facing seats. The poachers now got in, and just as they were about to drive off, having started the engine, Ishmael sprang forward, flashing his torch on his own face but with his .38 pistol pointing at the driver, shotgun slung over his shoulder.

"Ishmael McCulloch" he shouted. "Cut the engine."

"Shite! It's the bloody maanager" gasped the big man.

"Get out and get your hands up" ordered Ishmael. "Now get that doe tied onto the side seat. Not the one the Bren is on," he snapped, moving close enough to control what they were doing with his flashlight on them.

"And whoever makes a move to that Bren is a dead man."

Just to make sure they understood, Ishmael fired a round between their two heads.

"It's all right, Mr McCulloch" called out the driver hastily, "we'll no be tryin' anything."

"You're dead right, you won't" answered Ishmael. "Now get into the front, the two of you."

When driver and passenger were in their places, Ishmael jumped into the back and, keeping his revolver in the nape of the driver's neck, ordered them to drive down the glen.

"There are still five rounds in this pistol. Any funny moves from either of you and you're two dead men" he said through clenched teeth.

As the Land-Rover moved ponderously down the track to the glen Ishmael glanced at the body of the doe. It had bled profusely, and there were several gashes where bullets had torn through its neck. Its tender body was badly mangled by the wheels that had driven over it.

"You filthy bastards" Ishmael spat out. The poachers remained silent, conscious of the pistol barrel just behind them. But suddenly a figure loomed in the misty trajectory of the headlights. The big fellow leaned out of the window and shouted

"Run for it, Archie! It's the Maanager."

The driver momentarily extinguished the headlights in the gloomy glen, and when he put them on again the figure had disappeared.

"Who is it?" Ishmael demanded. "Is it the local ghillie?"

There was no answer.

"Try shouting or putting out the lights again and you've had it. I'll say you threatened me with the Bren and killed you in self-defence. D'you get it?"

Again there was no answer.

"Is that quite clear?" said Ishmael, letting them hear the revolver being cocked.

"Oh aye, Mr McCulloch, we'll no be tryin' anything" answered the big man again in a trembling voice.

When eventually they reached Succoth Farm, after many a perilous swerve towards steep precipices with the ungainly load of the Land-Rover, Ishmael called Sheena out, knowing the shepherd would still be recovering from his trauma. Sheena came running down the short path to the gate.

"Oh, Mr McCulloch, did you get the poachers? Aye, I see you did." She seemed quite unflustered. And not surprised.

"Sheena, please phone the Dingwall police and tell them to get here urgently."

"I will thaat" answered Sheena, hurrying back into the farmhouse.

While they waited the big fellow said he needed to get out for a call of nature.

"Don't you move" snapped Ishmael, "you can piss yourself there or risk having your cock shot off."

The big man didn't move and seemed to contain himself, muttering angrily.

After some twenty minutes a long white Rover police car arrived with flashing blue light. Ishmael put his .38 into his parka pocket again, but kept his licensed shotgun slung over his shoulder.

Two burly policemen handcuffed the poachers, bundling them into the back of the police car, after giving them a thorough search for concealed weapons.

"You're all wet, you filthy bugger" exploded the sergeant as he searched the big one. "Put the tarpaulin over the back seat" he ordered the constable. Ishmael couldn't help laughing; the smirking constable meanwhile loaded the Bren gun into the boot.

"Thaat's a good night's work you've done, sir" said the sergeant. "We'll be up later in the day to take a statement and collect the Land-Rover. We'll be checking for fingerprints, so just leave it locked."

They drove off with their captive cargo.

When the police car was about twenty yards up the road the big fellow managed to get his head out of the window and screamed

"We'll remember you, Mr McCulloch."

DESOLATION

When the police car was out of sight Ishmael recounted to Sheena as briefly as he could the events at the top of the glen. He refused her offer of tea partly because he was cold and his memory of that damp sitting-room; and partly because he did no want to excite the shepherd whose epileptic fit had been so recent. But most important, Ishmael wanted to get back to his cottage to let Shiel out of the house where he had been incarcerated for some twelve hours.

Quickly he got into the substitute Land-Rover, which he had left at Succoth Farm and drove hurriedly to his cottage. On reaching it he was surprised to hear no welcoming bark. Rapidly entering the porch into the living-room he found the collie lying stretched out on the floor, his mouth half open and his teeth clenched. His body was warm but his eyes were glazed. Poisoned. Ishmael knew at once and rapidly fetched a glass of water with abundant salt, attempting to pour it down Shiel's throat. He forced the jaws open, but they were already stiffening and the water ran uselessly from his mouth. It was too late. He was dead.

Ishmael immediately phoned the vet at Kinloch. Although it was six in the morning his ancient Austin arrived in ten minutes in clouds of steam.

"I'm very sorry" said the moustachioed vet, " there's nothing thaat can be done. They must have given him a very strong poison to haave acted so quickly. If you'd been here an hour or two earlier you could possibly have saved him. I'm not sure. Salt and water would have emptied the stomach. But if it's very strong you need to get it within an hour at most."

"Aye" said Ishmael "and I've got carbon powder to absorb poison but it's no use giving it to a dead dog. They must have thrown something poisoned through the broken window." Shiel had been alone who knows how long without food.

"It's too baad" the vet commiserated "thaat a highlander should do such a diabolical thing. The trouble is thaat animals trust us."

"Will you do an autopsy for me this morning?"

"Certainly I will" said the vet, quite distressed himself. "Come along to my place at ten. You can't miss my house. It's got Tigh a Vet on the gate. You speak Gaelic, do you? No, of course not. Thaat simply means the vet's house. And you'll see a collection of old cars in the garden. As I think I told you, I keep three or four in the hope thaat one of them will go. The Land-Rover's on its last legs too."

When the vet had gone Ishmael drank half a bottle of whisky, pacing up and down the long room, hot tears streaming down his craggy face. Then taking his still faintly warm collie in his arms he threw himself on his bed and slept fitfully until nine.

"To think that only yesterday he saved my life" he said out loud on wakening.

NEMO ME IMPUNE LACESSIT

The vet held up Shiel's stomach for Ishmael to see. It was scarcely the size of an orange.

"Yes, whoever it was gave him chicken laced with poison. It's a chlorine-based agricultural product, I'm almost certain. But I'll get it off at once to the poisons laboratory in Inverness."

Ishmael carried Shiel back to his Land-Rover, laid him down on the passenger seat and drove back to Succoth Farm.

"Good morning again, Sheena. I've come back to ask a favour. Is John here?"

"No, he's up on the hill with the sheep, but if there's anything I caan do for you I'll be very glaad."

At that moment there was barking of collies and baahing of sheep, and the gangling old shepherd tottered through the doorway, back for his midday dinner having corralled the sheep until afternoon. A couple of collies came bounding past him, nuzzling Ishmael as a remembered friend.

Ishmael told them about Shiel's poisoning. Sheena clasped her hands over her skimpy bosom with a gasp of dismay, while the shepherd collapsed into a rickety armchair.

"Thaat's terrible, terrible" the shepherd intoned in a deathly voice, wringing his gnarled hands, his head dropping onto his right arm. "I don't know what to say, Mr McCulloch" he burst out in a fury. "It's terrible the rascals there are here. It caan never be mended, oh no, never, never. It'll be thaat keeper aand those ghillies thaat haave got a grudge against you. Humiliated they were, but they haaven't the courage to face you. A lot of low cowards they are."

"Aand to think thaat we were talking" intervened Sheena, "them poisoning your beautiful dog, maybe while we were waiting for the police to come and take those shameless and cruel poachers to prison."

"What's thaat about the poachers going to prison?" demanded the shepherd.

So Sheena recounted to the shepherd what Ishmael had told her briefly.

"Och, thaat's wonderful, wonderful what you haave done, Mr McCulloch. But it caanae bring baack your wonderful collie. What is it we caan do for you? If only there is something."

"Well, as you know" began Ishmael, "my cottage belongs to the estate, a house without a garden, and I fear that if Shiel was buried outside on estate land those evil men would desecrate his grave. So the favour I have come to ask is whether you could consider having him buried in your courtyard?"

"Oh, mercy, Mr McCulloch, you needn't haave asked," the shepherd began. "Of course we'll be honoured to haave Shiel here" the shepherd and Sheena answered almost in unison.

"What about the corner of the courtyard in the lee of thaat beautiful aspen?" asked Sheena.

"I don't think there could be a more beautiful place" added the shepherd, "with yon rivulet running on the far side of the tree and under the wall through thaat wee tunnel. Would thaat be all right, Mr Mc Culloch?" the shepherd asked, deeply moved, and anxious to alleviate Ishmael's grief.

"Yes, that would be ideal."

"I hope you will be able to catch the culprit and he gets the punishment he deserves" said the shepherd.

"The punishment that awaits the killer of my dog is death."

★

Ishmael's return to his cottage was dreary. No welcoming bark, no jumping up affectionately. He was convulsed with anguish and rage. Why, oh why had he gone up the glen at night without Shiel? Why hadn't he shut him in the upstairs bedroom? If he had taken him with him …

Absolutely overcome by remorse, he poured a double dram, pacing up and down that long draughty sitting-room. How could he find the culprit? Could it have been the keeper? But he had several dogs. Would he not fear retaliation?

Ishmael would never do such a thing, but what about the

mentality of these people? And those grinning ghillies, above all that Archie. He wanted to kill them all. He even thought of going and killing them at once. In that way he would be sure of getting the evil coward. "The cursed thing is, as the vet said, that animals trust us," he muttered. "How would a dog realize that a man was giving it food to kill it, to let it die in agony? Imagine the expression on the human face as he did that."

Ishmael kept looking at the corner where Shiel used to lie on his rug, half –expecting to see him, over and over again as he paced back and forth.

"I wish I could be buried with him. I know that from this time life will never be the same. Why did I ever come to this benighted place?" he said to himself. As Sheila had warned, it was beginning to drive him mad. He did know that if he was to live he must get away from Loch Mhor, at least for some time. But what he would do, and when he would come back he was not at all certain. What was certain was that he would have vengeance for his dog. But he also knew that he must get out of this drunken torpor that had overtaken him. That required also some hope, some plan. And for the time being he had neither.

The whole day was passed in this way, although Ishmael began to shiver. He ate nothing but only drank more and more whisky. Yet it was neither cheering nor inebriating. He did manage to phone the factor, telling him he would be off work for some time. And told him to get the windows repaired without delay. Eventually he dragged himself upstairs and slept for hours, only to waken in the middle of the night, when he resumed his morbid marching up and down the cold sitting-room.

Early next day the vet telephoned to say the poison was confirmed. It made no difference. Ishmael knew it already. But he went to Dingwall and got some posters printed offering £500 – more than he could afford – for information leading to the conviction of the criminal. He distributed them in the local pubs, shops, post offices and hotels. When he came to the Kinloch Inn the front door was locked. The owner had gone to Inverness. On going round through the yard to the back door he came across a ghillie with the publican's wife lying on top of an upturned boat. The wife's skirt was pulled right up and she was moaning. Ishmael quickly turned back, pushing a poster under the hotel front door. The ghillie was Archie Gillespie.

On returning to his cottage from these rounds Ishmael could see the Royal Mail Land Rover, bright red, approaching through the trees.

"Afternoon, Mr McCulloch" said the cheery post woman. "Very sorry to hear about your lovely dog."

"Would you like a quick dram, Jeannie?" Ishmael asked, yearning for even a minute's friendly company. In spite of his determination to live a solitary life.

"I'll no be saying no" she was not slow to answer, handing him a small parcel.

"Will we have it outside in the sun, Jeannie? My house is very dismal."

"Lovely."

"Will you keep your ear to the ground, Jeannie? I'm offering £500 for information."

"If I hear anything, I'll let you know. And I won't be wanting any money. That was a bonny collie, and I'm upset myself. Slainte. Well, I'd better be getting on with my round or they'll be asking what I've been up to."

Everyone knew Jeannie loved her dram and kept a wee flask in the post Land-Rover.

The packet contained a copy of Kilmeny from Sheila, with a very agitated note saying Shandon's yard was under siege. "It's a sit-in, with hundreds of workers taking it in turn to occupy the place. There's even a notice on the gates saying:

'Mr. Shandon, NO ADMITTANCE, KEEP OUT.
NO WORK WILL BE DONE IN THIS YARD
UNTIL WILLIE DEUCHARS IS REINSTATED.
THE EMPRESS OF THE CLYDE AND THE QUEEN
CAN GET F....D'.

That was all. Ishmael wondered whether Sheila had substituted the blanks in the final word.

ELLA'S CONSPIRACY

Meanwhile, although Sheila went to the university every day she couldn't concentrate on her medical studies. She kept drifting off into a dreamworld of her own. She hardly ever saw her father these days. He had withdrawn into himself and kept himself apart, pacing up and down the veranda looking over the sea and disappearing through the first convenient doorway whenever his wife or daughter appeared. He had taken to talking to himself, muttering imprecations about the recalcitrant workmen and his useless manager. He had also taken to drinking copious draughts of whisky and puffing furiously on his gnarled old pipes, biting through stems at an alarming rate. He took his meals by himself now, but after a few bites he would push the plates away leaving the meal more or less uneaten.

The doctor had called, taken his blood pressure, and finding it at an alarming rate ordered Shandon to stop drinking alcohol. He might as well have ordered a lion to leave a carcass.

Every other day there was a headline in The Glasgow Herald bemoaning the strike. The latest headline was

SHANDON STRIKE DESPERATE
LORD SHANDON REFUSES TO BUDGE
YARD LIKELY TO CLOSE IN BANKRUPTCY.

Headlines in the tabloid press, which mercifully Shandon did not read, were infinitely more lurid and even menacing.

But when Sheila cut across Shandon's walk in the grounds, he accosted her.

"What was the party at Dalry like?"

"I hated it. Had to leave early because it made me feel sick."

"So the Scottish aristocracy isn't good enough for you. Is that it?"

Sheila didn't answer.

"Your mother tells me you've been meeting that good for nothing fellow who came here expecting to get a job. Is that right?"

"I haven't been meeting any good for nothing fellow, but a man who is worth a hundred of the simpering creatures I met at Dalry."

Shandon snorted and abruptly turned away to attend to a ghillie who was waiting for instructions.

Sheila went back to the house and shut herself in her bedroom. She gazed out over the water where she had first encountered Ishmael on the shingle of the shore. Her reverie was interrupted by a light tap on her door. Her mother came anxiously in.

"Are you feeling all right, Sheila dear? You look so pale and you aren't eating your meals. You don't seem to have any appetite. Shall I call the doctor, do you think?"

"No, mamma. You know I don't eat when I'm happy."

"Is it that Ishmael or whatever he's called?"

"Listen, mamma, 'that Ishmael or whatever' is the most wonderful man I've ever met, apart from Dadda. Do you know that he dealt with a local gang of poachers at Loch Mhor? He speaks of it as though it was nothing, but I've come to realise that it's a very dangerous job he has up there. The man who was manager before him left suddenly because he was terrified, they say, of an Inverness gang who have been killing deer with a machine gun. Get them in the headlights of a Land-Rover at night and mow them down. But Ishmael is determined to rout the lot of them. It's said that the Inverness gang are very dangerous and ruthless. And it's suspected that they have an informer if not a real accomplice locally. Probably one of the estate ghillies. I'm so afraid of what may happen, mamma."

She broke off tremulously, putting her arms round her mother, tears pouring down her cheeks.

"And yet Mamma, though I'm frightened, I'm so happy at the same time because he is what he is. I think he's going to ask me to marry him. I've begged him to do that."

"My dear little whimsical Sheila, you didn't do that, did you darling?" said her mother, hugging her daughter tight.

"Yes, I did mamma. But even if he doesn't ask me, I don't care. It's so wonderful just to know him. You must meet him."

"Let me think a little, precious," said her mother looking at Sheila pensively. All of a sudden she let out a little shriek of laughter, and with sparkling eyes turned and left the room.

Ella went straight down to the verandah, where she knew she would find Shandon pacing furiously up and down, his pipe glowing and a stream of smoke escaping in his wake.

"Shandon" she said, "don't try to shake me off. I've got a marvellous idea that may save the yard."

Shandon halted abruptly and stared at his wife in amazement, those steely blue eyes fixed on her as she managed to get her arm through his and they walked up and down together.

"You haven't taken leave of your senses, have you?" Shandon broke out in a hoarse whisper. To see his wife smiling at him in the circumstances really did concern him for her mental well being. They had been under such strain, not speaking to each other for days.

"Listen, Shandon" – she never used her husband's first name – "I've got a proposal to put to you. You know that young fellow Ishmael McCulloch who came for an interview and you threw out. Well, listen to this. In the short time he's been manager of the Loch Mhor estate…"

"You're not telling me he's got a job?" burst out Shandon incredulously.

"Shandon!" said his wife, stopping abruptly and stamping her little foot, "would you kindly give me your undivided attention for two minutes and don't interrupt! Not only is he manager of a huge estate, but he has already had a gang of poachers sent to prison." Ella allowed herself a little licence here, the poachers having so far been arrested, no more. "A gang that has been plaguing the highlands for years. The police are useless. The excuse is always the same, as you know. 'We know who they are, but we haven't got enough evidence to arrest them.' Well, Mr McCulloch has done just that in a matter of days."

"All right. Good for him! I had a feeling I should have taken him on. It's just that the interview went wrong. He made it impossible for me. I wish him all good luck. He must be a brave young man."

"That's just it" said Ella. "All is not lost. If you can swallow your pride and offer Mr McCulloch the job as manager – from all I hear he's got the toughness that's needed to bring the men round."

"Aha!" snorted Shandon, "I can see you've been talking to Sheila. It's a conspiracy between the two of you."

"Not so!" retorted Ella. "Sheila knows nothing of my proposal. And I'm only going by hearsay. But you have seen Mr McCulloch. You have heard what he's done. And you, and only you, can take the decision. Things are desperate, and as Shakespeare said, in such cases desperate remedies are required."

"To blazes!" growled Shandon. "Petticoat government! Is that the idea? Get to the kitchen, woman, and organise the servants. Don't try to interfere in my business."

"All right, all right Shandon. You know best. I was only trying to help."

And she did make for the kitchen, with just a suspicion of a smile once out of Shandon's sight. For she knew her scheme had taken seed. It was essential now to leave Shandon to think it out by himself.

★

Next morning Ella was sitting quietly doing embroidery in her boudoir before breakfast when Sheila burst breathlessly in.

"Just look at this, Mamma!" she confided, showing Ella a big paragraph in The Glasgow Herald stating that the Manager of the Loch Mhor Estate had captured deer poachers armed with a machine gun.

Ella hugged her, and without a word tiptoed down to the dining room, where she left the newspaper open, as though casually, by Shandon's place at the head of the dining table.

SUICIDE? ... NEVER FEAR

"You're not giving in, are you? What's this, Ishmael?" the doctor burst out on barging through the door of Ishmael's cottage. "I've only just heard the awful news. I'm truly sorry."

"I don't care about anything except revenge. But how am I to know who did it? I've never in my life had a dilemma where I can't act."

"What have you eaten today?" demanded the doctor.

"An oatcake."

"God damn! Is that all? I'll have to give you a jag. You're trembling."

So saying he hurried down and then ran up the steep stairs again with his little doctor's bag, a mini-gladstone.

Ishmael observed without comment the doctor's agitation about what was, after all, his own infirmity. Having jabbed Ishmael in the backside he left with strict orders to lay off alcohol.

"No alternative. That was the last of the whisky I have in the house" Ishmael answered ruefully, pointing to an empty bottle.

As soon as the doctor had gone Ishmael began shaking violently and a cold sweat broke out on his back. He leaned out of the window to call Stevenson back but it was too late. The Alvis had gone.

Ishmael picked up the two broken parts of the glass phial from which the injection had been drawn. Inscribed in capital red letters was the warning CAUTION. THIS MAY CAUSE SUDDEN DEATH. IN NO CIRCUMSTANCES TO BE ADMINISTERED WHEN THE PATIENT HAS ALCOHOL IN THE BLOODSTREAM.

Still trembling notably Ishmael methodically searched the cupboards upstairs and downstairs until at last he found a half-full bottle of whisky that must have been left by the previous manager. He poured a large part of it into a heavy glass saying both defiantly and with resignation 'SLAINTE!' and drank it straight off.

The shaking went and he began to feel much better. Fitfully, he got better and worse, lying on his bed and hearing voices with

American accents in the trees outside his window. 'Why those accents?' he wondered.

As Ishmael slept fitfully during those alcoholic days and nights there was a roaring coming nearer and nearer his cottage as a huge menacing lorry ground to a halt by the door. Then silence. A whisper in the silent moonlight.

"Sadie! Sadie! It's me, Pedro come to see you."

Ishmael hurried out, .38 pistol bulging in his pocket.

"Excuse me, sir. I am Pedro, Spanish lobster lorry driver. Sadie no here now?"

"No, there's no Sadie here, but come in. Join me for a dram."

Pedro jumped eagerly down from his lofty cab, explaining

"I am coming see my family. I have big family at Kinloch. And Sadie one of my girl friends too," confided the side-burned Pedro as he swallowed his Glenmorangie lolling in a big armchair. "In Spain no easy have girlfriend. Church and Franco very not like that. Boy and girl fined 5 pesetas by Civil Guard for kiss in Murillo Gardens in Sevilla."

And so Pedro willingly divulged that he drove round the highland coastal villages buying up lobster to be stored in that gigantic freezer lorry while he visited his Scottish paramours.

"Spanish finished all lobster, so I must come here."

It transpired that Sadie was the wife of the previous manager and Pedro would call in on his way round the coast, knowing that the wretched manager would be sozzled in the Kinloch Inn.

"He no come back before morning, so Sadie and me have little meeting before he come back" he giggled.

Pedro narrated too his family connections in Kinloch. He had fathered numerous slightly swarthy offspring now highly respectable members of that community with jobs as builders and 'security' men on the oil platforms and one even an employee of the Nature Conservancy at Inchnadamph, who wore a gaudy kilt of dubious authenticity. The older 'damas,' now rather past their prime and somewhat grizzled, Pedro did not forget, going out to his lorry for a moment and coming back with a big bag of mantillas, fans and other trinkets, which he proudly displayed to Ishmael.

"Have you got a wife in Spain?" asked the bemused Ishmael.

"Yes, I have wife very good, but better no having the same soup every day. Boring and Scottish woman very boring too. Like have Spanish man" giggled Pedro. "They got husband also boring, very, very boring."

After another couple of drams Ishmael queried "How did you come to know about Scottish lobster?"

"Used to be lorry driver to Aberdeen. We so much whisky had we drunk we no know to turn right to south or left to north. So we are putting our hands in back of lorry and if touch fish, we know go right to south. No fish, turn left to north."

Pedro's head now began to sink onto his chest and in a moment raucous snores reverberated round the room. It was just after five in the morning and concerned that Pedro might miss further assignments Ishmael shouted "Wake up, Pedro. Time to go."

But the somnolent Pedro moved not a muscle except for a benevolent grin that expanded over his chest to the accompaniment of those snores, dreaming perhaps of his Scottish conquests. As a last resort Ishmael took up his bagpipes and skirled

"Hey Johnnie Cope with your hounds so early," the army reveille, right above Pedro's lolling head; whose only effect was to increase the breadth of that self-satisfied grin, so Ishmael retired to his bed as it was now half-past five in the morning and at once fell asleep.

Two hours later he was awoken by the roaring of that monster lorry as Pedro set off without a word. Soon after the lorry had left two disappointed highland lassies turned up at Ishmael's cottage.

RESUSCITATION

Next evening the doctor came again with a loaf of bread, butter and cheese. Besides a copy of last week's Glasgow Herald. There was the paragraph saying 'POACHERS CAUGHT RED-HANDED AT LOCH MHOR ESTATE.' And inevitably Stevenson had brought a bottle of whisky.

It was fortuitous that the doctor should come this day for, to his amazement, Ishmael had received a letter by the mail Land-Rover at about two o'clock that afternoon. It was from Shandon. Ishmael put it into the doctor's hands. Meanwhile he walked up and down the long sitting room, tottering occasionally. This is what the letter, badly typed on an old Imperial, said.

SHANDONS
Shipbuilders
Greenock
STRATHCLYDE

Dear McCulloch,

      Sheila has given me your address. I will come straight to the point. Things are desperate here. It's anarchy. Led by vicious shop stewards under the influence of that communist Tyas.

The yard is closed down. Or rather it's occupied. What they call a 'sit-in.' They won't let me into my own yard. Suicide. It's about lay-offs. 200 must go. We can't afford to pay them. The yard is heavily over-manned. (The strike over Willie Deuchars is resolved.)

There is no man in the yard who could take on these troublemakers. Or elsewhere. I have interviewed a dozen applicants. One look at them reveals that they haven't got the guts required. Some are too obviously middle-class in manner, others sure to prove too cringing, too 'matey' with the men. It's a brave man who'll take the job, if only I could find one.

I believe you are that man. I need a man of your calibre who can be closer to the workers than an ordinary manager could be. The very term 'manager' is anathema to them. You would have as chief foreman a very loyal and technically first-class man in Johnnie Brown. He would keep you up to the mark on all technical problems. But he cannot face huge mobs of belligerent workers. That is not his temperament. I know you have experience of shipyards. But what is urgently needed is a man capable of confronting workers in a dire situation.

If anarchy can be overcome, you will be invited to join the Board of Directors; if it does not offend you to say so. I had second thoughts anyway after our interview at Shandon Lodge. Knowing your army record and now having read in the Glasgow Herald about your dealing with miscreants at Loch Mhor Estate, I have decided to write to you.

I won't try to coerce you. I know anyway that would be futile. But let me know soonest.

SHANDON

P.S. The 'Empress of the Clyde' is due to be launched by Her Majesty the Queen on August 31st. The work is nine tenths done, but she can't possibly be put down the slipway as she is. The men know what is to be done. It is a question of getting them back to it.

"What do you think?" asked Ishmael impatiently.

"Go and don't go. If you go, it may be a disaster. And you lose your job here."

"If I go, it won't be a disaster. And they can't get anyone else here. Who'd take the job? Who could do it? I'm minded to go, sort the yard out, see the Empress of the Clyde launched, and then come back here."

"Come back here? Are you mad, man? Why come back here?"

"It would be cowardice not to. I've got to get Shiel's poisoner, or poisoners. And I want to clean up the poachers. You may not believe it, but I like the Highland atmosphere. I do not want to be absorbed into the Glasgow bourgeoisie. Can you imagine living in Bearsden? Shandon's yard is a challenge. It's just what I need now. I don't want to – I don't intend to – lose my hold on life. And there's another reason I can't tell you about."

"Oh, Christ! I can imagine what that is. It's a wee lassie. Right? Let's have a wee dram to that," he said, solemnly opening the bottle he had brought.

Ishmael couldn't help marvelling. The doctor might prescribe deadly medicine, but he, just by being his inimitable self, helped to haul him back to life.

"I'm not saying" Ishmael answered, "but slainte to you and slainte to her and slainte to me. Providence knows I need it. For her I would do anything."

"I knew it!" the doctor laughed triumphantly. "But what's this about Providence?"

"Because so far as there's any benevolent force in this miserable world it's providential. You know as well as I do that the more scientific discoveries are made, the more certain it is that our existence is meaningless. That there is no purpose to it all."

"Jesus! Let's give it some purpose then. And who's responsible for all those birds' songs and their beauty? You'd better take that offer of Shandon's, and quick! Before I take it myself. I wouldn't half like to get away from the yammering Pharisees of the Free Church that infest this place."

Ishmael marvelled again. The thought of the intellectual doctor facing a mob of angry shipyard workers with a harangue interspersed with literary quotations and no doubt copious drams was wonderful.

'It's for your bodily and spiritual health, chaps, that I recommend you return to work.'

The doctor laughed. And at last Ishmael laughed too.

When the doctor had gone, Ishmael made himself a cheese and onion sandwich and filled a tankard with McEwan's Export ale. He really was coming back to life, he reflected. But continually he glanced into the corner where Shiel's rug still lay. 'I may be coming back to life, but life'll never, never be the same. Even if I get the bastard that poisoned him. That won't bring him back to life. I miss him terribly. I can hardly believe I'll never see him again. Christ! He was my friend. And he saved my life.'

SHEILA EVER IMPULSIVE

Unknown to Ishmael, Sheila had boarded the overnight London to Inverness train in Glasgow and was on her way to Loch Mhor. Impulsive as ever, she had felt a foreboding about Ishmael's life in the Highlands.

'I'm seeing everything just as though I were Ishmael' she thought to herself, enthralled by the quaint little highland stations as the train sped northwards: Dunblane, Auchterarder, Gleneagles, Dunkeld, Ballinluig, Pitlochry, Blair Atholl, Dalwhinnie, Newtonmore, Kingussie, Tomatin. They all looked so innocent, small houses huddled together, divided by pines and larches. Here and there a smallholding between stations, darkened by overshadowing woods; collies rounding up sheep, glimpses of lonely lochs and hurrying burns.

All these features were the same as Ishmael had seen. But Sheila saw them from an empty first class compartment, often standing up, her face pressed against the window. It was all a land of romance to her; unreal, as though she was reading a fantasy.

As the train approached the highland capital, Sheila made her way to the buffet car where breakfasts were being desultorily served by waiters in grubby uniforms. The train stopped at a lonely crossing where she saw a ghillie come running out of the woods with a little basket of eggs, which he handed over to the railway chef, who was leaning out of the galley window, a cigarette dangling from his lips.

"Thaat's the eggs for Lord Dalry's breakfast, miss" confided the waiter as he poured Sheila's coffee. "Thaat's him sitting over yonder at the end of the buffet car. He says he cannae abide London eggs, so the chef's supposed tae boil yon for His Lordship. He gets a good tip for doing thaat an' all. But he'll no be getting his estate eggs. The chef'll be haavin' thon. His Lordship'll get the London eggs as usual. He cannae tell the difference."

TRANSCENDENTAL

"Where would you be going, dear?" asked Jock, driver of the old Wester Bus at Achnasheen. "Kinloch…thaat would be for the estate maanager's house, did ye say? Would you sit aat the baack dearie, as I've got folk to get off at Kinlochewe."

Glen Docherty, 'glen of evil scouring,' had been menacing when Ishmael came down through the yellow-black clouds from the 'Field of Storm,' but today Loch Mhor shimmered in the distance, its islands with their ancient Caledonian pines clearly visible. Sheila was still in a dream when the bus bumped to a stop at the ramshackle Kinloch post office. When she asked the way outside the post office hut to the manager's house on the estate she got some queer looks. But Sheila didn't notice, so taken was she with her surroundings.

"Take the traack in the lee of the hill yonder on the far side of the loch. It's a long way down" they said, all competing to give information, looking doubtfully at her light shoes and the tiny overnight bag she carried. Nevertheless, Sheila set off blithely, leaving the curious locals to speculate.

"She's a bonny lassie. Will she be staying with him or whateffer?"

"He's a dour one to be haaving a laass like thaat visit him an' all."

"Thaat's what I'm thinking. Uhu."

"Yes, uhu, oh yes, thaat's right enough."

When Sheila eventually reached Ishmael's cottage, stung by nettles, scratched by brambles and bitten by midges in the shade of the trees, she was quite exhausted. But there was no sign of life. She called out and after a minute or two the left hand dormer window upstairs opened and a bleary-eyed figure peered out. It had been Ishmael's first night's sleep since the poisoning and he had slept the sleep of the dead.

"I've been worried because I hadn't heard from you" Sheila shouted anxiously in her high-pitched voice. It was early afternoon. Why would he be in bed at this time?

"Is something the matter? Aren't you well?"

Ishmael staggered down the steep stairs and took Sheila in his arms. He didn't say anything.

"How you smell of whisky!" said Sheila, without reproach but with some concern. She noticed that his right eye had shrunk, was smaller than the left; seemed to have retreated into its socket. They went in and Sheila gasped on seeing the disorder and the filthy state of the place.

"I must clear up" she said and then, "if you like, I'll make some lunch. What have you got?"

"Eggs and cheese. And bread; that's all."

"Why don't you lie down again until I've put things right? If you give me an hour, I'll call you."

Ishmael, bedraggled and unsteady on his feet, was only too glad. He felt so heavy that he could hardly keep awake. When Sheila called he found she had made up the bed in the other cramped dormer-windowed bedroom and left her little overnight bag on it. On going downstairs he automatically looked into Shiel's corner. The rug had been removed, and the whole place dusted and generally tidied up. She had changed the places of his books, parka, shotgun and boots, though the whole place was certainly cleaner. But all this irritated him intensely. He wished she hadn't come. Why had she come? He would have invited her if he had wanted that. He knew he wasn't looking well and he didn't want sympathy. He had already made the effort to get on the road to recovery and only needed a little time. He had actually intended to give her a surprise when he came to Glasgow in response to Shandon's plea. But now he was angry. Above all at the removal of Shiel's rug.

Sheila was conscious of her visit being unwelcome and wished she hadn't come herself. Even more so when the cheese omelette she had made stuck to the pan, and the only broken, somewhat blackened fragments appeared on the plates.

"I'm terribly sorry" she cried, putting her arms round Ishmael's neck. "I'm afraid I'm not very domesticated. I hope I'm not a nuisance here. I did want to help."

Ishmael could only acquiesce, and after a dram began to feel almost his old self.

"Listen, Sheila, I'm much better now. Why don't we go for a walk up to Lochan Shuna this evening? If you feel up to it."

"Where's that?"

"We'd need to take the Land-Rover and go up the gully by the burn at the side of Slioch. It's steep and hard, but the atmosphere up there is … what can I say, transcendental."

"Oh then let's go" Sheila agreed joyfully, "I'm sure I can manage it, only my shoes aren't much good. But just a minute! When I was clearing up – forgive me – I'm sure I saw a woman's or a child's boots in that cupboard beside the kitchen sink."

They were mouldy, but otherwise good Spanish fell boots, light canvas with rubber soles.

So they set off, Sheila pretending not to be tired by her long walk from Kinloch; Ishmael forcing himself along the route to recovery. Ishmael was aided by a heavy black cypress staff, but quite exhausted now by the hard climb, they were astonished as they got to the high ridge to find that Lochan Shuna was surrounded by the incandescent white of a late snowfall gleaming in the light of evening sunshine.

The atmosphere was as Ishmael promised: transcendental. A stiff breeze was blowing but otherwise there was absolute silence, apart from the lapping of the hurrying waves on the rocky shore of the loch, surrounded in isolation by distant white mountain peaks. It was as though they were near the heavens.

"I think this is the most beautiful place I've ever been to" Sheila said dreamily. "I can just imagine Kilmeny here."

"I'd like to die here" retorted Ishmael.

"Oh no, no" protested Sheila, "live, live. Live some moments like these and let your soul fly and we shall meet in the heavens, then return here. Not in death, but in life."

Ishmael muttered "But of course I didn't mean to die now, but when it's all over."

"Nothing's ever over. Only transmuted. What's the matter? What's wrong? Do you wish you hadn't come to this place?"

He told her how Shiel had been poisoned. And his foreboding, his certainty, that life could never be the same again. How could there ever be glad morning?"

"I must get them, kill them" escaped from between his lips.

"But how can you fight an invisible enemy? A shadow" said Sheila plaintively. "How can you ever know who it was?"

"That's just it. Christ! Seventeen days have passed, and I've done nothing. No response to my offer of £500. That means they must all be in it together."

"Who?"

"The three ghillies. And maybe the keeper. I may have to kill them all to get the evil coward. They're all in it, one way or the other. They hate me. I'm the incomer who's disturbed their lazy, petty criminal existence. They haven't got the brazen effrontery of the Inverness gang. They'll act as look-outs, they'll tell where the deer can be easily killed and how the best salmon can be netted. But they're only curs. Camp followers. They've no courage. That's why they act behind your back. Why they poison an innocent animal."

"Oh, Ishmael, will this ruin everything, for ever? Can't you forget?"

"Forget!" said Ishmael enraged. "How like a woman! A pragmatist! Of course women have no sense of honour. Can't you understand, I'm a marked man. I've got to avenge Shiel's death. I will not forget. I will have vengeance. However long it takes to find the criminal. Vengeance is mine."

"But the law will find you guilty of murder."

"Who is the murderer? Is a very intelligent, affectionate, brave, loyal creature, who would never betray, who is innocent, is he worth less than a lascivious, treacherous, dissimulating human being of low cunning, a coward who betrays an animal's trust? And if the idiot law, which is only the product of human minds, can't differentiate, then it must be left to the individual to decide. It is my mission to avenge this evil."

"Are you going to be all your life obsessed by this?"

Sheila looked at Ishmael doubtfully, but said no more.

"Who would have thought a highlander would do such a low, unmanly thing" muttered Ishmael again.

"Perhaps you've idealised the highlanders. There'll be every kind there, just as in the lowlands or the cities. But please understand, Ishmael, I'm with you and I am desperately sorry about Shiel. In a way I wish I had known him. But that would only have made it worse. He was your only companion."

"Friend" Ishmael retorted.

"But am I not your friend?" asked Sheila sadly.

"You are more than a friend. As he was. It's not ephemeral" he added vehemently. "It is eternal, indestructible, independent of our corporeal state. It transcends nature, it is above and beyond reason."

They embraced as though in a trance as clouds shadowed the sun in absolute silence.

After some minutes Sheila asked "Oh Ishmael, couldn't you get away from this place?"

"And leave my dog here? No, I couldn't do that. But I'll tell you now what I decided the day before yesterday. Your father has written to me asking for help with the strike at the yard. And I have sent an answer saying I'll get that ship launched. If it's the last thing I do. Or the penultimate. It's a challenge and I need something tangible I can face to get back to life. But I've made clear that once the Empress of the Clyde is launched I am free to do whatever I will. It'll only be a matter of weeks. And then I intend to come back here. And somehow I will kill Shiel's killer."

"But Ishmael, that is wonderful! Oh, what can I say? You'll come to Shandon Lodge! You'll be one of the family."

She threw herself on Ishmael's neck. But he fended her off. Roughly.

"That I will not."

"I'll find my own lodging and do my job as a shipyard worker. I'll be my own man. Independent. Though I'll do all I can to get that ship launched. In any case, if the workers knew I was staying at the Lodge they'd be convinced I was only a puppet, a lackey. And that would make it impossible to win the men over. To get them to see it's in their own interest, and in Scotland's interest, to get the job done. I'm not going to hoodwink them. And I won't have any personal contact with your father until the ship's launched."

"Oh heavens, Ishmael! I don't know whether to laugh or cry," said Sheila, doing both, tentatively putting her arms up to embrace him. This time he did not repulse her. On the contrary, he held her tight in his arms, the wind rustling through their hair.

"I love you so much, Ishmael" she cried, "but I am so afraid. Why am I always timorous about you?"

She kissed his eyes in that enchanting way of hers, and passed her hand over his flinty face. It was torment to Ishmael. He didn't say he loved her. He knew anyway it wasn't necessary. But like her, he wondered where this was going to end.

'I'm getting in deeper and deeper' he reflected. 'I should never allow her to get mixed up in the evil of this place. Here, high up the mountain, it's pure. Primeval. Down below it's a trough of perdition, like the bogs.'

"You won't change your mind about going to the yard?" Sheila asked after a long silence.

"No, I won't do that. But I won't change my mind about returning either. Think, Sheila, what life would be like down there. Quite apart from the malevolence, have you thought what this place will be like in winter? Interminable snow, rain and damp, with dreary grey skies. And dark. Life in a wretched hovel, with more or less illiterate neighbours, except the doctor and the vet. Though the shepherd and family are wonderful. And my pay is miserable. Maybe the first months would seem a romantic idyll. But think of the long years. And the dullness of it all. I came here because I want – wanted – to be alone. Close to the elemental."

"Nowhere would be dull with you, Ishmael! Nowhere!"

They lapsed into silence again. There was the most glorious sunset over Loch Mhor, the clouds reflecting from the sky the incandescent beauty that made Sheila tearful. But Ishmael was flinty-faced, withdrawn, distant, reflective.

Without a word Ishmael broke away and marched onto the great white plain surrounding the lochan and in gigantic letters inscribed in the hard snow SHEILA with the heavy cypress staff.

"Let me have it a moment" Sheila implored, and rushed to write in the snow below her name LOVES ISHMAEL.

"There" she called out, "let the heavens take note of that!"

Suddenly Ishmael hugged her, kissed her, held her in an iron grip while they remained silent, the wind now up, driving the white crested waves of the lochan ever harder as though they had some mysterious secret purpose. A transfiguration.

And then, taking Sheila by the hand, Ishmael said cheerfully "We'd better be getting back, or we'll be caught by the dark. The way down in the gully is slippery and dangerous, even in daylight. There are bogs on either side of the so-called track only about two feet wide, and the rocks are slimy and precipitous."

"Just like life!" Sheila laughed. And they descended.

PEEPING TOM

When they got back to the cottage it was quite dark under the alders and once inside Ishmael could see that Sheila was exhausted.

"I'll sleep in my own room, if I may call it my own" she said, and flitted upstairs.

Ishmael poured himself a big dram, inevitably glancing at Shiel's corner. Where there was now no rug.

'Just as well' he thought, 'sorrow is not the same as morbid moping.'

He had sat there for perhaps an hour, the only light coming from the full moon and the faintly glowing fire, when there was a scream from upstairs. Then there was a bang and a man's curse. Grabbing his pistol, Ishmael raced upstairs and burst into Sheila's room. Just then there was a skittering sound on the slates of the steep roof by the dormer window, and then the noise of a great splash.

In an instant Ishmael was at the window. What he saw in the moonlight left him astonished. Quite clearly he observed the keeper, pork pie perched on his dome, struggling out of the water butt below the window, and once free running off towards the trees.

Ishmael fired the .38 close behind McCrone, then to the left of him, then to the right, so that the keeper dodged this way and that until he disappeared in the undergrowth.

Turning to Sheila, who was sitting trembling on the edge of the bed, he asked what had happened.

"I didn't think I could be so stupid. I was just reading a little with the bed light on when I saw a grinning face in a pork pie hat reflected in the glass outside. Instinctively I noticed two hands holding onto the window frame, so I banged the window shut. The rest you know. I'm sorry I screamed. It gave me such a fright."

"That was the game-keeper" said Ishmael grimly, putting an arm round Sheila in her nightdress with embroidery lovingly done by

Ella. "You don't need to worry. He won't be coming back, though he's known to be a peeping Tom."

Sheila began to laugh, a little uneasily. But she begged Ishmael not to leave her alone. And there being only one narrow bed in the room, they occupied it together.

OH CHRIST! WHAT IS IT?

Ishmael woke early in the morning to find himself alone. He could hear a delicate treble voice singing slightly out of tune, and leaning out of the window saw Sheila half-walking, half-dancing through the trees and bracken, going down towards the loch.

"What the devil have I done to deserve this?" he said aloud, staying where he was until the sound died away by the loch side. "Oh Christ! Oh Christ! What is it?"

Suddenly coming to as though he had been in a trance, he followed her, soon catching up and taking her to a deep bay where they swam in the shade of the alders. Already it was hot. Sheila looked strange to him with her hair all wet and glistening plastered close to her skull like a seal's.

When they came back she would not have breakfast, so Ishmael decided to take her to the Badachro hotel for lunch. It was such a magnificent early July day that can only be found in the Highlands. As Sheila's feet were blistered from her long walks yesterday and the ill-fitting boots she had found in the cottage, Ishmael took her in the old Land-Rover.

They walked for a time in the fresh breeze round Badachro bay and then sat at a white table on the hotel lawn by the sea, the breakers crashing benevolently. When they had been sitting there for a while there was the roaring noise of a car and then a loud, jolly greeting from behind Sheila's back.

"Good to see you, old boy! And who have we here?"

"Sheila, the notorious doctor!" laughed Ishmael getting up and pulling out a chair. "The church is trying to get him out of the Highlands."

"Well, the highlanders look like getting the church out" said the doctor, appraising Sheila's physiognomy with evident approval, "they had a congregation of three last Sunday. And that was a good day. Yet the minister lives in a twelve-room manse. What was that wonderful remark – by Marlon Brandon, wasn't it in – 'On The Waterfront' – 'A gravy-train rider with a turnaround collar?' The biggest load of hypocrites you ever saw, ha! ha! ha!"

The doctor settled for a large John Collins. "Don't tell my wife" he nodded to Sheila who was having her favourite apricot juice. Ishmael, in the slightly chill breeze, a hot toddy.

"Where is your wife?" Sheila asked.

"Where she should be! Don't you know the Spanish proverb?
La mujer y la sardina,
A la cocina!

And he doubled up with laughter, Sheila looking slightly taken aback. But Ishmael was really glad at that moment of the doctor's boisterousness. It released that steely tension that gripped him. That sense of wonder and apprehension at what might destroy it. Having gulped his John Collins, the doctor insisted on ordering another round. Sheila looked beseechingly at Ishmael and somewhat askance at the doctor. But to her surprise, Ishmael asked for a lager and lime.

"A keely's drink" he said, "but infinitely refreshing and … well, as the doctor's here … doctor's orders! I've got to get down to two big drams in the evening; though you've no idea what it costs to get rid of the shakes."

"D'you think you'd like to live here?" the doctor asked, turning to Sheila, who blushed scarlet, the paleness of her face making it all the more remarkable. And her consciousness of that making her whole visage burn.

"I'm sure she wouldn't, in the long run" intervened Ishmael, trying to relieve her embarrassment.

"I can answer for myself, you know" Sheila corrected him "and the answer is that if I decide to, I will."

She hurriedly excused herself, running into the hotel, saying she'd be back in a few minutes.

"Sorry, old boy! I've put my foot in it. It's so unusual to find a sensitive young woman these days. I haven't seen one blush for I don't know how long. Brazen hussies all nowadays! Don't know what things are coming to. Something wrong with our society, old boy! I read in the paper this morning that women buy over a million vibrators a year. In England, of course, poor dears. Electric they are!"

"Sheila will never have heard of one. I must say I hadn't either."

"Don't you believe it. The age of innocence is gone. Pace you, Ishmael. There's nothing our girlies don't know these days. 'Sex is the new religion' they shriek. Carry condoms in their handbags. Boyfriends give 'em vibrators to take on their solo holidays. Perhaps they are innocent, ha! ha! ha! Sell 'em in the big fashionable London stores, according to The Times. Would you believe it? Of course, this is the age of automation, isn't it? Instead of 'our servants can do our living for us' substitute machines. Ha! ha! ha! Oops, here she comes!"

"Cynical snake! Muttered Ishmael out of the side of his mouth. He was inwardly easy, but determined not to wreck this rare moment of ... Well, there she was, radiating innocence.

"Heard you had a visit from the peeping Tom!" the doctor laughed raucously.

Once again Sheila flushed, but when she told him how she had slammed the window on his fingers and his fall into the water butt complete with pork pie hat, the doctor's own face turned purple with hilarity.

"I'll have that round the Highlands in no time. Ha! ha! ha! If only I'd been there we could have had that pistol practice."

But Sheila begged him to say nothing. "I didn't want to hurt him. It was quite spontaneous. I'm ashamed to say I was terrified. "Thank goodness Ishmael came in to the rescue." And she instantly coloured again.

They had a very convivial lunch, the doctor pleased to see the touching attachment of the tough Ishmael and the timorous, delicate Sheila. Ishmael was grateful now for the doctor's ribald jollity, banishing incipient solemnity between Sheila and himself. Even if at times embarrassing. That lunch was one of those encounters which remain indelible on the flux of things. All was not awful for a time.

The doctor insisted on taking them for a drive in his long, lean Alvis, round the coast northwards to Gruinard bay, Sheila sitting beside him, her ringlets reformed in the Badachro ladies' room flying in Ishmael's face as he sat behind.

"Ishmael," she called out, "you know when I was trying to tidy that tiny shed at your cottage, all I could find were wire wheels, an engine and what looked like a gear-box. The engine had a plaque saying 'Speed Twenty'."

The car screeched to a stop on a precipitous bend.

"Don't tell me!" shouted the jubilant doctor. "They'll be Alvis parts. This is a Speed Twenty. Engine! Gear box! Wheels! Just what I need! Can't get spares. Name your price, old boy."

"Listen!" said Ishmael, "You'd better pull into the entrance to the inn there before we cause a deadly accident. I hadn't realised they were Alvis parts. Offered Archie Gillespie £5 to get rid of them. 'I know a man who could dispose of them,' he said. 'A man in Wester Ross.' What would they be worth? He was going to pocket that."

"Cheap at £500."

"Well damn it! The ruddy thief! You can have them for the bottle of whisky I was going to give that rascal. Said he'd prefer that to the fiver. Isn't there an honest man in the Highlands?"

They celebrated at the Gruinard Inn, on a cliff top overlooking the sea. Sheila looked radiantly happy, and when they got back to Ishmael's cottage that night she came over to him, put her hands again on his rough face and said, once more kissing his eyes

"Thank you, Ishmael, for this day. And yesterday."

They had a rudimentary supper and Sheila, exhausted physically and emotionally, clambered up to her little bedroom and fell asleep at once. Ishmael went down to the shore of the loch and the skirl of a lament for Flodden on his bagpipes echoed over the water as the sky darkened and a high wind got up. Sheila heard the lament in a dream and wept.

★

Next morning, on the way to Inverness, as the old Land-Rover passed the turning for Achnashellach before Achnasheen, there was a smell of burning. Hamish glanced at the water gauge. Normal.

"Look over there" Sheila called out, catching Ishmael's arm so that he stopped the Land-Rover. And there he saw it. The Achnasheen hotel was a smoking, blackened ruin. There were groups of people standing round it, staring incredulously. The wind was reviving flickering flames here and there, and there was that sickening stench of guilt that accompanies burnt out buildings. "How did it happen?" Ishmael asked the Indian Jew, who was standing wringing his hands outside what had been the dark, gloomy bar.

"Last night. The wind. Who knows what it can have been in this place" he muttered disconsolately. "And the insurance had just run out. We were too hard up. I knew I shouldn't have talked about it to the customers. Somebody had a grudge. Wanted to get it cheap when I bought it. 'Bloody incomer' he called me. We're ruined."

There was no consolation that could be offered so they hurried on to Inverness across the wild, melancholy country, arriving just in time for Ishmael to hustle Sheila onto the Glasgow train.

"When will you come?" she asked, leaning out of the window as the train trundled off.

"At the end of the week. I've told your father in my note."

Two days after Sheila had left Jeannie brought Ishmael a letter. There were only two lines, in Sheila's enormous spidery writing on paper with her name printed at the top.

> Ishmael, now, as never before,
> I know I love you.
> Sheila.

Ishmael read it, and paused thoughtfully for some minutes. It left him perplexed.

However, he had a lot to do before leaving for Glasgow. Peremptorily he told the factor he would be away for a month or two. The factor hummed and hawed, but he knew, and Ishmael knew that there was nothing he could do about that. No one else could, or would, do the job. He left a work timetable for the ghillies in preparation for the grouse season. And instructions regarding stalking.

As for the gamekeeper, McCrone himself called at Ishmael's cottage that evening. His attitude veered between sheepishness and truculence.

"I thought it was strange there should be a light in that room, Mr McCulloch. I just wanted to check up there were no thieves. You can't trust anybody these days, caan ye? It was strange, thaat's what I was thinkin' when I saw thaat light shinin' out through the trees."

Ishmael gave him a silent steely glare.

"It was not verra nice to be treated in thaat way, I'm bound to say, Mr McCulloch, when I'm only tryin' to do ye a good turn or whateffer. I caan tell ye I won't forget thaat."

"I won't either" Ishmael answered curtly. "Take this note of instructions. Now get on your way."

Disgruntled, Ian McCrone, who had been hoping to be invited in for a dram slunk off home, pork pie wobbling as he muttered his animosity towards his boss. Ishmael had not troubled to tell him about his temporary absence. But he was laying up trouble.

Next day he packed a couple of books and with his Gladstone bulging and his bagpipes in a bag he set off for Inverness and Glasgow.

★

PART II

HOUSE OF THE ISLANDS

Ishmael had decided to look for lodgings at Gourock, a busy little town on the west coast from which ferries cross the Firth of Clyde, and only a few miles from Shandon's shipyard at Greenock. Instinct took him to a big Victorian house in a garden overlooking the ferry terminal and the western isles across the water. Although it had no sign other than 'Tigh An Eileann' – 'House of the Islands' – in big letters over the porch, Ishmael guessed it was a lodging house. Which it was.

He was welcomed by a plump and friendly Indian woman in her early forties, with black oiled hair drawn back tightly over her head and sparkling, sloe-like eyes. She seemed to like the look of him and chatted away merrily in an educated English voice as she led Ishmael to a spacious room on the first floor with a view to the west. She smelt faintly of spices and oriental perfume and her smile revealed perfect ivory teeth. Having told him about prices, meal times and bathing arrangements, she closed the door from the inside, leaning back against it and silently contemplating Ishmael with an alluring smile. He felt slightly embarrassed, sure what this meant. He had never been alone in a room with a married woman who had not tried to seduce him. But after a moment or two, the landlady saying she had a pot on the cooker and dinner would be served in a quarter of an hour, slowly detached herself from the door and went downstairs. Not without a backward glance at Ishmael.

Going down himself a little later, Ishmael bumped into the landlord, a genial but broken-down Lancastrian of about sixty, who wasted no time in telling him he had been a cotton mill manager in India.

"'arry Feckles is the name" he announced, taking Ishmael's hand and laughing loudly for no apparent reason. "Dinner's joost abaht ready. This 'ere's the dining room, Mr McCulloch."

In that cavernous dining room there was a long polished wooden table sparsely populated by three young Chinese and a solidly built blond German in his late thirties. There was, besides, a small table set apart beside a French window with a Spanish-style balcony with a canopy. This table was occupied by a large, craggy-faced spinster who introduced herself to Ishmael.

"Miss Jacobs" she rumbled in a deep, throaty voice. "Save the Children Fund manager for twenty years. Must keep up the civilised formalities, young man, mustn't we?" she added, with a deprecatory glance at the Chinese. And she then let off a gurgling laugh.

The Chinese silently threw discreet glances in Ishmael's direction, while after some guttural throat clearing the German intimated that he was a shipping agent from Bremen studying for some Scottish legal qualification related to shipping. Meanwhile they all sat expectantly waiting for their dinner.

Suddenly the dining room door was flung open against the wall with a loud bang, and a young woman with a mop of curly red hair, a fat blotchy face with a gash of lipstick not too accurately applied and cider bottle legs protruding from a mini-skirt that barely covered a buxom bum flounced in, threw down plates of soup so that they splashed over the table, and bursting into tears, made her exit, slamming the door.

"It all depends on 'ow things is going outside" said Harry Feckles hurriedly looking in to reassure Ishmael.

"Just what I was going to tell the new gentleman" Miss Jacobs announced from her eminence apart, "If things are going well with her boyfriend Molly's …"

But she was cut short by one of the hitherto silent Chinese who addressed her solemnly.

"You talk too much, Miss Jacobs."

Everyone looked at Miss Jacobs in the appalled silence. But she emitted another of her rumbling laughs. Just then the Indian proprietress came slowly in bearing plates of hot pot, which she deposited in front of the German, and then Ishmael, who sat opposite. She beamed at Ishmael, explaining that Molly, having one of her tantrums, had gone home. She made several more deliberate visits to and from the kitchen, serving the Chinese, whom she did not favour with her benign smile, and finally Miss Jacobs, saying that hungry men must be served first.

"Mein Gott, ve vere hungry at Stalingrad" the huge German exclaimed fixing his eye on Ishmael and tucking in to hot-pot, "ve dit ze det men eat, ve vere starving zo."

Ishmael asked whether they were Germans or Russians that he had eaten. And if both, if he preferred one to the other.

"Vell, ze Russians ver meat kwite gutt, zey hat ze foot to eat, but ze German rations finisht. Skin ant bone only. Ze Russian lek cut in very thin slices ant roast in ze fire not too bat vas."

"You disgusting cannibal" exploded Miss Jacobs, "remember who won…"

But she in turn was interrupted again, this time by an undersized Englishman with a bald head bursting loudly in with his hands clasped triumphantly above his head which he wagged wildly, letting drop on the table a shower of pound notes as he shouted gleefully

"Bringing home the cabbages!"

Sitting down next to Ishmael he explained that he had been to the races and won several hundred pounds on 'Rob Roy' in the 2.30.

"I told you all at breakfast" he grinned, "that that 'orse would win and win it did at long odds. Rob Roy at twenty-four to one at Motherwell it was. I put on twenty quid. There y'are, see" he ejaculated, letting what remained of his winnings fly all over the table.

"A fool's game" barked Miss Jacobs, "don't you listen to him. He'll lose it all in no time. Silly little man" she added gruffly, "he's been drinking."

Ishmael was not a little taken with his fellow lodgers, but wishing them all good night, he left the room to go upstairs for an early night's rest. He nearly collided with Harry Feckles who rushed out of a room with an unmade bed at the bottom of the stairs exclaiming

"Ahm ever so sorry, Mr McCulloch abaht our Molly. She's loovely when everything's a'right outside, but she's 'ad a bit o' bother wi' the boyfriend like. She's goin' out wi' 'im tonight, an' tomorra she'll be as right as rain. Needs a bit o' toochin' oop."

Which declamation Harry Feckles ended with a bronchial guffaw.

Early on Sunday Ishmael left the illustrious and slumbering Tigh An Eileann. He set off along the picturesque road by the confluence of Gare Loch, Loch Long and the river Clyde that breezy morning. Several ships, big and small, were sailing in and out and to the north, the peak of Ben Lomond reared above the low cloud.

'The mid-west of Scotland is just as magnificent as the Highlands' he thought to himself, striding along eastwards.

It was only a few miles from Gourock to Greenock, where the cranes of Shandon's yard loomed on the local horizon and beyond them those of Cunliths: the talisman of employment for countless southern Scots.

'GREENOCK, BIRTHPLACE OF JAMES WATT' the sign announced as Ishmael approached the shipbuilding town. 'How is it that the inventive Scots,' he reflected, 'are now so resistant to technical advance in the shipyards? Watt not only patented his own steam engine but projected the screw propeller that the world's shipping still depends on.' When Ishmael reached Shandon's he found the main gates free of pickets but plastered with posters, including one or two with the hammer and sickle. Just outside the gates was a colossal poster asserting

THE SCOTTISH WORKERS WILL TEACH THE BOSS CLASS A LESSON

It was adorned with a grotesque caricature of Shandon fiendishly grinning with a gigantic red nose and a fist full of £100 notes, while in the other hand he brandished a huge whip over a group of cowed workers, purporting to snarl

PROFIT FOR ME. NOWT FOR YOU

Another vast poster proclaimed
SHANDON KEEP OUT
SCOTTISH WORKERS SIT-IN

But it being a Sunday, no one was sitting in today except for two or three caretakers and Shandon's ex-General Manager, who came running up with a haggard expression as soon as Ishmael entered through a side gate. The main gates being padlocked with colossal chains. Inside the yard Ishmael noticed an enormous placard showing Shandon with bare buttocks being assiduously licked by the bowler-hatted General Manager himself. No wonder he looked under stress! But the General Manager that was didn't wear his bowler hat this morning, looking peculiarly insignificant. His thin, pinched face expressed doleful hopelessness. He hadn't even dared to remove the offending cartoon.

"Good morning to you, Mr McCulloch" he said with a watery smile in exquisite English accents. "I'm afraid there's nothing that can be done. We'll never get the 'Empress of the Clyde' completed in time. Indeed, I don't think we'll ever get it finished at all. I fear you are wasting your time coming here" he whined. "It's anarchy. And it's the same at Cunliths and half the yards. John Brown's, Yarrows, Harland & Wolffs. They've all been on strike for weeks. All the yards will be closing like a falling pack of cards."

Ishmael felt a strong urge to give this cringing figure a good kick up the backside. Which, of course, he resisted. He was accompanied by the whimpering creature on a tour of inspection of the yard.

Right in front of them rose the majestic spectacle of the 'Empress of the Clyde.' But walking the length of the berth – they had begun at the sea end of the slipway – Ishmael observed that there was no bow to the boat.

"How is that?" he asked the chief gaffer.

"Well you see we only have sixty ton cranes, so the ship has had to be built in sections. You can see the rudiments of the bow section over there."

"Aren't the cranes mobile?"

"No, I fear they aren't. It's all a question of investment, you know."

"Just like Cunliths years ago. What century are we living in? The nineteenth?"

Going over to inspect the bow section Ishmael saw that there was extensive riveting.

"Don't you do welding?"

"Yes, we do some, but Lord Shandon, you know, believes in the traditional methods that have always served us so well in the past.

We have built some of the greatest ships on the Clyde."

"Well if things go on like this you won't be building any more, quite apart from the strike. What techniques do you think the Japs and the Germans are using? Are they antediluvian like Noah's Ark, or is it only us?"

"Ah, but are their ships of the Clyde-built quality? Clyde-built's the Roll-Royce of the shipping industry and the shipping lines will always buy quality."

"It looks as though the 'Empress of the Clyde' is first class quality, though I will look it over from stem to stern. But is Rolls-Royce keeping up to date with the latest technological developments?

Or is it still using the motors of years ago, excellent though they were? People won't buy forever just for the name. And what about price? Are our ships as cheap as the Japs? Or are our prices now uncompetitive, because of over-manning? And a topical question: do we keep to the contractual date? Or are our ships always delivered late?"

"Well, as I said, Mr McCulloch, we'll never keep to the contract date for the 'Empress of the Clyde'."

"It seems to me you are contradicting yourself. One minute you say Clyde-built will last for ever, and at the same time you lament that the industry's on the way out."

"Yes, but …"

"Yes, but nothing. We haven't the time for futile speculation. And I'm telling you the 'Empress of the Clyde' will be built on time."

"That's impossible …"

"Do you want to bet? A case of whisky to a bottle. If it's on time, you give me a bottle. If it isn't, I give you a case. How about that?"

"I'll take you on, but I shouldn't. It's like taking sweets from a child."

"We'll see about that. Now where's the canteen and the wash rooms?"

"There aren't any. Lord Shandon wouldn't allow canteens as they're places for plotting strife, he says. As for wash rooms, we haven't got the money. This isn't a five star hotel you know."

"Is that so? We'll see about that too."

Ishmael spent the rest of the day inspecting the hull of the

'Empress of the Clyde,' the hold, decks, cabins, bridge, galleys, public rooms and equipment. He could see that the quality was undoubtedly first class, even if it included an anomalous mixture of riveting and arc welding. He noted down what had to be done. There was a lot to do, but he was sure it could be done in time. Provided, of course, he could get the men back to work.

By the time he had finished it was getting late. The gaffer had left for home hours earlier. Which was a relief. Ishmael could well imagine how he would have antagonised the Glasgow workers. Above all with that English, public school accent. Not to mention his bowler hat. Ishmael couldn't help a sardonic smile as he passed the poster with the gaffer attending to Shandon's posterior.

Exhausted by his day's inspection Ishmael called in at the Highland Fling before tramping back in the gloaming to the House of the Islands. The pub was empty and about to close. Condescendingly putting up a double dram and a chaser, the barman complained that the strike at Shandons was good for trade during the week but a disaster at weekends.

Ishmael said nothing. He was reflecting that it was as well he had insisted on having no contact with Shandon until the date of the launch. And that he had rejected Sheila's entreaties to stay with them at the Lodge. Now, as always, he was determined to be independent. And he knew it was the necessary condition for the 'Empress of the Clyde' to be completed and launched on that date when the Queen was to preside. It was all still arranged, and at Ishmael's demand had not been cancelled.

"Terrible trouble they got there" the barman volunteered, when Ishmael banged down his whisky glass for a refill, "there'll be a full turnout o' the strikers the morra tae meet the new general manager. He's in for a rough time. I feel sorry for him."

★

On reaching Shandons in the morning, two hours before the strike meeting, dressed in dungarees and his old tweed jacket, Ishmael was at once accosted by the ex-general manager.

"Your bowler, Sir" he said, proffering the hat obsequiously to

Ishmael, "and, eh, wouldn't a dark suit be more fitting? There's a gentleman's outfitters in the centre of the town. It's only five minutes away."

With a glance of contempt at the wretched gaffer, Ishmael grabbed the bowler and marched rapidly to the end of the slipway, past the towering superstructure of the 'Empress of the Clyde' and kicked the bowler hat high into the air so that it fell into the oily waters of the Clyde. It floated away whirling round and bobbing up and down ignominiously.

Ishmael then called the foremen to a brief meeting telling them to stand by the proposals he would make when addressing the men. Or else. He ordered the head foreman to get a three-shift rota made out immediately, two hundred men on each.

"What times, sir?" asked the astonished functionary in a weak whining voice.

"Six a.m. to two p.m.

Two p.m. to ten p.m.

Ten p.m. to six a.m."

Ishmael answered curtly.

"But we've never had a three-shift system, sir."

"Well, we're having it now. Get cracking."

The foremen looked at Ishmael doubtfully, one grinning behind his hand and nudging his neighbour.

"He's only a bairn" he whispered, "you'll never get the blokes tae obey."

Faced by Ishmael's cold stare, he removed his grin and his hand, suspending judgement. But just then Ishmael caught the eye of another foreman, a small man who was looking at him sideways with clenched teeth. He appeared strange, even insane. However, short of time, Ishmael dismissed the foremen with orders to report to his office ½ an hour after the meeting.

When they had left, Ishmael made a phone call to the man with the lopsided face at the Glasgow office. His last words before hooking up the old-fashioned receiver on the wall were:

"Don't argue. By twelve tomorrow without fail, or you'll be for the high jump. Get Shandon's authority and get on with it. Immediately. Is that quite clear?"

The strike meeting was arranged for half past ten that morning to coincide with the opening of 'The Highland Fling' at ten. It was already packed. The pub had a dirty 100-yard terrace frontage on the murky Clyde waterfront, with ancient green tiled tables and wicker chairs. It was jammed in between Shandons and a warehouse by the railway line that served Shandons and Cunliths at Port Glasgow.

It now being a quarter past ten Ishmael edged his way unremarked into The Highland Fling, fighting his way through the throng. Having ordered his dram there was a tap on his shoulder.

"What brings you here, my friend?" asked a gritty old voice.

It was 'Cloth Cap.'

"And you?" Ishmael asked.

"I've just come alang tae see who this new manager is" 'Cloth Cap' answered. "Ye ken I'm retired the noo. He's got a right job on. They're takin' bets o' ten tae one he will nae last the day."

Ishmael downed his dram, which 'Cloth Cap,' winking at the barman, had paid for, and shook his hand, saying

"I'll be seeing you after the meeting if you're in here, and we'll have another. But excuse me now. I've got an appointment."

The barman and 'Cloth Cap' exchanged puzzled glances as Ishmael left.

STRIKE

Ishmael plunged through the milling mob of workers in the yard and rapidly mounted the launch platform in front of the 'Empress of the Clyde' with its missing bow section. He was faced by about six hundred sceptical, leering faces. About to address them, he was met by mocking heckling.

"Where's yer bowler? Hey, ye cannae speak wi' oot yer bowler!"

This produced roars of laughter, but when it subsided Ishmael tried again to speak. This time he was halted by screams of

"Pip! Pip! Are ye gaun tae hunt a fox the day?"

Ishmael gesticulated for silence. Then a booming voice called out

"Sugar foot!"

When the laughter and jeers made it possible, Ishmael stretched out his arm with his forefinger pointing at the huge man who had insulted him.

"Hud yer wheesht! Or come up here and I'll sort you out, you big cissy."

"Get him, Billy!" roared the mob. "Get the f….bastard! Go on, up ye go an' knock him aff yon platform. C'mon, Big Billy, we're waitin' on ye!"

'Big Billy' was an enormous man in his forties with the bulging biceps of a riveter. Slowly he made his way to the platform ladder and cumbrously climbed it to raucous cheers, towering over Ishmael. It was a case of David and Goliath, but Ishmael called out

"C'mon then, let's see what you can do!"

'Big Billy' advanced to the middle of the platform and swung a colossal fist wildly at Ishmael who ducked under it and gave 'Big Billy' a hard left and a right to the solar plexus that left the giant gasping. What neither 'Big Billy' nor any of the spectators knew was that Ishmael had been welterweight boxing champion at Glasgow Academy and had nearly killed a man in a bout in the army.

Ishmael didn't pause. He closed in, taking advantage of 'Big Billy's' breathlessness and hammered a terrible tattoo on his liver, which brought Billy to his knees. Unknown to Ishmael he was suffering from cirrhosis of the liver, like so many other shipyard workers, from chronic whisky drinking. Ishmael hurried to support the giant as he tottered against the platform guard rails, when to his amazement Billy reached out his arm and gasping shook Ishmael by the hand. The handshake was the only thing that hurt Ishmael.

There was uproar amongst the crowd, some cheering, others urging 'Big Billy' to have another go. But the general verdict was that it must be stopped. Ishmael caught sight of 'Cloth Cap' among a sea of other elderly cloth caps waving to him from the back. He clapped Billy genially on the back and when the pandemonium had died down offered him his hand. They shook hands again to cheers, even if there were some dissenting howls.

Ishmael then got 'Big Billy' a chair intended for spectators at the launching ceremony, and prepared once again to address the workers. This time he was listened to in silence.

"You're on strike because two hundred of you are to be laid off."

At once there were enraged protests, but Ishmael raised both arms for silence.

"The two hundred will not be laid off, in spite of over-manning" he shouted. At once there were delirious cheers. Again raising his arms for silence, he continued

"But the condition is that you work a three-shift system until the 'Empress of the Clyde' is completed. And completed on time."

There were angry murmurings from the crowd, but they subsided in order to hear what was planned for them.

"Two hundred men on each of the three shifts will avoid having six men on a job that one or two can do. And it will make the work go faster. That's now urgent. And it will save those two hundred jobs until the 'Empress of the Clyde' is launched.

If it is launched on time, it's certain other orders will follow, and you'll all be in work. If it isn't finished on time, you'll all be out of a job. The yard's now got a name for overdue completion and new orders won't come here unless we can show we can do it as well as the Germans and the Japs. Clyde-built quality's the best in the world. But delay and restrictive practices are pricing us out of the market."

Ishmael's address was interrupted by the shop stewards, who demanded to be heard. He had no option but to let them speak. When he signalled assent, a pinch-faced man called Tyas jumped onto a bollard with a huge megaphone and shouted

"It's a con. You know, the usual. Strings attached tae everythin'. We're gonnae stand on our principles: nae man in this yeard's gonnae lose his job tae suit the gaffer's profits. They dinna think o' the worker that's got a mortgage on his hoose, that's got a wife an' bairns tae keep. An' I'm tellin' ye this three shifts is a con trick tae get ye back tae work till the ship's feenished, an' then what? It'll be three-shift systems forever. Have ye worked night shift? If ye have ye'll know it ruins yer digestion. Ye cannae sleep during the day, an' ye never get tae see yer friends. They call yon the grave-yard shift. An' a rotating system's worse. Yer body doesnae ken if it's comin' or goin.' One week yer dinner's in the morn, next week it's in the afternoon. And the next it's at night.

I'm tellin' ye, boys, don't touch it. It's the thin edge o' the wedge stuck intae us. It'll kill us, so it will. It'll break ye."

Tyas was a forceful leader and a clever speaker. His declamation was greeted by cheers and angry shouts of solidarity. But knowing his timing to a 't,' Tyas jumped off the bollard to allow another union leader to oppose Ishmael's plan. And another. And another.

The tone of these harangues became more and more overtly political, and had considerable success in their rabble-rousing intent. Ishmael realised that if he didn't stop them in their tracks he would lose control of the meeting. He returned to the front of the platform and raised both arms for silence, but was met with a further barrage of catcalls and jeers. He could see that the protests were by no means universal but coming from certain well-defined sections of the crowd, led by Tyas and the three other union activists.

Ishmael turned up the volume of the loudspeaker and let out a tremendous bellow demanding silence. But still the cliques under the control of the shop stewards kept up a barrage of barracking. Ishmael was wondering what more he could do when all of a sudden there was a hush. Looking round, to his astonishment he saw that

'Big Billy' Kennedy was standing behind him in the centre of the platform with an arm raised above his head.

"Ye say ye want a democratic workplace" he yelled to the leaders, "but whit ye want is a dictatorship run by yerselves. Shut yer gobs an' let's hear whit the manager has tae say."

A sullen silence continued. Ishmael took the front of the rostrum again, this time to a volley of cheers. He looked to see where they came from. It was from the back, amongst the older workers. He could see 'Cloth Cap,' in a sea of other cloth caps, enthusiastically waving encouragement. He wasted no time in taking up his address again and changing tactics. In view of the political assault by the union leaders he decided to confront them head on. If reason couldn't win the day, maybe an emotional appeal would.

"Stand up at the front, the union leaders so everyone can see you" he called. Some advanced arrogantly, others sheepishly, but all looked taken aback.

"Face the men" Ishmael ordered. "Now raise your arms with palms open. Look at their hands" he urged the rank and file workers. "Soft, white, aren't they? Have these workers' leaders ever done a day's work in their lives? They talk about the rigours of shift work. But how do they know? What have they ever done except sit in luxurious offices with leather armchairs and heating. While you have to face the cold and the rain, the deafening noise and the fumes of the yard. And whose money are they living on, with their big, fat salaries? Who pays for their life of luxury? You do! They wallow in luxury on your union contributions. And they are going to wreck Shandons. One of the greatest shipyards on the Clyde. That's what they want, because their motives are political. Their boss is in the Kremlin. Haven't you seen the hammer and sickle on two of those posters at the gates? They want Scotland to be a communist satellite like Poland, Romania or Czechoslovakia. Their idea is that no one should have anything that everyone can't have. So they want to destroy this yard, once the most prosperous on the Clyde. Their game is to make it unprofitable by gross over-manning and when it sinks, then have a political take over. When it's rock bottom bankrupt.

And what'll happen to you? You'll lose your TV's, you'll lose your cars. Those of you that have got houses will lose them. How will there be money from a bankrupt shipyard? And if you pay rent you'll be evicted. They'll have every family living in one room like the Russian working-class. In flats without heating. We'll all be equal then. Equal in squalor and misery. But they'll be the boss class, your union leaders, just as in Russia. They'll be the ones with limousines and shofoors. They'll be living in mansions in Glesga, with summerhouses in Helensburgh.

While you'll have nothing. Not even jobs because by then the Germans and the Japs will have your jobs. The great shipyards of the Clyde will go under. You're already paid more than double what the Japs get. And the Koreans are coming up. They'll not even get a quarter of your wages. So whose ships will the great shipping lines buy? The technologically advanced and cheaper ships built in the Far East and several European yards still, or the expensive Scottish ships still using riveting and arc-welding that never keep to the contracted date? It's impossible to pay you more in these times. And keep on six men to do what a machine can do in a sixth of the time. The union leaders keep telling us we must invest in advanced technology. But when it is installed, they refuse to allow it to be used.

I'm telling you, for all its good quality, Clyde-built will be a thing of the past if the political apparatchiks have their way. Have you no eyes that you can't see what's going on? Have you no ears that you can't listen to sense, to what's in your own interest? Do you want to see the de-industrialisation of Scotland? Because when the shipyards close, the steel mills will close. And what will Scotland be left with? Red Robbo's destroying the British motor industry and its many factories and outlets in Scotland. The Germans, Japs and Koreans are jumping in over our industrial corpses. Yet a few years ago the British motor industry was the number one exporter in the world. And so was the British ship building industry until a few years ago. We surpassed even the Americans in both fields.

Have you no pride in Clyde-built? I don't need to tell you the great battleships and warships that beat the Germans were built here during devastating German air raids. Many of you built those ships. And many of you built the great liners, the envy of the world, such as the 'Queen Mary' and the 'Queen Elizabeth.'

Do you want to lose all that? Or are we going to get the 'Empress of the Clyde' built, and built on time? It can still be done. And as I told you, there will be no lay-offs. The two hundred men marked for dismissal will be employed on the three shifts. Vote for them. Save their jobs. And your own. It's for you to decide. Take the vote, shop stewards. And no hanky-panky.

Yes, means we work.

No, means we're finished."

A cheer went up from maybe half the men. Many of the old hands were in tears. The others remained sullenly silent.

"Christ!" said Ishmael to himself with a wry grin. "I've turned into a demagogue! I didn't know I had it in me." Ishmael had brought out all the fearsome language picked up in the H.L.I. barrack room, which amazed the strikers and even shocked some of the older hands.

The vote was counted. And checked. It was 304 to 296 for going back to work. Ishmael had worked the miracle and won them over. But by a grimly slender margin. There was a tremendous roar of triumph by those in favour. But Ishmael raised his arms once more and the men became silent.

"Work begins the day after tomorrow. The foremen will post notices this afternoon with the shifts allocated. I didn't want to tell you before the vote" he called out jubilantly, "but from tomorrow two canteens and four washrooms will be assembled. They'll be 'Portakabins,' quickly assembled buildings and they'll be ready the day after tomorrow when work begins.

The canteens'll be dry, and there'll be no howfs in the yard. But of course, out of hours, there's 'The Highland Fling.'"

There was a really rousing cheer this time. Ishmael shook 'Big Billy's' hand again and off they went to 'The Highland Fling.'

★

ALL HELL LET LOOSE

The new shift system began at 6.0 in the morning but Ishmael arrived an hour earlier to supervise the final arrangements. The day before had been a hectic rush with all the shipyard plumbers and electricians to get the washroom and canteen bases set up besides the arc lights for night work. When the hooter sounded at six the two hundred workers trudged in with billycans clanking at their belts. The Portakabins had arrived and the men stared with awe at the impressive array of huts.

"He's a guy guid organiser, this new maanager" and other similar comments were made as the men took up position at their multifarious tasks. By 6.30 the yard was organised pandemonium. The din of hammering, drilling, riveting, the groaning of the vast cranes swivelling, the foul smells of effluent and the fumes of welding filled the thick air. The yard was like a huge infernal cave.

Ishmael did a tour of inspection with Shandon's chief foreman, descending into the bowels of the ship where the boilermakers were rounding off their work. The fumes and dust here were almost asphyxiating and the murky atmosphere of the hubbub was punctuated by bronchial coughs and on getting close to workers what sounded like terminal wheezes. There was a stench of urine and, turning a corner they came across a boilermaker relieving himself into a bilge pump sump, which stank.

"Why don't you use the new toilets in the wash rooms?" Ishmael angrily asked the worker, sheepish at being caught in the act.

"Well, ya see sirr, there's them auld reekin' toilets in the yard an' all, but by the time I've climbed up an' outa the hull it might be too late. An' onyway, I'm workin' in a team, an' if I go we all lose money on piece work. Whit's mair, the gaafers haave a shithoose clerk tae time us in an' out the laavy."

On coming up for air and stopping at a section of the bow being welded there was a scream of pain as a welder collapsed backwards, one hand clamped over his eyes. He had not had his protective goggles on when he looked at the start of a weld. Blinded and in agony, he writhed on the ground before being carried off on a stretcher. But no question of being taken to hospital.

"It's 'flash' he's got, sir" the foreman told Ishmael. "It'll be days afore he caan see again an' he'll suffer as though his eyes are filled wi' sawdust."

"Aye, I know that, I've seen it happen at Cunlith's."

"An' he'll no get ony sick pay."

"He will," Ishmael countered "I'll see to that."

When they came to the riveting section Ishmael could see Big Billy driving his team of six, muscles bulging as he manipulated the very heavy rivet gun. Even with that clumsy gun, Billy could do over six hundred rivets a day; none too many in the tight time schedule. The team was so absorbed in their onerous and high speed work requiring great dexterity that they were unconscious of their manager and chief foreman's presence.

The apprentice 'rivet-boy' who had to take the white hot rivet out of the brazier and put it into the aperture for the gun to fire it, with a falsetto curse dropped the rivet onto the ground when his tongs slipped.

"Come on now, Willie, wake up, boy" chided Big Billy, "didn't ye sleep last night or whit's the matter wi' ye?"

"I was wi' a lassie" boasted the callow youth, "so I didnae sleep."

"Away ye go," bawled the scrawny woman 'hauder oan' – holder on – from the other side of the plate, "If a laassie lifted her skirt tae ye ye'd run an' tell yer mother she tried tae pee on ye."

She followed this up with a cascade of unprintable obscenities related to fitting the red hot rivet into the aperture, amid ribald guffaws from the old hands; until Big Billy cut them short.

As they moved on the foreman shouted to Ishmael above the racket

"The wummen we haave working here haave the filthiest tongues. Outdo the men every time. Though thaat Sadie is one of the least foul-mouthed."

"I suppose they feel they've got to hold their own against the men" Ishmael retorted.

It was coming to the end of the morning shift and Ishmael was curious to see what the local caterers he had contracted were offering. By the time he got there a milling crowd was at the entrance, waiting for the hooter. When its harsh and dismal moan let them off the men surged in. Self-service provided tattie pies and beans, fish and chips, haggis, tatties and neeps, besides a fry-up of egg, sausage, bacon, black pudding, beans and tomatoes with chips. All options included an outsize mug of tea with a stack of sliced bread and marge. The prices, as Ishmael had stipulated, were moderate.

"All fried except the pies and haggis" Ishmael exclaimed, "bad for their arteries."

"Excuse me, sir" said the foreman as they watched the workers cram food down their throats, "it's a deal better thaan spending all their pay in The Highland Fling, where they usually go straight off the minute the hooter goes. Half of them are suffering from malnutrition and then the alcohol goes for their livers. At least they'll get one square meal a day."

When they came out, hearing the baahing of sheep from one of the washrooms they crossed over to see what was going on. There were twenty showers in each hut, and in the nearest of these that strange baahing was followed by the mooing of cows. Looking in, they could make out about twenty bodies in the shower stalls through the clouds of steam, who now changed their refrain to the grunting of pigs and neighing of horses. So did the exhausted boilermakers, riveters, welders and crane drivers amuse themselves. It might have been a stable, a pigsty or a byre.

"Just bairns they are" the foreman laughed. As they turned to go a worker with a towel round him panted up to the foreman and said jubilantly

"It's the first hot bath I've haad in ma life, d'ye ken, Jimmy!"

"Practically none of the tenements they live in" confided the foreman when they were outside, "practically none of them haave bathrooms. There'll be a kitchen sink aand a laavy at the stairhead aand thaat's it."

The afternoon shift was pouring in when Ishmael saw a B.S.A. 350 c.c. motor cycle propped against a wall with a ragged bit of cardboard dangling from its handle bars advertising 'FOR SALE £50.'

"I'll take it" said Ishmael to the welder about to mount it and go home.

"Done, sir" said the elated worker, so Ishmael got cash from the office and paid him on the spot.

"He'll be needin' the money, sir" the foreman said. "There's thaat many o' them in debt. They drink their pay aand then they haave tae pawn their belongings."

"Aye, and I'll be needing the B.S.A." Ishmael replied. "It'll save me the long walk to Gourock. I haven't the time now. I'm going to do the rounds of the afternoon shift. Be seeing you tomorrow."

★

It was with Jock Gow, that half-crazy looking foreman who gave sidelong glances with clenched teeth that Ishmael did the check up on the two o'clock to ten shift. Jock was not a man to use two words when one would do and seemed both morose and sceptical as they inspected joiners, electricians and plumbers doing final work before the great ship sailed. Everything seemed to be going well as they surveyed the work of welders, pressers and caulkers. But when they came to the riveters, things were going hopelessly slowly.

It was the Tyas team that was making practically no progress. It didn't take Jock Gow long to realise they were deliberately going slow. He began by grabbing the rivet gun and demonstrating how it could be done in double quick time, the ponderous tool seeming light in his strong hands. As he did so, he gave the riveters those deadly looks sideways and made the rivet man get it white hot out of the brazier in a flash and the whole team working as they had never done before, himself again and again firing the heavy gun in perfect sequence. The whole team except Tyas.

Tyas himself managed to be the odd man out and both Jock and Ishmael could see that he was attempting to contrive an accident. Jock lifted an elbow to his face, as though he would hit him.

"What's the game, eh? Ye doan't want the ship feenished on time, dae ye? You an' yer malingering crowd. Just watch it!"

Tyas backed down, and Ishmael knew that Jock wanted to give Tyas his books on the spot. Sack him. But he could tell that Jock was weighing up the trouble the sacking of a shop steward at this point would cause. Another strike. Just what Tyas wanted. Then the ship would never be launched.

But the look Tyas gave both Ishmael and Jock as they moved on, Jock having put the fear of hell into that group, was ominous.

With otherwise relatively minor mishaps in a yard notorious for serious accidents the first day of the new shift system passed off well. Ishmael had thought of staying over the night shift too but Jock Gow protested

"Are ye maad, maan? Ye cannae dae twenty-four hours an' expect tae see things is going as they should be. Away ye go now, get tae yer bed the nicht an' leave it tae me. I caan dae two shifts as well aas I caan one. An' ye'll need tae be on top form the morra."

In spite of, or perhaps partly because of, Jock Gow's not altogether respectful attitude to his boss, Ishmael could see that Jock was a man he wouldn't find in a thousand. He decided, as he left the yard with Gow in charge, that he would promote him to chief foreman.

After working those two consecutive eight-hour shifts at Shandons Ishmael rode off on his old BSA 350cc to the House of the Islands.

It was a cold wet night and Ishmael was glad to accept Jock Gow's admonition to go home after two shifts to keep up energy for tomorrow. The rain was now torrential and by the time Ishmael got to the House of the Isles on that oily old motorbike he was soaked to the skin. It was nearly eleven o'clock.

Going straight up to his bedroom in the silent house he had just pulled off his wet shirt when there was a tap on the door. Before he had time to answer the handsome Indian landlady entered bearing a huge cardboard box fastened with red bands of tape. She paused breathlessly, putting the package on the bed, gazing with undisguised admiration at Ishmael's naked torso.

"This came for you by special delivery" she said with that ever-alluring smile that was both suggestive and maternal. When she had left, with her habitual backward glance, Ishmael took out of the box a large packet wrapped in cotton wool containing a porcelain figurine of an angel, which was broken and a variety of other expensive trinkets. Dismayed, he then withdrew from the bottom of the box a luxurious fleece-lined leather jacket and a printed card with Sheila's spidery scrawl.

'Ishmael. May your spirit fly to heaven and back and may the jacket keep you warm these cold wet days. Sheila.'

Ishmael was enraged. He could imagine her walking elegantly round R.W. Forsyth's followed by an obsequious manager, as she indicated one capricious purchase here, another there. He was minded to smash the decapitated figurine and the other expensive trinkets. As for the fleece-lined jacket, he decided what he would do with that.

But once dry and warmly dressed he went down to the dining room where his supper had been left cold on the table. He was surprised to find the big German sitting at the table devouring a plate of ham.

"How is it you're here so late?" Ishmael asked.

"Vent to see 'Othello' at ze Citizen's Theatre in Glasgow."

"Did you go alone?"

"Vell, yes I did, ant no, I didn't. I inwite French nurse to meet me at ze door of ze Citizen's but ven I arrive she is not zere. I wait a qvuarter of an hour ant zen I go in by myself."

"Aren't you very strict about time? Women are always late."

"Ja! She vould be painting herself ant putting on ze perfume to haf ze goot shcmell. Never vait for ze woman. Just a qvuarter of an hour."

"You're hard on them, aren't you?"

"Gott im Himmel! No. Ze voman live ze powder puff life. Ant ze Englishmen ant ze Americans zey pander to zem. Ze voman is not equal to ze man. All ze history not is wrong. Othello says about Desdemona, look ze programme

"She lov'd me for ze dangers I hat pass'd

Ant I lov'd her that she did pity zem."

Zis vas ze basis of ze chivalric relation betveen men ant vomen. But now ze vomen vant all ze rights vithout ze responsibilities. Do ze vomen fight on ze battlefields to defent zeir country? Do zey do ze heavy vork in ze mines or ze oil tankers? Do zey do ze dangerous vork of ze firemen? No, no, zey haf ze powder puff life. Ze easy vork fit plenty of money. Ze voman is not a serious zing. As your Shakespeare is saying in 'Othello'

'You rise to play, ant go to bet to vork.' Hein? Ha! ha! ha! I haf it written on my programme."

At that moment Harry Feckles looked into the dining room in his baggy olive green cardigan and carpet slippers, alarmed at the sound of the German's boisterous laughter.

"Is everythin' a'right then, Mr Schleicher?"

"Ja! Ja! Zank you Mr Feckles."

When the landlord had retreated, Peter Schleicher looked up from the remains of his ham at Ishmael.

"Ze vife send him. It's a vitch! Ze other lodgers hier zey call her Lady MacBeth. She find ze Chinese vashing ze socks in ze betroom ant she is shouting

"Disgusting! Disgraceful! Very bat schmell! Go out of ze house if you are repeating zis."

Ishmael had noticed that Peter had a big green book with the title 'Law of Contract' beside him on the table and asked him if he was studying law for some exam.

"Ja! I must study ze Scottish law in Glasgow. As I zink you know I am shipping agent in Bremen ant ve haf many contracts vit ze Scottish."

Embarking on a dish of peaches, Peter asked

"By ze vay, how is ze ship going?"

"We're desperate for time. The principal trouble is the riveting. It's a slow process: one man manipulating the riveting machine and another on the reverse side of the steel holding the rivet in place. What they call the 'hauder oan.' And it's what's causing most delay."

"Haf you not ze 'Gravimax' machine? It can do ze vork of six men."

Ishmael explained how antiquated the equipment at Shandons was, and how resistant to change the men, the union leaders, the foremen were. Not to mention the Proprietor.

"How can I get a 'Gravimax?' I don't think they exist in Scotland. In fact I've never heard of them."

"Possible only exist in Germany at ze moment. Ze new invention. If you like I will send a telex to my office in Bremen ant you ze day after tomorrow vill it haf if you give me ze address."

The situation being even more desperate than Ishmael was prepared to confess even to himself, he readily and gratefully agreed. And so it was that exactly two days later a brand new 'Gravimax' arrived at the Manager's office at Shandons. German efficiency! Ishmael smiled a moment as he opened the parcel and thought of Peter's 'ekzactly a kwarter of an hour.' And wondered what happened to the French nurse.

★

First thing in the wretched cold damp morning Ishmael looked for Willie Deuchars, reinstated on general duties. When Ishmael accosted him he started guiltily, having a quiet smoke. But when Ishmael presented him with the fleece-lined leather jacket he wrapped it round himself in tears.

Going over to the riveters, as might have been expected, the introduction of the Gravimax brought out all the mulish stubbornness of the riveters. The Gravimax was demonstrated by the fearsome Jock Gow to a group of sceptical workers, under the influence of Tyas, who shouted angrily

"Ye're right. It'll do the work o' six men. An' what'll haappen tae they six? We ken well enough. They'll be oot."

"We're no haein' it" was the general verdict."

Ishmael and Jock tried to din into the workers that the Empress of the Clyde would not, and could not, be finished on time at the rate they were going. It wasn't simply the number of men on the job, but the speed with which that job would be done.

Tyas convened a meeting of shop stewards, who vetoed its use.

"Gravimax means the maximum number of graves for riveteers" called out a wag. But the silly slogan took hold and turned into a war cry. Things went from bad to worse. The mass of riveteers now refused to work at all, unless the Gravimax was hurled into the Clyde. And so two valuable days more were lost in the internecine squabbling.

But the Luddites had opposition. Big Billy, the hero of the yard in spite of his bout with Ishmael, formed up a hefty group of supporters. He took the Gravimax and showed them how much safer it was than the old teamwork of catch-boys, heater-boys, puter-ins, hauder-oans, besides left and right side riveters. With all the potential for accidents at each stage.

But reason wouldn't win the day, Ishmael could see. The two groups, those in favour under Big Billy, and those against of Tyas's powerful resistance, were headlocked like two rams. The situation was so desperate that a winning formula had to be found. And Ishmael found it in the middle of the night at Tigh An Eileann.

The riveters were all guaranteed their jobs and would be paid at the maximum piece-work rate achieved at the yard, even though some were transferred to welding.

Ishmael pointed out that riveting was anyway on the way out, and that the future was in welding. The Empress of the Clyde was to be the last ship using rivets at Shandons.

Meanwhile, three more Gravimax would be expedited urgently from Bremen, and the four men using them, would be paid at the same maximum rate as those transferred, plus bonus pro-rata on piece work.

Appealing directly to the men, in the face of opposition from the shop stewards, Ishmael narrowly won them over, with the invaluable support of Jock Gow and Big Billy.

Peter Schleicher dispatched another telex, and two days later the three Gravimax guns arrived.

SHEILA COMES TO TIGH AN EILEANN

When it seemed almost certain that the Empress of the Clyde would be launched in time, Ishmael invited Sheila to come to Tigh an Eileann one Sunday.

Sheila was all in a flutter, wondering what this could mean. She hadn't seen him since her visit to Loch Mhor. But while she was apprehensive, she was elated. Her intuition told her this was a crucial moment. So, unusually for her, she took extraordinary care of her appearance. Even debating with herself late on the Saturday night what she should wear. First trying on this dress and looking critically in the long mirror in her bedroom; then rejecting it in favour of another. In the end it was nearly three o'clock in the morning before she could decide, tripping about her bedroom to the strains of Vivaldi's Concerto in C Major for Diverse Instruments with Mandolins.

When she did appear that Sunday at midday at the House of the Islands she wore her dark green dress and a little gold collar with emeralds round her slender neck, her quaint face even paler than usual after a sleepless night but none the less fetching, her black ringlets setting off her pallor.

The Indian wife opened the door in astonishment, but welcomed Sheila with her warm smile, showing her into the communal sitting room while Harry Feckles called Ishmael.

In a moment Ishmael appeared, and he too was taken aback by the simple loveliness of Sheila, her innocence allied to the shining intelligence of her dark brown eyes.

"You have resuscitated, Ishmael" she exclaimed with wonder at the change from his desperate appearance at Loch Mhor.

"I had no alternative. But I've become something of a machine."

Just then the gong sounded loudly for lunch, the buxom Molly giving it the full enthusiastic force of her plump right arm.

"Hello, hello!" rumbled Miss Jacobs from her separate table, "have we a new lodger here?"

The Chinese shot discreet and rapid glances at Sheila, while the boisterous German Peter Schleicher looked at her in undisguised admiration. Sheila was a little shy and nervous but Peter soon established a jolly conviviality that included our friend 'bringing home the cabbages,' Mr Frank Eason, who gurgled, half drunk

"Ye're a wee smaasher, laasie!" in his acquired Glaswegian.

Before Sheila could acknowledge this compliment Molly burst in, as usual banging the dining room door against the wall and triumphantly planting a huge ashet with a vast whole cod in the centre of the table before Peter Schleicher, who usually served the other lodgers.

Molly first stared open-mouthed at Sheila, then ogled the blond German, obviously in good form after her Saturday off and having, perhaps, been 'tooched oop' by her boyfriend.

But suddenly there was a roar from Peter as he beat his great fist on the table.

"Schtinke! Schtincke! Schtinke!"

And there was a stink. The great fish was reeking, obviously more than a little 'off.'

In the consternation that followed, Molly burst into tears, which ran in rivulets down her heavily made-up cheeks, and flounced out of the room with a scream. The Chinese silently formed their mouths into the letter O, while Miss Jacobs reprimanded the German for

"Most unseemly behaviour!"

Sheila let out a peal of laughter, perhaps on account of nervousness, which caused Miss Jacobs to scrutinise her through her lorgnette.

And then, inevitably, Lady MacBeth appeared with a countenance as black as thunder. But when she realised that it was the big handsome German who had caused the commotion she changed in an instant to smiling apologies, and tinned salmon mayonnaise was rapidly substituted.

"It was my husband who went to the market and those fishwives must have bamboozled him" she laughed in velvet tones, gazing benignly at Peter Schleicher.

Sheila and Ishmael set off on a walk that afternoon towards

Greenock, but as soon as they had glimpsed the magnificent superstructure of the Empress of the Clyde on the horizon they turned back.

"That's enough on my day off" said Ishmael. "Come on, we'll go for a ride on my motorbike."

So they roared off from the House of the Islands along the shore of the Firth of Clyde, Sheila riding pillion, clinging on to Ishmael's waist. She had never ridden on a motor cycle before and the incongruity of her elegant get-up on that oily old machine emitting clouds of black smoke gave Ishmael perverse satisfaction.

While for Sheila it was a breathless adventure as the wind unravelled her ringlets.

"Are you going to…?" she shouted in Ishmael's ear.

"Yes, I am. I want you to marry me, Sheila, and I want to marry you. You'll have to live on egg and chips."

"I know! I know! I know!" Sheila screamed rapturously.

"No sacrifice! No mission! No martyrdom! I'm not Schweitzer!" shouted Ishmael. But he got a tremendous slap from Sheila's right hand in a moment of hatred. Hamish swerved. A car was coming and the B.S.A. headed downhill through the trees towards the shore, throwing them both clear to tumble to a halt.

"Oh Ishmael! I'm terribly sorry" gasped the trembling Sheila, picking herself up and running towards him, who seeing that neither suffered more than a few bruises, took Sheila in his arms and hugged her with such strength that she would have protested had she not been so happy. Her moment of hatred changed in an instant to rapture.

"I'm so very sorry" Sheila whispered, her head on his shoulders.

"You were right, Sheila. Don't be apologetic. What does it matter?"

And he laughed, looking at the picturesque bruise over Sheila's right eye.

Ishmael picked up the battered B.S.A., the motor still running, which had nothing worse than twisted handlebars and an impressive dent in the petrol tank. They walked through the trees to the shore with all the relief of what might have been.

"When Ishmael? When?"

"As soon as you like, once the ship's launched."

"Should I ask Mamma and Dadda to make arrangements?"

"Arrangements! That sounds grim. But yes, do whatever has to be done. It isn't important."

DEATH IN LIFE

At last the yard was working at full capacity. But the din, smells, fumes and filth everywhere were almost intolerable. Besides the ever present danger of lethal accidents. And yet this was the life of these hundreds of grey-faced men, half deaf, with 'yellow finger,' bronchial, some with incipient lung collapse from asbestosis, others with rotten livers from whisky. Many of them, in spite of the prohibition, got their whisky in the yard, and when Ishmael came across a 'howff' or drinking den, the lookout having failed to see him coming, he had to order its closure. But he knew they'd re-open it in another place in no time. How else, he reflected, could a life time of labour in this bedlam, with the rain and the cold in winter, the constant threat of management lock-outs, strikes, lay-offs and sackings at the whim of a petty foreman, how else could life be bearable. With the pittance of pay and the squalor of home life in the tenements.

As he made his way from the welding of the great bow section to the riveters, he saw a circle of men apparently playing some kind of football. When he got closer he was sickened to find they were kicking a big live rat from one side of the circle to the other, the wretched creature surrounded by grinning faces. Maddened with rage, Ishmael broke up the circle, offering to sack any man who wasn't at his work immediately. They dispersed sullenly and the rat lay gasping on the ground, one of its eyes knocked out if its socket but hanging on, blood oozing from its mouth. He did the only thing he could, and ended its agony with the heel of his boot. One rat in an infestation of hundreds, some so big and fierce they killed yard cats.

Ishmael worked night shift too, so that the men knew he could and would do it. And so that he could make sure there were no slackers and dodgers. One night a crane sling carrying sheet metal for the bow section broke, the steel crashing amongst a group of workers in the circle of the arc light. By a stroke of providence it hit no one. But it was only good luck this time.

There were two more accidents, one affecting Ishmael. As he passed below a group working high on the bow section a rivet fell with a glancing blow to his head. He suffered only a nasty cut but didn't even bother to get it dressed or disinfected. It happened to be Tyas's group. Who knows whether it was accidental or malevolent? For that reason many managers wore virtually bulletproof bowlers.

Hatred between management and workers was endemic in all shipyards on the Clyde.

The other accident was serious but miraculously not lethal. When at last the bow section had been hoisted into place and joined to the ship's hull all that remained was painting. And when it came to painting EMPRESS OF THE CLYDE on the bows, the painter slipped off the greasy planks of the precarious roped cradle hanging from bollards and would certainly have been killed if he had not fallen onto a bale of mattresses on the quay side, ready for the liner's cabins. As it was, he ended up with several broken ribs and his left knee was jerked out of joint.

The result was that the painters refused to finish the job. All that remained was to complete EMPRESS O…, which was when the unfortunate painter had fallen. There was only one thing for it. Ishmael grabbed the spray gun apparatus, clambered over the side and shimmied down one of the ropes to the shaky trellis. It took him a couple of hours to finish it. It was just as well he didn't look down. The drop to the quayside was 80 feet.

But the ship was ready at last, and the myriad trades: upholsterers, plumbers, electricians, carpenters, French polishers and others who had to put the final touches to the ship had completed their tasks. Once launched there would still be much to be done aboard, but that would be, apart from the turbines, primarily cosmetic. And the Empress of the Clyde was to be launched tomorrow.

★

THE AMAZING FEAT OF THAT 'REMARKABLE YOUNG MAN'

It was a beautiful late August morning. The City of Glasgow Police Pipe Band were playing a pibroch on the quayside in front of the Empress of the Clyde, which was decked out in St. Andrew's and union flags. So too was the launch platform from which Ishmael had harangued the workers and had his bout with 'Big Billy.'

At the front of the platform stood Her Majesty the Queen, dressed in a navy blue skirt and jacket and, for once, without an extravagant hat. Today she wore a matching navy blue balmoral, which became her well, with a pheasant's feather fastened in the silver cap badge. On her right was the Queen Mother in her familiar powder blue outfit and net veil, giving little waves and smiles in the direction of any cameras she happened to see. And there were many.

To the left of the Queen, the characterless Secretary of State for Scotland, dressed in an ill-hanging kilt, was flanked by the Lord Provost of Glasgow, rubicund, beaming and slightly drunk, festooned in chains and seals of authority. Shandon towered over the orotund Lord Provost, who delivered a lengthy eulogy of the Queen and Shandon's yard, while Shandon and the chairman of Cunard, the new owner of the Empress of the Clyde, exchanged pleasantries.

Behind them motley Scottish aristocrats were hobnobbing with the Duke of Edinburgh, the scholarly Duke of Argyll doddering absentmindedly among his peers while the brassy Duchess ogled the smooth government Minister for Trade and Industry whom she had reputedly seduced, like legion others, in the ducal castle at Inveraray. A security camera had been installed but did not reveal the head of the lover. The duke's millions had given her a wonderfully gay life and she exuded the joy of living. Although the government had dispatched the Minister for publicity purposes, it had contributed almost nothing to the fortunes of the Scottish shipbuilding industry.

The six hundred workmen who had built the 70,000 ton liner thronged the quay below, and thousands of 'ordinary' Scots lined the banks of the River Clyde, including 'Cloth Cap' (Jimmy Anderson) and 'SNP' (Sandy Logan.)

When the Lord Provost's preamble eventually came to an end, a call for silence was made over the public address system, and the Queen gave a short speech praising the shipyard management and workers, and the Cunard Line for their faith in 'Clyde-Built,' acknowledged to be the best quality world-wide.

She then pulled a little lever, which sent the traditional bottle of champagne smashing against the bows of the ship, and it began its slow progress down the slipway.

Ishmael was below supervising the work of the carpenters who winched away the blocks that held the ship upright, the holding chains slowly and steadily loosening to ensure the safe progress of the great ship into the water.

There was a terrifying moment when one of the blocks obstinately refused to move owing to a jammed capstan, which might result in the ship entering the Clyde lopsided, and possibly turning turtle. But the foreman carpenter, at Ishmael's urgent command, rallied his team who with crowbars, sledgehammers and axes, succeeded in freeing the recalcitrant block in the nick of time. A highly dangerous manoeuvre, which could have cost them their lives.

None of this was evident to the cheering spectators, though the yard workmen were only too well aware of the threatening disaster, and the drowning of those on board. An occurrence not unknown on the River Clyde.

But once the Empress of the Clyde was safely and majestically afloat and being pulled westward by tugs, the shipyard workers joined in the cheering, waving their cloth caps, some gnarled old hands in tears. And even a few of the younger ones.

While the V.I.Ps on the platform began to look forward to the regal lunch in St. George's Square, Shandon pointed out the figure of Ishmael to the Cunard chairman, recounting

"The amazing feat of this remarkable young man."

For the first time for years a Shandon ship had been launched on time.

"Keep him on" said the Cunard chairman, "and we'll be back to you for our next order."

Lady Dalry, standing just behind them heard every word, and craned her elegant neck over the guard rail to observe this 'remarkable young man.'

★

Ishmael was, in fact, invited to that regal luncheon, but sent a message to Shandon declining. He had received the official invitation, which included the menu. In deference to Her Majesty's well known predilection for the use of French in culinary matters, and the foolish Scotch belief that the French were great admirers of their country (hence the idiotic plates on the back of Scottish cars proclaiming 'Ecosse') the whole menu was in French, though the courtiers and civil servants had had difficulty with the first item.

Cock-a-leekie soup was translated as 'La soupe du coq qui fait l'eau'. Ishmael scanned the next dishes, screwed the invitation up, and threw it into a litter bin, spitting out,

"Petty British snobbery."

ISHMAEL AS ALWAYS INDEPENDENT

When the formalities were over and those invited to lunch with the Queen were being driven away in limousines, Shandon's chauffeur was sent to collect Ishmael who was standing at the back of the throng. He told old Tam he would make his own way to the Lodge, in his own time. He was to join Ella and Sheila for late afternoon tea at Shandon Lodge prior to the ceilidh at 8.0 p.m. Meanwhile he was to have kicked his heels at the Lodge.

On the contrary, he wandered the streets of Glasgow, passing the elegant ladies in fussy veiled-net hats tapping along in their high heels to tea at Trerons, Coplands and Pettigrew & Stevens, where superannuated musicians forming trios and quartets played Strauss waltzes while cakes, scones and empire biscuits were served on three-tiered stands. In Sauchiehall Street Ishmael came across a tiny old man brandishing a bunch of flowers, calling out "Primrosees, primrosees, lovely primrosees" to the giggles of incredulous boarding school boys, who knew better English, thronging round him. If only to put an end to this performance, Ishmael bought the primroses, pushing them into his pocket and forgetting about them. He then dropped into The Highlandman's Umbrella for a pint and a stovie before riding his battered BSA to Shandon Lodge.

'Cloth Cap' and 'SNP' were established at the bar. But the moment they saw Ishmael 'SNP' came breathlessly running up to him gasping "In the name of Robert the Bruce, Ishmael, Jimmy says you fair scunnered the strikers at Shandons. F… marvellous the way ye brought them round. Aand we were both aat the launching o' The Empress of the Clyde. But of course ye didna see us. You were thaat busy wi' getting the ship launched."

"Ye worked wonders" said 'Cloth Cap,' who immediately ordered three drams and chasers. "Here's tae ye, Ishmael!"

"I'll says thaat an all, Ishmael, ye wonder worker" burst out Sandy Logan, jumping up and down with excitement. "Listen,

Ishmael, we've got a by-election at Edinburgh, Leith on Friday week. Will ye no come an' gie us support aat yon meeting: old ware-hoose, corner o' Dock Street aand Commercial Street. Ye will come, will ye not? An' gie us a spell-binder aas ye did aat Shandons. We're desperate. The Labour baastards'll win out-right if ye dinna come tae the rescue. Just belt it oot, Ishmael, afore our official caandidate gets on yon plaatform… ye will, will ye not, Ishmael? An gie him a guid warmer-up. He's no very strong aa speaker, tho' his heart's right wi' us, aand wi' auld Scotland."

Ishmael ordered a round of Glenmorangies and looked closely at Sandy Logan, while Cloth Cap's eye winked at him from behind.

"I'll need to think about it" said Ishmael distantly. "As you know, while I'm in this world I'm determined, in spite of Jimmy Anderson (who winked again in response) I am determined to be an island and I will not become a member of any political party. But … but as the cause is for Scotland I might act as a supporter. Corner of Dock Street and Commercial Street you said, Friday week. Time?"

"12 o'clock midday."

"I knew you'd do it" whooped Sandy Logan, "I kenned ye would."

"I said I'd think about it, think it over, Sandy. And if I decide to back you, I'll be there. But don't bet on it. If I'm not there it'll be for personal reasons."

"Ye're right tae think aboot it carefully, Ishmael, bide yer time, maan" said Jimmy Anderson looking cautiously over the rim of his glass.

And with a solemn 'Slainte' from all three, Ishmael left them to make his way to Shandon Lodge and the Ceilidh.

*

When he eventually reached the Lodge he was taken aback by the enormous marquees in the grounds, dwarfing even the huge doocot by the drive. Innumerable flunkeys were scurrying about one or two pausing to eye the incongruous figure carrying a Gladstone bag and tramping resolutely towards the house. Ishmael had brought his highland outfit and bagpipes for the ceilidh that was to be the prelude to the wedding tomorrow.

Before he got to the Lodge itself Ella spied him from what they called the summerhouse, a romantic retreat by a stream two or three hundred yards from the main house, in a leafy bower of aspens. She darted out to waylay him, putting her arm through his, saying

How is it we've never met. And tomorrow you take my daughter, you buccaneer!"

Immediately she took a strong liking to Ishmael and he to her. That mischievous sparkle in those black eyes and her conspiratorial chuckle as she told him she had avoided the Lord Provost's reception and the regal lunch at the near cost of a divorce from Shandon, gave them an affinity he had not expected from her family.

They sat at a rustic table on the verandah of the summerhouse, which Ishmael noted with some misgiving was as big as his mother's house in Lentilloch. Just then a taxi drew up at the main house and Mrs Irene McCulloch and Seonaid, both dressed in McCulloch tartan dresses got out and were received by Sheila wearing, in turn, the McCorquodale tartan with a little glengarry perched rather incongruously if fetchingly above her ringlets. There had been a heated dispute with Ella about these, Ella wanting Sheila to put her hair up. But Sheila steadfastly refused, saying her face would look like an old maid's. Secretly, she feared the impression such a sudden change might make on Ishmael though he had seen her sleek head when she swam in the bay at Loch Mhor.

There was much embracing and kissing of cheeks before Sheila led them over to the summerhouse, where they all sat down to a scrumptious tea brought out by two smiling maids in black and white uniform. Ella kept them all merry with jolly anecdotes, while Seonaid managed a few bantering sallies at Ishmael's expense, causing her mother to reprove her in mock-scolding tones. Ishmael remained silent, much observed by Ella, and with some trepidation by Sheila, who turned disconcerted glances towards him continually.

All of a sudden a great cloud of dust enveloped the drive as Shandon roared up in his old Austin Sheerline. He strode over to the summerhouse, exultant at the morning's triumph and the royal luncheon at the Town Hall. It was probably the greatest day of his life.

He shook hands with his in-laws to be, kissed Ella and Sheila, playfully cocking her glengarry to one side, where it suited her better, and warmly taking Ishmael's hand, which he had not shaken since that fatal interview. They all sat down again, much fawned on by Sheila's dark red Irish setter, Kim. After a perfunctory cup of tea, Shandon levered his great weight out of his wicker chair, saying he had a matter to attend to briefly. The Austin roared off again, leaving them all to the sort of desultory conversation of new acquaintances, with much appraisal and sizing up on all parts.

"Did you bring any salmon or venison?" quipped Seonaid facetiously to Ishmael who grimaced and reminded her he hadn't been at the estate for over a month. But Seonaid insisted on presenting him now with a long silver-mounted skeandubh wrapped in tissue paper, in sisterly affection for his betrothal. Sheila was overwhelmed, and kissed the skittish Seonaid, who embraced her warmly. And so the late afternoon passed, all parties a little nervous, Ishmael longing for a dram. Eventually he got up and going into the house got a flunkey to pour a very large whisky from the array of bottles in readiness for the ceilidh. Fortified, he rather unwillingly rejoined the women, making much of Kim, who had readily taken to him.

And then there emerged an apparition. The most beautiful Bentley convertible Ishmael had ever seen drove sedately to the house, its long, straight, sleek wing lines resplendent in a deep burgundy colour, setting off the sumptuous white leather seats to perfection. They were all amazed to see that the driver was Shandon. He parked the limousine and came over again to join them.

"Just a little something I had to collect at tea time" he said nonchalantly, winking at Ella, who was as surprised as any. It was a Bentley Continental.

"Bringing home the cabbages" muttered Ishmael with an ironic smirk.

Shandon then went to supervise preparations for the ceilidh, and Ella took Mrs McCulloch and Seonaid to show them round the house. Which left Sheila and Ishmael slightly nervously alone.

"How funny that your father should so casually slip off at tea time and come back with that magnificent Bentley" laughed Ishmael for something to say at this awkward, indeterminate time. Ishmael was astonished to see an ugly black shadow cross Sheila's face. He knew what it meant but he could not take it up. How was he to express now his shock, his repugnance at an unvoiced suspicion, an accusation that could not be less just? He had been painfully aware of her wealthy background and loathed it.

Time and again he had warned Sheila of his circumstances, of his probable perpetual poverty, which he not only did not mind but had chosen.

"You'll have to get used to egg and chips every day" he had insisted. To her romantic delight.

The insinuation of her expression, however fleeting, was unworthy of her. He seethed inwardly, clamming up and becoming morose. The more he thought about it, the more it enraged him. And as anger that could not be expressed, he felt it choking him. Abruptly he got up and walked off, Sheila hurrying after him, throwing her arms round his neck and beseeching him to tell her what she had done wrong. Which made it all the more impossible to remonstrate, without belittling both of them.

He shrugged off her arms and walked rapidly out by the loch, leaving her to go back disconsolately and only half comprehending, into the house. He hated the sight of her glengarry now, at that pert angle, and it wasn't until half an hour later, after the start of the ceilidh, that Ishmael could bring himself to make his way through the throng that had now congregated in the marquees, in the grounds and in the house itself. There were hundreds.

He headed for the house, repelled by the milling hordes pouring into the marquees. No sooner had he entered than he bumped into Shandon and Ella.

"We've been looking for you everywhere" boomed Shandon. "Come with us for a moment. We've got something to show you" added Ella, noting the look of exasperation on Ishmael's face, "I think you'll like it."

"This way, old boy" Shandon said genially, leading the little procession to the west wing.

'What in the name of the devil can it be now?' Ishmael said to himself querulously, beginning to wish he hadn't returned from his trudge along the seashore. 'Why didn't I just go?' he asked himself.

'No one would have missed me with this mob.' And then he thought of his mother and Seonaid and relented, as they passed along a glass-covered passageway leading to the west entrance. 'But I definitely don't want to see Sheila' he added to himself as a final thought, following the exuberant Ella, who kept turning to him with her jolly manner and saying teasingly

"What d'you think it is? Can you guess?"

"There! What d'you think of that?" said Shandon, flinging wide the double doors opening onto the west drive.

Ishmael could hardly believe it. He had expected some onerous obligation, perhaps an agreement to be signed or an autograph photograph of the Queen with the Empress of the Clyde. But there, in all its splendour, was a gleaming black pre-war Railton convertible, its vast engine shrouded by a long high bonnet and a heavy chromed radiator cowl.

"But you've bought two cars!" exclaimed Ishmael. "Or is this for you, Ella?" he bantered, at a loss for what to say.

"No, it isn't for me" answered Ella with her mischievous smile, "it's for a young man who longed for one in his army days in the Far East."

"But how did you know?"

"Woman's intrigue" bellowed Shandon. "Sheila told Ella, and Ella inveigled her husband, as usual, into carrying out her wishes."

He laughed heartily, clapping a great hand on Ishmael's shoulder.

"It's all yours, my boy. I had the devil of a job finding one in good condition, but I don't think it'll let you down. It's only done thirty-three thousand miles and we had it overhauled by the Rolls-Royce works. We were able to get the few genuine Railton parts that were the better for changing" he added.

"What can I say? This is what I've wanted for years. The only car I dreamt of in Korea. They sent out copies of 'Performance Cars.' How can I thank you?"

"It's just a wedding present" Ella rejoined, "and you saved us the usual headache of thinking 'what would he like?'"

"No, it's not just a wedding present. It's a symbol of my appreciation of all you did at the yard, Ishmael."

Shandon beamed, so that the dour, rough lines of his face seemed not to know where to move in this unwonted levity.

"Our thanks and blessing to you, Ishmael" said Ella. "Let me kiss you, my dear. Let's see if I can make Shandon jealous!"

And she put up her little arms, embracing Ishmael and planting a rapid kiss on each cheek while Ishmael hugged her. And shook hands again with Shandon. It was the reconciliation of the former antagonists, but Ishmael was still embarrassed.

"It's too good for me. You have been too kind. But I'll try to deserve it."

"That's enough" barked Shandon "Get into the car, old boy, and give it a trial. See if it's any good."

So Ishmael drove off along the west drive with the requisitely satisfying roar, and some grinding of gears before he got used to double de-clutching. Not to mention a near miss when he discovered that the brakes needed to be applied with full force a good hundred yards before the power of the monster could be reined in. He drove along the Gare Loch, past Finart and the whole length of Loch Long before turning back, taking the few sedate motorists he encountered by surprise as the Railton thundered past, disconcerting two old ladies in a Morris Minor and astonishing one or two farmers ambling along in Land-Rovers. He had got it up to its maximum of 100 or so miles an hour on the one long straight stretch of road, feeling breathless exhilaration as the wind streamed through his hair. By the time he parked again at Shandon Lodge the temperature gauge was high, but Ishmael's morose mood had gone.

But as he walked through the covered passageway and past the vast marquees, intending to pick up his Gladstone bag from the summerhouse and change into his kilt, he was held up by the mass of guests blocking his way, including his ex-colleagues from prep-school at Lawers House, so he remained as he was for the time being in his old tweed jacket, open-necked khaki shirt and brown flannel trousers. Particularly as he observed that his old schoolfellows were got up in comical highland dress with white socks and black bow ties.

Ishmael's father had removed him from Glasgow Academy and

sent him at ten years old to the upper class Lawers House where he found himself amongst the Scotch 'aristocracy,' in effect the plutocracy: sons of brewers, new-rich motor bus magnates, steel millers and ship-builders.

One day, as the good-looking boys at Lawers House as usual congregated round the ever popular and somewhat swarthy master, 'Gambo,' on their way to the rugby playing fields, Gambo stopped the little troupe, singling out the ugly Ishmael.

"Do you know, McCulloch, when I was with class 4A yesterday I asked them 'Who is the most unpleasant little boy in the school?'

"And do you know, McCulluch, the answer was unanimous. They all answered *unanimously*, McCulloch."

'Unanimous' was a new word to the young Ishmael, one he would never forget; and forever despise.

And of course the troupe of boys, including Gambo's handsome favourites, on their way to 'rugger' relished that epithet, one they would never let Ishmael forget. Ishmael knew then that he was apart; and did not regret it.

But on his father's death at Dunkirk his widowed mother had been forced to send him back to Glasgow Academy, unable to pay the plutocratic fees at Lawers House. Which was a stroke of luck for Ishmael, who felt an affinity with the Glaswegians as opposed to antagonism towards the plutocrats, with their posh English, which they were further to refine at English 'public schools,' those hives of expensive private education.

"I say, who's that oik?" queried Julian as Ishmael pushed past.

"God only knows" simpered the Hon. Crispin, Viscount Dalry's son "Probably an under-gardener, heugh, heugh."

"That's putting it a bit high" giggled Giles of the gaiters, "by the looks of him I'd say he was a lavotrah cleanah, don't you know?"

"Quite wrong, chaps" the Hon. Hugh McNab corrected. "He's actualah our Sheila's betrothed, would you believe!"

"Must have taken leave of her senses" chortled Crispin.

"Heah, heah!" echoed Julian Colquhon in prime parliamentary mode.

"Gosh! If only the boys of the Bullingdon were heah we'd have him in the pond in no time" asserted the Hon. Hugh, thinking of his simply splendid Oxford thrashes. "Sartorial solecism! Eh?"

"I don't think I'd try if I were you," said the modest John Robson, who happened to overhear this exchange as he himself tried to edge his way through the throng of the aristocracy. "He caught a gang of armed poachers in the Highlands single-handed and had them begging for mercy."

"Christmas!" said Crispin. "I say, weren't you Sheila's, what shall we say, fiancé?"

"I was never quite that" answered Robson resignedly, "and I cede to the better man. For if Sheila's chosen him, then that's what he is."

And he passed on.

"Bloody wet!" laughed Giles, while Robson was still within hearing.

"Wight evewy time" crowed Julian.

"Not to worry" answered Crispin, "there are as many fish in the sea as eva came out of it, heugh! heugh! though not all of them have her expectations, eh!"

At that moment Ishmael and John Robson met at the far exit from the marquee, both relieved to get away. John offered Ishmael his hand and his congratulations, saying

"You're a better man than I am, Gunga Din!"

Ishmael was as surprised by the quotation as he was embarrassed by the eulogy, but he said to John

"Sheila always speaks very well of you. Admires you. Listen, why don't we get away from these spoilt puppies with their kilts and white socks, looking like leggy girls, and find ourselves a dram ot two?"

"Just what I was looking for" agreed John, "but I couldn't get near the booze for the crowd."

So they walked amicably over to the house and into the main hall where John pointed out to Ishmael the great shipbuilders congregated there.

"That's Stephen, there's Scott and Connell together. Oh, and Lithgow's just behind them, talking to Viscount Colville, the steel magnate."

Sir James Lithgow might have been a copy of Shandon: a big, distinguished-looking man with a red face and a big puce nose, the remnants of ginger hair in greying tufts curling round his ham ears.

Lady Colville, in a broad black straw hat and a becoming turquoise silk dress was chatting to Lady Dalry, who was absentmindedly as it were, casting an eye over Ishmael, who had at last succeeded in getting a double Macallan from old Tam. John Robson, prudent as always, limited himself to a brandy and dry ginger ale.

"Never take more than two" he confided. "You never know what you might do after that third drink!"

"Ah! There he is!" screamed Seonaid across the gathering of industrialists. "Ishmael! Where have you been? Here's poor Sheila been waiting for you and wondering whether she'd see you again!"

Sheila came up to Ishmael and John, blushing deeply at finding them together.

"All the best, Sheila" said John, "here's to your health, both of you."

They thanked him, admiring his generosity and his brave front in the circumstances. Sheila knew well that John loved her selflessly and the meeting was painful. But John showed no sign of the very real chagrin he felt after all these years. He was conscious that he was something of an object of derision to those who knew of his assiduous attentions to Sheila and who had taken it for granted that he was to have been Sheila's man.

"Let her go, just like that!" they said. "No fighting spirit! Allowed his fiancée to be lifted from under his nose!"

Others, mostly women, commented on 'the capricious nature' of Sheila, "always was a whimsical girl!"

"Turned down a good, solid man with an assured future for a Glasgow keely. No good can come of that. You'll see."

"Lost her head, she has!"

"And just look at the way he's dressed!"

Ishmael had, indeed, after observing Scotland's young aristocrats, and now the Lentilloch burghers in their fancy dress, decided not to change into his highland outfit. So there he stood in his shabby tweed and open-necked shirt amongst black-tied conformists with the ridiculous combination of kilts, white socks and grotesque ornamental sporrans that no ancient highlander would ever have worn.

Seonaid sneered at him in her provoking, mock-serious way, while Sheila hovered uncertainly, wishing that Ishmael would not make such a spectacle of himself and incur the ridicule of his inferiors.

'Why,' she wondered, while Ishmael was engaged in conversation with Seonaid and his mother, who had now joined them, 'why does he deliberately choose this boorish act of non-conformity and the morbid challenge of his Loch Mhor life. He could- can now – become a director of Shandons. In spite of all his renunciation of the material world, he raves about cars. His rebellion is a perversity.'

And as soon as she had reached that conclusion, she repented. 'Of course he's worth a hundred of any of them. It's I who am perverse, victim of my upbringing.'

Ishmael, who was unaware of this and was looking round at the Lentilloch burghers, with Seonaid's acerbic commentary, lighted on the figure of Rutherford, the solicitor who read the lesson in Sunday's church service, while simultaneously having an affair with a Lentilloch teenager, and had now got himself up in kilt, black tie and monocle. They were all, in their way, comic.

Ishmael did not feel any class antagonism. He merely found the aristocrats, the shipyard owners with all their power and arrogance, and the Lentilloch burghers funny in their different ways. They did in fact form three distinct classes, and between themselves there was snobbery of various kinds: the aristocrats despising the industrialists as parvenus and the burghers as nonentities. While the diligent burghers looked on the shipyard owners as vulgar new rich and the aristocrats as ineffectual social butterflies. The shipyard owners themselves agreed about the aristocracy, whom they knew had never done a day's work in their lives; and pitied the burghers as little men who hadn't got the courage and imagination to take a risk.

Ishmael simply had the consciousness that he didn't belong anywhere. He had none of the fashionable pseudo-affinity with the so-called working class. He was, he supposed, in a class of his own. Of no particular breed. A mongrel.

CEILIDH

Highland dancing was now being organised outside the marquees, the pretty young girls being infinitely more adroit than the young men, breathtaking in their highland dress as they performed sword dances and the highland fling, accompanied by the Duke of Atholl's pipe band from his small private army.

When twilight fell there was a call in the great hall:

"Ishmael! Ishmael! Come on man, let's have you on the pipes!"

So Ishmael, scruffily dressed as he was, stood on the little dais at the end of the hall and enthralled his audience with a rendering of 'The Black Bear' that reduced Sheila to tears. Ishmael followed that with 'Hey Johnny Cope with Your Hounds So Early,' ending with 'Highland Laddie,' getting wild applause. He was then presented with a quadruple whisky in a quoich by Shandon's handyman-chauffeur-butler old Tam, which he took by both handles and downed with relish. Observed with concealed curiosity by Lady Dalry.

There were now recitals of Gaelic songs, poems and charms, necessarily translated into English. Ella moved all with a song about a love-lorn lassie of the Hebrides who was pining away until the wind told her that Duncan, her lover, didn't come because Calum, a secret rival from the neighbouring fishing hamlet, had told Duncan Lorna loved another man from Uist, where she had gone on a journey to buy wool. The lassie begged the wind to tell Duncan the truth. So Duncan challenged Calum to a duel with claymores. But the rival was deadly cunning. When Duncan said "I will choose the time: dawn; you may choose the place." Calum chose a spot where the sun at dawn came through a hole in a rock. So Calum kept his back to the rock and when the sun suddenly shot through the hole, Duncan was dazzled and Calum, seeing his rival blinded, plunged his claymore into Duncan's heart. Then Lorna cursed the wind for betraying her, but the angry wind made her mad, and she wandered forlorn by the sea until she died.

Ella had learnt this song in Gaelic as a child in the Outer Hebrides but so bright was she that she translated the ballad impromptu into English, yet with the beautiful lilt of the native Gaelic speaker. When the frenzied clapping had died down, Sheila shyly mounted the dais and gave a recital of her beloved Kilmeny that she knew by heart. So carried away was she that her voice was tremulous and even the stolid burghers of Lentilloch were moved to question momentarily the norms of their routine existence.

> Kilmeny looked up with a lovely grace
> For Kilmeny had been, she knew not where,
> And Kilmeny had seen what she could not declare,
> A land of love and a land of light
> Without sun, or moon, or night,
> Where the river swa'd a living stream
> And the light a pure celestial beam;
> When she spake of the lovely forms she had seen
> The land of vision it would seem
> And a land where sin had never been,
> A still, an everlasting dream.

Sheila had made her own arrangement of James Hogg's lines.

As soon as the recitals were over, some of the congregation, mostly young but including some middle-aged, got going with wild Scotch country dances. Sheila took no part in these. Nor did Ishmael but he now joined in the general and irresistible conviviality. Yet always the horror of Shiel's poisoning destroyed any joy or tranquillity that he might have felt.

And the gnawing question of what was to happen between himself and Sheila was reaching its climax. It was now past midnight and at midday they were to be married in the local Church of Scotland at Shandon. Though he was an atheist Ishmael had no objection to that, to him fictitious ceremony. What was the difference between that and the cold ritual in a registry office? That sacrifice, if sacrifice it was, he was ready to make for Sheila. And for her family and his mother.

He withdrew by himself, re-filling his quoich and going out

under the stars to that pebbly beach where he had first met Sheila, pacing up and down in his habitual restless way. He thought of that shadow that had crossed Sheila's face only hours earlier. And it was borne in on him that in the long run Sheila could not stand the life at Loch Mhor. He, likewise, could not stand the life as a director of Shandons, hobnobbing with those plutocrats. He would be bought. For the rest of his life. He did not belong. And he would be true to his mission to avenge Shiel's death.

Sheila had been accustomed to having everything she wanted. As he remembered her pledge "We'll fight in the mountains." A wry smile broke out on his face. And what about her last note? "Now as never before I love you." What then, of what went before? And those printed cards…. Those expensive presents.

He reflected on Lady Dalry's unmistakable look of longing that had momentarily passed over him. And the innumerable married women who had done likewise. Of course Sheila was different. She had true innocence. And yet. Her background, her insouciant leaving £400 in her expensive bag in the bus, all indicated that she took material wellbeing for granted. And who could blame her?

But he feared her whimsicality, her ideal notion of working in Schweitzer's leper colony. The grand romantic gesture.

Her morbid attachment to the tomb of the young airman in the Necropolis. Was she not trapped in a world of make-believe? Of Alice in Wonderland, of Kilmeny? And was he himself a figure of fantasy to her? He recalled how she had smiled to him that morning after the swim in Loch Mhor, calling him "master."

And what if he was put in prison for life for killing Shiel's poisoner? Or poisoners. Because kill them he would when he found out who it was. He must – he would – find a way of getting at the truth. But how? That was the question. Never had he been up against a dilemma he could not resolve. As Sheila said, he was attempting to fight a shadow, a chimera. But having dealt with the Shandon impasse he must now face that spectral horror. It had to be done. And Sheila could not be party to it.

Suddenly he brought himself up short on the shore, the bright lights and music of the ceilidh recalling him to the present. He must confront Sheila. He walked back to the Lodge with measured, unhurried steps and had no sooner gone through the main door than he met her, tremulous and anxious.

"Where have you been, Ishmael? I've been looking and looking for you and I couldn't find you. It was like a dream I had when you were at Loch Mhor. Oh, heavens! It'll soon be time for supper and dadda's going to toast our health and happiness. In front of everybody. We must be there."

Ishmael at once felt a sense of dread in the pit of his stomach. And a vile dry taste in his throat and his mouth.

"Sheila, where can we talk for a few minutes by ourselves?"

Sheila looked at him with alarm, but said

"We can go into the morning room. There's no one there and the doors are kept closed."

They entered and sat together on a small green sofa.

"What is it, Ishmael?" Sheila asked fearfully, moving close to him and putting her arm round his waist. Ishmael did not, could not answer for some time. He then sat back, looked her in the eyes, and said

"We can't go on."

"Why not, why not, why not?" Sheila implored.

"Because it wouldn't last" Ishmael answered with a set jaw. "Your world is not my world. And I have to carry out my mission."

"You're slipping away like a snake" said Sheila. "Then go, Ishmael. Go! I will not plead with you."

Ishmael made to embrace her, but she recoiled rapidly, got to her feet and ran out of the room.

Ishmael sat stunned for a moment. Then he too got up, and he went into the great hall where a gargantuan supper was being served. He stood momentarily undecided behind the tables, un-noticed by the diners who were preoccupied with plates of lobster and caviar, smoked and fresh salmon, and steaming dishes of venison.

Their attention was called by Shandon, who rose peering slightly myopically at the assembly, just a little inebriated like everyone else except the solid John Robson. He stood on the small dais at the end of the hall from which he could see over the myriad heads and from where he could be seen and heard in his great bull's voice by everyone.

"Ladies and gentlemen" Shandon boomed, lifting high into the air an ancient family goblet of engraved glass by the base, as though to appraise the quality of the huge dram of malt whisky therein.

"Ladies and gentlemen, I have the honour and the great pleasure of proposing the toast to my daughter Sheila and Ishmael Mc Culloch on the occasion of their betrothal, in anticipation of their wedding at twelve midday today, in ten hours' time. I ask you, ladies and gentlemen, to raise with me your glasses …"

He held his glass high, but he got no further. At that moment there was a deafening report and the goblet in Shandon's hand was shattered. In the moment of shocked silence that followed, Ishmael, who had demolished the glass with a single shot from his old .38 pistol, called out

"The wedding's off!"

Immediately there was universal pandemonium. When some semblance of order had been restored there were loud exclamations of "A lunatic!"

"I told you so!"

"I knew it!"

"He's unstable!"

Shandon's face had become suffused with purple, and it looked as though he might have a stroke. Ella rushed over to calm and console him, while John Robson came forward and supported him as he tottered to the study. Sheila was nowhere to be seen.

Seonaid and her mother frantically searched for Ishmael. They found him in the morning room lying on his back on the floor and kicking his legs in the air with demonic laughter. They rushed to find Sheila; when they returned Ishmael had disappeared. They looked everywhere, even going to the summerhouse, where all they found was his brown flannel trousers. His kilt, bagpipes and Gladstone were missing. Otherwise there was no trace of him.

The ceilidh broke up in uproar. The good burghers of Lentilloch transported themselves home in high dudgeon, none more so than the lawyer Rutherford, whose monocle had popped out of his eye at the sound of the pistol shot.

"A bounder, I tell you" he complained to all who would listen to him – who were not many. "I always knew he was a good for nothing. A Glasgow keely!"

And so ended the ceilidh. Poor Sheila retreated distraught and inconsolable to her bedroom overlooking the sea loch, throwing herself on the bed, and crying convulsively. Ella had rushed to be with her, to try to calm and cheer her, but it was to no avail.

Shandon did have a fit. It was a fairly severe stroke. But John Robson had the presence of mind to call an ambulance, and before long Shandon was out of danger in intensive care at the Western Infirmary, watched over by the petrified Ella.

After the fiasco of the ceilidh Ishmael disappeared. No one knew where he was. But after some days he had a secret meeting with the leaders of the Scottish National Party in Edinburgh.

Following the launch of Empress of the Clyde and his chance meeting with Jimmy Anderson and Sandy Logan at the Highlandman's Umbrella he had meditated on the possibility of joining the SNP but had decided against that. Yet the idea of a new Scotland, the possibility of a new beginning impinged on his consciousness to the point of obsession. At last he had an ideal to pit his strength against.

So he decided to give all his heart and support to the SNP, while refusing to become a member, maintaining his determination to 'be an island.'

SCOTLAND THE BRAVE

It was raining torrentially in Edinburgh, Leith, a biting east wind blowing in off the North Sea. A by-election meeting of the Labour Party was coming to an end in a disused warehouse on the corner of Dock Street and Commercial Street, packed with cloth-capped Labour supporters in a smoky atmosphere so thick you could hardly see the far end of the building where men were slumped half asleep on broken-down chairs.

The Scottish National Party, as always short of funds, was waiting to take over the gloomy hall at a knock-down price once Labour's meeting ended, and the Labour candidate, in his triumphant peroration roared 'Tartan Tories,' 'Tartan Tories,' 'Tartan Tories' to wild acclamation from the Labour supporters leering at the impatient crowd hanging round the doorway.

Sandy Logan was getting very nervous as Ishmael had not turned up. When all of a sudden Ishmael in Black Watch kilt leapt onto the platform and marched up to the snub-nosed Labour speaker who backed away at once.

"What the devil did you say about tartan Tories" he yelled. "You sneaking little traitor to Scotland. At least we're proud of our country, and we don't kow-tow to the English. It's past your time, so get off the platform before I throw you off."

There were wild cheers from the SNP supporters who came charging in from the Rabbie Burns howf across the road. The Labour speaker quickly hopped off the platform as the bedraggled Labourites surged out to the Rabbie Burns.

Ishmael had been invited as 'guest speaker' at the SNP meeting, as 'warmer up' for the political candidate by Sandy Logan, the only SNP man who was a member of Parliament. So it was arranged that the three should sit at a long table, Sandy on the right, Ian MacGillivray pro-tem on the left and Ishmael in the middle. Though Ishmael insisted on standing.

Sandy explained to the congregation that Ishmael had saved the situation at Shandon's shipyard by winning over the strikers and getting the Empress of the Clyde built just in time for the launch by the Queen. The audience applauded. Then Sandy explained that Ishmael was not a member of the SNP, and had no personal political aspirations but that he believed in independence for Scotland and would do all he could to support the SNP cause.

APPLAUSE

"You say you support independence for Scotland, but what does independence mean to you, Ishmael?" called out Sandy Logan.

"First of all, it means absolute independence. But Scotland should have alliances, with Canada, New Zealand and Australia, which are teeming with Scots. And also with Scandinavia. And notably with England on the basis of absolute equality. I'm thinking of a defence alliance. But we shall not enter into the kind of alliance that Great Britain has with the United States of America, the so-called 'special relationship' whereby we are the junior partner ready to embark on foreign adventures to support the American empire. A similar position to that of the Russian satellites."

"You mean that we should form part of a federation with England?" came a call from a grizzled old Scot in the body of the hall.

"No, I do not" Ishmael retorted. "A federation would of course mean something like the states of America: semi-independent but subject to the central federal government. I mean, as I said, absolute independence, so that we are not led into the type of adventure the British Government has recently been involved in at English instigation: the Suez adventure. And here again, we were let down by the 'special relationship' with the United States, who undermined the pound sterling and caused the weak Anthony Eden government to fall. Even though, as a major in the Argyll & Sutherland Highlanders told me, all the British had to do was to motor alongside the Suez canal, chasing Egyptian soldiers who ran like hell in front of them without firing a shot.
Loud laughter in the hall.

"And what about Scotland's independent defence forces?" queried Ian MacGillivray, the SNP candidate at the by-election.

"As you know" Ishmael answered, "The British defence depends on nuclear bombers at present. But there are plans to change from the V-bombers to nuclear submarines armed with nuclear missiles. I think here we should negotiate with the English, because these submarines would be based in Scottish waters. So we could negotiate from a position of strength for one of these submarines to be ceded to the Scottish government. I think the English would be very ready to accept that proposition because of the great cost of these submarines and because they would in effect be getting one free under our alliance.

"What other armaments would Scotland have?" came a cry from the back.

"The nuclear armed submarine would be our supreme defence weapon, but we ought to introduce National Service for both men and women, a highland brigade or division and a lowland equivalent. This would induce a sense of pride and after one year only of service the troops would pass to the reserve, and so within a few years we'd have a substantial army, air force and navy to call on in time of emergency. Women could be largely employed in the role of clerks and administration, besides forming social services in support of the old, infirm and orphanages. My idea is that as a small country we should be like Sparta or Switzerland, with every man maintaining his armament at home, ready to respond to unforeseen circumstances. We haven't time to go into details now, and you can argue over my proposals later."

MacGillivray now asked Ishmael for his views on education.

"We must make Scotland an international centre of excellence as it was in the time of Hume and Adam Smith, and the Edinburgh Review. I think we should concentrate on three universities: Glasgow, Edinburgh and Aberdeen and get them up to the standard of Oxford, Cambridge.

It is important that Scotland should not become parochial, but be cosmopolitan and bring the best brains to teaching that can be found, even from abroad."

"And where are we going to get the money for that?" asked Sandy Logan.

"From Scotland's oil off the coast of Aberdeen. The English are careful to call it 'North Sea' oil. And have you noticed, it costs more to fill up your car with petrol in Inverness than in London? With the oil revenue Scotland can be the lighthouse of Europe. And we shall have the Scottish pound just as the Australians have the Australian pound."

"Apart from oil, what are Scotland's principal resources?" called out Sandy Logan.

"One of the most important things for Scotland to do is to resuscitate the shipping industry. We might just be in time to do that and return to building world-class ships like the Queen Mary and the Queen Elizabeth. But conditions in the yards will have to be enormously improved. Scotland can again be a major World shipbuilder.

Apart from that, we must 'internationalise' (to use a horrible term) the whisky industry, develop fish farms, forestry (planting the ancient indigenous trees besides the conifers,) and also develop our farms. But we must not develop what the Americans call 'mega farms' in which animals are regarded merely as creatures to be exploited every minute of their lives before slaughter. Those animals are not regarded as sentient beings and spend all their lives cooped up without freedom to roam the fields, in fact scarcely permitted any movement… The Americans have reduced life to a question of money."

"Could you tell us your ideas about the social life of the Scots under independence?" asked Sandy Logan.

"Increase and develop our wonderful festivals.

"The most important thing is that Scots should feel they belong to a great independent society. There should be no titles, no knighthoods to create social division. Nevertheless, I think ancient titles should be preserved as harmless, and in time these will have less and less significance. Scotland must not become a dictatorship. We should develop the old insistence on honesty whereby a Scotsman's word is his bond. For that reason Scotsmen were preferred as bank managers, known for their honesty.

"Sandy Logan is signalling that my time is up. So I will just say finally that the division into posh-speaking upper class and the rest must be remedied, and I confess that I don't know how that can be done in the near future, but if we develop our universities into great ones equal to Oxford and Cambridge that will in time have its effect. It's not right or healthy that some are ashamed of Scots dialect, as the upper class Russians were of their own language, speaking to each other in French. Some of them couldn't even speak Russian at all, pre-Revolution."

"Don't underestimate Scotland. This great country has been one of the most inventive in the world. Remember Watt's steam engine, and his projection of the screw propeller for ships. Stephenson's locomotive, the 'Rocket,' capable of between 12 and 20 miles an hour, so amazed people that the English government minister dispatched for the opening ceremony was run over by it declaring that that speed was impossible for a machine. (Laughter)

Then we had 'Tar McAdam's' tarmac now universal world-wide, John Boyd Dunlop's pneumatic tyre, Alexander Graham Bell's telephone, Kelvin's wireless telegraphy and Logie Baird's television. And remember the Scotsman who discovered penicillin, and saves the lives of countless millions world-wide. Alexander Fleming.

In the Arts Scotland's zenith was in the late eighteenth and early nineteenth century with Robert Burns, Walter Scott, Lord Byron and Robert Louis Stevenson, not to mention the two James Thomsins."

"What aboot Scottish composers?" came a cry from the middle of the hall. I've niver heard of any of yon."

"Nor have I" answered Ishmael laughing, "but it's said that the Italian Donizzeti was a Scottish emigrant Donald Izat, and that Edward Grieg was also, his name being changed from Greig."

"Painters. Were there nae great Scots?" came that same voice from the middle of the hall.

"It is affirmed by many distinguished critics" answered Ishmael, "that Raeburn was the greatest British portrait painter."

"It is important to remember that Scotland was an independent nation for centuries" Ishmael eagerly called out in crescendo, ignoring Jimmy Logan's signal that his time was up, "and it's time we were an independent nation again and not just an appendage to England. James VI of Scotland ruled England as James Ist. Finally, don't forget our great national heroes, William Wallace and Robert the Bruce, who fought for independence. And the triumph of the battle of Bannockburn. Don't let it all go. This small nation has the heart and history of a great nation. Remember that the great Scottish patriot William Wallace who fought to defend Scotland from the English invaders, was taken in chains to London where he was hanged, drawn and quartered, and his head displayed in public on a spike."

Ishmael turned about, withdrew his bagpipes from the Gladstone bag on the chair, and gave a memorable rendering of 'Scotland the Brave,' which received wild cheers and applause.

PART III

RETURN TO LOCH MHOR

After a week or so Ishmael returned to Loch Mhor and resumed his duties as though he had not been away. After a predictably grumpy encounter with the factor, who informed him that he had dismissed Gillespie who, wonder of wonders had been arrested by the police on evidence that he had been acting as lookout for the Inverness poachers. Ishmael remembered the driver's switching off the Land-Rover lights on the track up the Glen to Lochan Shuna and the warning shout to Archie. Though with the thousand 'Archies' in the highlands it was amazing that the plodding police had actually made an arrest. To no avail. Archie was released on bail, as were the two Inverness rascals, who had all been allowed an appeal on a 'technicality.' The usual story. And now the factor had been obliged to re-employ Gillespie as a ghillie. Ishmael felt a momentary shudder at this news, but shrugged it off. He had to make arrangements for the grouse shoots.

When he called the gamekeeper and the ghillies together they were sullen and surly; except for 'big' Angus, who was as generous in proffering the half bottle of whisky from his deep pocket as ever, welcoming Ishmael with his wheezing laugh and a huge hairy paw in handshake. Gillespie eyed Ishmael through half-closed slit eyes, and his greeting was almost a snarl.

"Got me put in the Inverness clink for a month. Innocent I was. How the hell did they know it was me in the glen? Impossible. I was in the Kinloch Inn bar. The lassie'll tell ye. Aand there's folk here aas is going to pay for it" he added.

"If you can't do more than yap your mouth off like a whoorie why not try to be a man and hud your wheesht." Ishmael retorted, menacingly. "You're a coward, and you know it." He feinted a move towards Gillespie, who retreated.

"Aye, get on wi' ye, Archie" said 'Big' Angus, "ye haad a graand time in the jug. Ye's got better grub thaan ye ever haad in the hotel bar, cooked for ye by the owner's wee wifie."

Gillespie couldn't suppress a smug grin at the reference to his prowess 'wi' the wummen,' but that didn't stop him boasting

"I do for thaat Edinburgh eediot o' a so-called husband what I done for plenty others."

The other ghillies sniggered appreciatively but to Ishmael's surprise the keeper reprimanded them.

"Don't be listening to his tales now. Aand you, Archie, put your steel helmet away and don't be giving us any more of your bull-shit. Aas for you two, you should know better thaan to play up to a rascal that'll be inside again aand out of his job afore ye caan turn round."

Was this, wondered Ishmael, some kind of subterfuge by the keeper? Ishmael knew that the factor had only sacked Gillespie in his absence on the orders of Major Tooth, who would not allow any convicted men on his estate. But he had been quick to re-instate him the moment the appeal was accepted. Better the riff-raff you know ….

"This braggadocio is some kind of camouflage to deceive me" thought Ishmael. He was as sure as he could be that the keeper was in with the poachers: the locals, and even maybe the rascals from Inverness.

Whatever the keeper's reason for the display of authority, McCrone was even more surly than Gillespie and more churlish in his attitude, fingering his throat as though it still hurt from that head-lock of Ishmael's. But McCrone's moods were still changeable, oscillating from servility to truculence. As though he hadn't the guts to back his boasts.

It was the same in the pub at Kinloch, where Ishmael called before going back to his cottage. When Ishmael entered there was once again that silence and men's backs turned towards him. No one would speak to him. He was a pariah. Not that he wanted to get into conversation with those 'turnip heads.' But for the look of the thing he had made a banal remark to those at the bar beside him. Even the barmaid, usually so 'fresh,' served him with glacial coldness, as though she couldn't quite find any reason for refusing to pull a pint for him.

And the doctor didn't appear. As Ishmael made his way to his cottage he recalled the drunken muttering of the highlander on the Glasgow to Inverness train:

"What am I coming home to?"

He came home to a damp cottage with mouldy unwashed plates in the kitchen and without electricity: cut off by Hydro Electric for non-payment of three months' bills. Opening a drawer he found Shiel's rug bundled into it by Sheila. A grim reminder. As if he needed it.

It being evening now he called at Succoth Farm. Knocking at the door there was no response. So he walked through the courtyard to the shimmering aspen in the lee of which Shiel was buried. The aspen leaves had already taken an autumnal tinge, rustling in the light breeze. Ishmael stood there silently for some minutes, and then intoned out loud

> "Shiel I have never forgotten you.
> I have come back to avenge you."

Then he turned back to the farmhouse. Sheena was now waiting in the doorway.

"It's right glaad I aam to see you baack, Mr McCulloch. Will you be coming in for a wee while?"

When they were taking tea inside Sheena asked Ishmael about the 'lassie,' and how he had got on in Glasgow. But Ishmael said nothing about Sheila and parried her curiosity with a few general remarks.

"You'll have heard how the poachers got out of jail, aand thaat Gillespie was charged aand 's out too. Aand there's been quite a lot of activity up the glen since you've been away. Aat night, thaat is, Mr McCulloch. I've been hearing Land-Rovers coming down in the small hours. Aand thaat keeper, he does nothing. In with them, I think he is."

"I daresay" answered Ishmael. "I've come back to find out. About that and the killer of my dog."

"I'm not thinking 'big' Angus haad anything to do with it, Mr McCulloch, but thaat Gillespie is a right evil one. Aand thaat other one too, you know who I mean, is one I don't trust. No, I don't trust him at all, no more than I do the keeper."

"Well" said Ishmael, "I'll have my own way of finding out."

Sheena turned her head slowly to look carefully at Ishmael, and paused, before saying "Will you, now, Mr McCulloch? Yes, I think you will. Thaat's what I'm thinking."

179

Ishmael was going to look for the shepherd on his way back to his cottage but met him wandering, almost doddering along behind his immense flock of sheep with his eager collies in the setting sunlight.

"Down dogs, down" ordered old Anderson, who shocked Ishmael by looking much older than when he had left not so long ago.

"Oh, Mr, McCulloch, it's verra pleased I am to be seeing you here again. And how did you get on in Glasgow, if you don't mind my asking?"

"Fine, thanks, Mr Anderson. And you, how have you been keeping?"

"Well, to be quite honest with you, Mr McCulloch, none too well. The fits haave been coming on me more frequently, aand I've a bit of a job on the hill sometimes to keep my baalance."

"Have you not seen the doctor?"

"Thaat I haave, sir, aand a better doctor there is not in all the highlands. He'll come out aat night or any time Sheena rings him, though I tell her not to be bothering him. Aand he's given me some pills thaat haave calmed me down. Calmed me down they haave, Mr McCulloch. I've been thaat worried the faactor would get rid of us or whateffer, Mr McCulloch. The ghillies haave been complaining again, saying it's evil spirits I haave."

"I'll shut them up" Ishmael said with a determination that reassured the shepherd. "And if they don't shut up, they'll be the ones to go. As I told you, it's my responsibility, not the factor's."

"Oh well, I'm not wanting to be the cause of any maan losing his job, Mr McCulloch, sir, believe me, sir. But knowing you are here again, just knowing thaat, I feel safer, if you know what I mean. Och, Mr McCulloch, sir, I mustn't be forgetting. Do you mind yon puppy of mine, Fionn her name is. If you'd like to haave her now, she's well enough weaned from Jess thaat you could take her tonight. If thaat would be suitable. She's a very bonny pup, aand verra bright, though I say so myself, if you'll excuse me, Mr McCulloch."

"Yes, John, it's very good of you. I would like to have her"

Ishmael answered, thinking now that he could bear to have a collie again. "She's a bitch, after all, and wouldn't make me compare her with Shiel all the time. I wouldn't take a male collie again, though."

So it was settled, and after a brief discussion of the outstanding problems with the sheep, Ishmael went to his cottage. The shepherd brought his new companion that night, when the sitting room was illuminated by a Tilley lamp. She was of course typically puppyish in her ways, frisky and given to rushing about, tearing up any cloth in reach and noisy. But though he was glad to have her, Ishmael felt certain rumbling pangs looking at her white ruff and the pattern of her black and white coat, reminiscent of Shiel.

"I'll never let her out of my sight" he said to the grateful shepherd. Grateful that Ishmael accepted his offering. "And if I have to go anywhere, with your permission I'll leave her with Mrs Anderson and the girls."

"Thaat would be graand, Mr McCulloch, it would indeed. Oh yes, aye, it would thaat. We'd be only too pleased to look after her for you, thaat we would."

And the old man – not so old in years but beaten down into premature age by hard life and illness – stumbled off home in the twilight.

HIGHLAND DOCTOR AGHAST

Ishmael was pondering one evening soon after his return all that had happened in Glasgow and Shandon Lodge when there was a loud knock on the cottage door. It was the doctor, large as life and jolly as ever.

"Well, well, you're back, Ishmael. And what happened in those weeks you've been away?"

Ishmael recounted the triumph of the Empress of the Clyde, at which the beaming doctor demanded a hefty dram in celebration.

"Here's to you, Ishmael, Slainte! old fellow. I knew you'd bring it off, though I knew how difficult it would be and what tremendous risks there were. It seems to me you thrive on great challenges, but I don't think this place is big enough for you. Beware you don't rot. Now tell me why you haven't accepted the top job they offered you at Shandons."

When Ishmael had narrated his 'incompatibility' as he called it with the boss class, the aristocracy and the 'plutocracy,' the doctor nodded with perplexed sympathy.

"And what about Sheila?" he asked, eagerly expectant.

But when Ishmael had explained, in his laconic, taciturn way, what he saw as the insuperable obstacles to any marriage, and had recounted the events of the ceilidh, the doctor was aghast.

"Are you crazy, man? That you've thrown everything up and broken the poor girl's heart to return to this horrible dump? When you could have been living in a modest house, if that's what you insist on, and could have continued as manager at Shandons even if you rejected the directorship you were offered.

And you've thrown the Railton they bought for you in their face. Imagine the joy it gave them to do that for you. I've got to say you've made it look as though you're a bounder. Just what all the Lentilloch burghers will be saying. But most of all, think of the Shandons. You'll have ruined them. Shandon will never be able to run that yard with all the commies in the unions, those idiot demagogues who'll wreck the workers' future. And Sheila's life, like her mother's, will be destroyed. Finished. And why have you done this? Because of your principles? What principles justify what you have done?"

"You don't understand, doctor. Imagine that when I made a harmless joke about her father leaving in the middle of teatime and coming back forty minutes later with a magnificent brand new Bentley Continental an ugly black shadow crossed Sheila's face. You must know what that meant. How could I go on with the recollection of that? She a millionaire's daughter, and I a penniless hired manager. If it isn't right you can't go on with it. Of course as you know she is innocent, quite unlike the typical modern girl. But remember that the bitch is in all of them. The typical marriage today is a question of who can devour who? And then a legal battle for money. I know of a case where a man had to live in his Mini car, and when he asserted his right to have a visit from his children the woman applied successfully to the courts to have that visit annulled because he hadn't got an adequate place to receive them. She got the house. And in the same newspaper I read of a 16-year-old girl who stamped on an old man's head as he lay on the ground and killed him."

"Yes, but you can't judge Sheila by the worst type of woman" the doctor interrupted.

"You tell me" said Ishmael passionately, "how many cases are there of poor men marrying millionairesses? A famous actress married I don't know how many millionaires. But when she was getting on in years she took up with an impoverished young man. Did it last? Of course it didn't. It may have been in part because the young man found out on living with her that all those artificial aids that women adopt: false eyelashes, bust boosters, hair pro-longers and all the rest of it couldn't help her when she was naked. But for whatever reason, and money was a big part of it, they couldn't go on."

"Yes, but Sheila doesn't need any of those artificial aids. And she's just about your age. And as you are aware, Shandon offered you a directorship at Shandons."

"Nevertheless, I'd still have been bought," Ishmael asserted.

After a pause, he asked the Doctor: "Do you think a woman can be a compensation for the nullity of life? Of the meaninglessness of the human predicament? Take the Spanish name Consuelo."

"Yes and no" the doctor answered. "The problem is man's tendency to idealise woman. And when something happens to question that ideal the man, like a child whose house of model bricks has developed a flaw, knocks it down. Kicks it over. With fiendish relish. Men come to women and say "Be my ideal." But how can they? Because the ideal would be based on illusion, irreality. You can see this tendency in modern pop music. A type of love based on a dream. Isn't everything now called a 'dream'? A dream relationship, a dream house, a dream kitchen, holiday. Whatever you like, it's a dream. And dreams are evanescent, phantasmagorical. There are no red cross knights today. But we should remember those canny crusaders when they set off for the Holy Land they got the blacksmith to fit their beloved with a chastity belt."

"Of course I realize" countered Ishmael, "that all this true love business is in great part simply Nature doing its work to ensure the procreation of the species. And that human copulation stripped of its idealized aura is no more than human bodies squirming. We, the physically most ugly of creatures – compare the beauty of animals, birds and fishes – idealize what they do naturally."

"You're a bit of a cynic, aren't you" laughed the doctor. "But tell me, do you think a woman is equal to a man?"

"Of course not" Ishmael replied. "They're related but intrinsically different. To state the obvious, women tend to be hysterical as the result of their physical difference from men, who tend to be aggressive where a woman may be quiescent. They are complementary yes, but equal no, no more than an orange is equal to a nectarine."

"But women claim to be intellectually, even artistically equal to men."

"In that case, how is it that, if the greatest art and human achievement is classical music, there are no great women composers? Is there a single woman equal to Beethoven? And we might add Bach, Mozart, Haydn, Schubert, Schuman, Berlioz, Tchaikovsky, Brahms, Vivaldi, Purcell and countless others."

"You've got me there" chuckled the doctor, "but what about Tolstoy's claim that women are morally inferior to males?"

"It would be difficult, wouldn't it, to find a male more depraved than Tolstoy in his early life, or more hypocritical in his old age, when he gave away all his possessions except in so far as he retained them by making them over to his wife."

"Oh mercy!" the doctor laughed. "Certainly historically women did not get a good press: Delilah, Clytemnestra, Goneril and Regan …"

"And not just historically" retorted Ishmael, "take the plethora of terms today exclusively describing women."

"What, for instance?" the doctor demanded.

"Hag"	"Bag" echoed the doctor.
"Crumpet" laughed Ishmael.	"Strumpet" capped the doc.

And so it went on:

"Coquette"	"Slattern"
"Harridan"	"Crone"
"Slut"	"Hussy"
"Whore"	"Squaw"

"Why squaw" asked Ishmael. "That's just an American Indian's wife."

"No, it isn't. Don't you know that the American feminists have insisted on changing the names of places such as Squaw Creek? They eliminate Squaw claiming that it means 'loose woman,' to say no more, in Indian lingo. In the same way as they have eliminated the word 'cock,' substituting the ridiculous 'rooster'."

"What is it they want?"

"What they've eliminated. And those clamouring feminists think themselves original. But Chaucer's Wife of Bath forestalled them by seven centuries with her determination to have the 'sovereignty' over her five husbands."

"Well, of course male poets are responsible for the idealization of women as angels, and giving them the names of flowers and the lovely seasons of April, May, June. Never heard of one called November, have you?"

"No, but take the beautiful lines of John Donne:
'Nor spring nor summer hath such grace

As I have seen in one autumnal face'."

"Mother Teresa comes to mind. And what if poor Sheila should join Schweitzer's leper colony in Africa?"

"Yes, and if she does I will be responsible. Or I'll be equally responsible if she doesn't" answered Ishmael gloomily. She is ethereal."

It was no good Ishmael trying to explain his certainty that, as he put it, 'it wouldn't last' with Sheila. And in any case he wasn't going to spend his life in a bloody shipyard. He had never undertaken to do that. He had only answered Shandon's call for help. To get the Empress of the Clyde launched.

"I've seen what it does to men after twenty years in that place. Half of them – more than half – are deaf from the racket of the machines, their faces are grey from inhaling fumes, and their fingers have no circulation in many cases from gripping vibrating tools for eight, ten, twelve hours a day. And of course they've no security of labour. The union bosses, like the obstinate, arrogant directors, are making sure there will be no future. For anyone. If I thought there was a fighting chance, a hope in the long run, I might pit my strength against it. But there's none. No hope. From being the greatest shipbuilding enterprise in the world, the Clyde workers, the shipyard owners and the government have allowed foreign yards in Japan, Korea, Germany and even Scandinavia to take the market from them. And they won't get it back. Because there isn't the will. Anyway, it's not my life. There's more to life than that."

"And where are you going to find it?" queried the doctor.

"Well, doctor, I'm going to surprise you, as I have surprised myself. Sometimes one discovers something unexpected about one's self as the result of some action in the past. Long before the ceilidh I spent an evening in the Highlandman's Umbrella in Glasgow, in Argyll Street, a pub, you'll know it, don't you. I met there an SNP MP, the only one there is I believe, with his friend, an old hand at Shandon's. Well, since then I've had at the back of my mind not only Scotland's tragic past, but its future.

After haranguing the strikers at Shandon's I discovered an emotional element I did not know existed. I had used a politician's emotional appeal to sway the strikers when logic failed. And yet it was to a noble end for the men, and for Scotland. It occurred to me reflecting on this that I could pit my strength to transform not just a striking crowd of men but a nation that has lost its way."

"Christ, don't tell me" interrupted the doctor, "that you're going to throw in your lot with that crazy rabble of Scots Nats."

"Listen, doctor and don't interrupt. Anyway, after the strike meeting, Jimmy Anderson, Sandy Logan's friend, came up to me and said "It was expected you wouldn't last the day, they had ten to one against you: being hooted out. It was a wonderful political triumph" he said, clapping me on the back, so delighted was he. And that set me thinking that maybe I could do something for Scotland.

"Well, then, after the launch of the Empress of the Clyde, when all the bigwigs were having lunch with the Queen at the Lord Provost's banquet, I dropped into the Highlandman's Umbrella, and who do you think there were there. Jimmy Anderson and Sandy Logan, the half-crazy M.P. for the SNP.

"Sandy came running up to me and burst out "From all Jimmy tells me about your winning over the strikers at Shandons, by Robert the Bruce ye'll haave to lend us a haand at Edinburgh, Leith, By-election. We'll need all the help we caan get."

"Now I'm going to surprise you again, doctor. After a meeting with the leaders of the SNP in Edinburgh, after the ceilidh that was, they asked me to support the prospective SNP M.P. candidate at Edinburgh, Leith."

"I wish I'd been there to see it" said the astonished doctor.

"Don't jump the gun, doctor. But you're right. I did that last Friday from the platform at Leigh."

"And how did it go down."

"Well enough, I think. But the point is I'm now dedicated to what is probably a lost cause. But in answer to your question 'And where are you going to find it?' that's it. And I'm going to surprise you even more, doctor. I want to reclaim all those centuries of old Scottish servility, to start anew, to wipe out the shame of Flodden and Culloden. To wipe out the gloating exaltation of the English poet Skelton in his tawdry triumph over Flodden."

"As you say, Ishmael, it may be a lost cause.

The trouble is those upper and upper middle class Scots are dyed in the wool Tories, and the so-called working-class will always vote Labour without thinking, as you know. But if there's anyone who can bring them round that man is you. Yet it'll take time. Are you ready to devote your whole life to it?"

"I can't tell you, doctor, how exhilarated I am at the prospect. It's something wonderful to live for, and to have something to live for. As you know I don't personally want political power and I will never become a politician. But with all my heart and soul I want Scotland to become independent and I will do everything, absolutely everything to bring that about."

"Let's have a dram to that, then" said the doctor jubilantly. "I hope I'll live to see it."

"And there's another thing" Ishmael insisted. "I'm going to avenge the poisoning of my dog. It's one of two or three. I've been thinking it out. What I'm going to do is get them one by one in a headlock and increase the pressure until the guilty one confesses. And then" – he paused for a moment and the doctor saw the set of his jaw and the passionate hatred in his eyes – "and then I'll make him drink the very poison he gave my dog. I've got it, the same as the poisons department analysis. A chlorine-based agricultural product. I'll keep up the pressure, make him open his mouth and pour it down his throat."

There was a terrifying gleam in Ishmael's eyes and a terrible determination in his expression.

"Oh, Jesus, you can't do that, man. This is grotesque. They'll put you in prison for life. And what good will that do?"

"Well, this life is a prison. No one gave us an option. We're flung into it. And I've got to carry out my mission of revenge. The law won't act.' And in any case, the imbecile law is only a man-made artefact. Do you think I can bear to see this vermin, these cowardly snakes, grinning in their cunning, and my Shiel dead? They have sentenced me. Not the other way round. And what …?" At that moment there were two shotgun blasts at the door. And then a tremendous crash on the roof. Followed by another. And another.

And by a stone smashing through the sitting-room window. Ishmael pulled out his .38 from his pocket and flung open the door. He could at first see nothing in the darkness but he heard the snapping of twigs in the undergrowth and the swishing of bushes as he made out the shadowy form of two or three figures running away. "Bloody cowards" he yelled, and fired three rounds low over their heads. He heard the sound of diabolical laughter receding in the direction of Kinloch. And then all was silent. By the light of his flashlight Ishmael saw that the telephone line had been cut right at the top of the nearest telephone pole, hanging down a couple of yards. Electricity too was cut.

By the glimmering firelight and with a trembling hand the good doctor poured himself a big dram, but he had been resolute. He had grabbed the shotgun, though he could find no cartridges in that split second.

"Christ, man! You'll have to get out of here."

"They will have to get me out of here" answered Ishmael tersely as he lit the Tilley lamp.

"Well, thank God we've survived that assault. Oops! Sorry, you're an atheist, aren't you?"

"I'm not drawn to kow-towing, obsequious, lickspittle worship. It doesn't matter where you begin, it's flattery, obeisance, in the hope of a reserved seat in Heaven. Like Caliban's 'Ban, Ban, Ca-Caliban, has a new master, get a new man.' Opportunism, the urge to prostrate oneself, partly out of fear. Take the Lord's Prayer, the paternalistic God – our Father, with his Kingdom, Power and Glory. The church organ is his brass band which stirs up the congregation to Hallelujah."

"Aha! old boy, there's no arguing with <u>your</u> brass band. A dram? But don't you believe in anything beyond our existence?"

"Well, take that tiny moth that is fluttering against the cracks in the shutters. D'you see how extraordinarily beautiful it is? It's got the aerodynamic triangular form of the Vulcan bomber. Yet it doesn't attack anything. Look at the delicacy of its feelers and its minute head and body. There's not only intelligence in its design but a wonderful aesthetic sense."

"You mean it's evidence of the Creator as artist?"

"That's about the only way you can look at it. But at the same time you could say it's pointless. It's so ephemeral."

"You mean evidence of the Creator as bored artist. Repetition ad infinitum? And isn't the world running out of species?"

"Certainly there is evidence, an admission by God, if Abraham's account in Genesis is to be believed, of imperfection in his creation. Hence the obsession with circumcision."

And while there maybe a diminution of species caused in part by human activity, humans themselves are multiplying by thousands of millions at an unsustainable rate. Can that be part of God's plan? If there is a plan."

With drams to hand, the doctor asked "Shall we perhaps have something to eat? Have you got anything, Ishmael?"

"Only eggs, cheese, bread."

"Hey, old boy, are you a vegetarian?"

"Can't stand the idea of the last sigh of an animal or the last gasp of a fish."

"You're right. It's disgusting. Yet I have a weakness for lamb chops, and fish and chips. You know we British carefully disguise from ourselves that we are brutal carnivores. Think of the language: beef, mutton, ham, venison. Nearly always French words. The Germans are not so squeamish with their 'fleisch'."

"And in every town there are 'abattoirs'," added Ishmael.

"Have you ever thought how many animals and fish the average person eats in a life time" queried the doctor.

"In a way I have. I had a dream of animals going into the ark with bites taken out by humans. Lambs without ribs, oxen with no tails, sturgeon without their reproductive system, eels skinned alive by the French and ducks and geese with their anuses corked."

"Yes, and now humans for a treat eat ostriches and kangaroos. How about scrambled eggs? My wife says I'm a good scrambler."

★

TWO GUNS BETTER THAN ONE

"I know I'm not needed" said the jovial doctor, "but I'll keep you company for another night. Two guns are better than one, and we can get some practice with that tin of peas."

And so, with guns at the ready, they passed two tense if convivial nights in the cottage. But no further attack materialised, although tramping sounds close to the building emerged on the second night. Which gave them the opportunity to discharge a volley into the bushes. There was no laughter this time.

It was as it were the all-clear, and the good doctor returned home, where he was severely reprimanded by his wife. "Just an excuse for more dramming" she scolded. Though she had to turn away to hide the involuntary smirk that had taken possession of her face.

"You're just an overgrown child" she chided, "neglecting your practice even if it was the weekend. Don't you forget the Free Church elders. They'll get you if you go on like this. And one of these days you'll do your innards in. Physician heal thyself!"

And so, as usual, their dispute ended in laughter. Which, observing the doctor's mock-penitent expression the indulgent wife could no longer contain. "Who but a fool would have married you? And who but an ass would have married me?" she concluded triumphantly. They then interlocked hands and arms and did a kind of portly jig round the room.

SUCCOTH FARM

When Ishmael called at Succoth Farm in the evening twilight he sensed a change of atmosphere as soon as he had passed through the porch in answer to a gruff call from inside. The jolly giggles of the girls had given way to a sombre silence, except for the howling of the wind round the house and the sharp insistent ticking of the steeple clock on the mantel shelf. The highland doctor was sitting silently by that clock, mini Gladstone at his feet.

There were two dark figures seated on either side of the peat fire, which gave out the usual acrid aroma. For some reason the lights were not on and the room was illuminated only by the dull flicker of the fire and such rays of sunset as penetrated the small windows. He became aware that they had risen to greet him, two huge shadowy shapes. As he took the proffered hand of the one on the left, which gripped like a vice, he could make out a great craggy face with a bent aquiline nose and a wild shock of hair which rushed upwards like a series of flames.

"Erik Anderson" a sonorous voice intoned, "pleased to meet you." And gesturing to the other form he added in a tone equally deep

"My brother, Michael. The doctor you will know."

Ishmael took the limp hand of the lofty gangling creature, who gazed at him mournfully from two extraordinarily bright blue eyes reflected by the fire light. His great forehead was half-concealed by a mop of black hair that hung over his face and collar, and as he greeted him in a high, piping voice, Ishmael could see enormous irregular teeth like a horse's that shone yellow between his sensual lips. He let out a little inconsequential laugh.

No move was made to put on the light and there was no sign of the shepherd and his family.

"Gone to the livestock auction in Dingwall" announced Erick. "Won't be back until very late."

"A power cut" whined Michael with his gentle intonation, as he moved to light a Tilley lamp in the receding twilight. Once again he let out a little laugh, almost like a whinny.

Ishmael sat down on a rickety armchair between the brothers, gazing at the glowing peat and glancing at the two in the warm light of the lamp. For a while no one spoke. Erik's head was vast. The bone of his crooked nose looked as though it would break through the taut skin stretched over it, like a cutting instrument. A scimitar. The whole craggy face was a blazing red permeated by small bluish veins like electric wires, beneath that fiery crown.

"You are the estate manager, I believe" he said, fixing a severe eye on Ishmael who sat taciturn and motionless apart from the shuffling of his brogues on the floor as though marking time.

"That's right."

There was a long pause before Michael's sallow, lugubrious face turned to Ishmael, moving uneasily in his chair, shrugging his shoulders under his jacket as though body and soul did not altogether coalesce.

"We got word that our father is very ill, so we've come home. But it seems he's not as bad as we were led to believe by our mother. Though she says he's liable to alarming ups and downs."

Again a long silence followed, broken by Ishmael.

"And what do you do?" he asked, looking at the gaunt figure of Erik, whose bearing betrayed inner turmoil.

"I'm a Jesuit priest" he retorted, as though the very terms disgusted him. "I work in the Gorbals trying to make something of those Glasgow Irish cut-throats. The friendliest people you could imagine. Though they'll wrap a sharpened bicycle chain round your neck with no bother."

He gave a throaty laugh, fingering his neck, which had a livid weal.

"And do you like the work?" Ishmael asked, almost sardonically.

"Hate it. But it's got to be done."

"Then why do you do it?"

"I've just told you" answered Erik with a withering stare. "But I won't be doing it for much longer."

"Why is that?"

"Because I've seen the darkness. It's not the Gorbals rabble. I'm glad to work with them. It's the Order."

"The Order?"

"Yes, the Order ... of Saint Ignatius Loyola. The Society of Jesus. Except for the black Pope and in spite of a few saints, it's rotten."

"Who's the black Pope?"

"The head of the Order. The Jesuit General in Rome. It's a pseudo-military organisation. The shock troops of the Catholic Church."

"What then is wrong with it?"

"What is wrong with it!" snorted Erik, as though the question was an irrelevance in the face of a self-evident truth. "Look, when I joined as a novice it seemed, of all orders the one truest to Christ. Jesuits are bound to poverty, self-abnegation, obedience and chastity. And the practice of the spiritual exercises devised by Saint Ignatius. For a number of years, as a novice, I believed I had found my true vocation."

"What then?" Ishmael asked quietly.

"I found that the Order is infested with power struggles and intrigue. Gluttony is the norm, and sodomy rife. Not to mention drunkenness."

"Christ!" said Ishmael involuntarily.

"You may well say that" Erik answered with a grimace.

"Are you then going to renounce your vows?"

"I am most certainly not going to renounce my vows of poverty and chastity. But obedience to evil I reject and will shortly leave the Society. I have already advised my superior and will soon be released from this horror."

"But not from the darkness" piped up Michael.

"And what will you do then?"

"He'll become a shepherd" interjected his brother, again with a shrill laugh.

Erik remained silent, his eyes fixed on the peat fire.

"And what about you?" Ishmael asked with quite some curiosity, turning to Michael. "What do you do?"

"As little as possible" Michael responded with a solemn nod.

"You damned fool" barked Erik. And then, apologetically to

Ishmael, "He took a university degree in Philosophy. Got a bursary to Aberdeen. Of course our father could never have afforded it. And he has frittered away his time and his life ever since. Wanders all over the world like a vagabond."

"That's not true" Michael countered, fixing those brilliant blue eyes on Ishmael from beneath his glossy black locks. "I don't believe in doing, but being."

"He's never done anything," said Erik angrily. "As for being…"

"I'm doing my doctorate thesis" Michael interrupted quickly. "I started it eight years ago."

"Have you not finished it then?" Ishmael asked.

"Oh dear, no, I haven't. The trouble is" Michael whined, "that when I lift my pen I cannae write." There was a pause. And then he added, "I think it's a sign of deepening of the mind." And he wagged his head sagely.

"And what's the thesis?" asked Ishmael.

"It's not just a thesis now" Michael responded absentmindedly, "it's a spiritual message."

"Spiritual message, my foot" Erik interjected furiously, "it's a lot of twaddle."

"Yes, but what is the message?" Ishmael persisted.

"SOD."

"SOD?"

"It's quite clear, isn't it?" responded Michael without irritation.

"I'm afraid it isn't. Why don't you clarify?"

"Society is based on deceit. It's a spiritual call to the masses to prepare for the great day."

Erik let out a contemptuous guffaw and left the room.

"I hope" said Michael impressively, ignoring Erik's interruption, "that the technical obstacles may be overcome in the next ten years or so, if I may employ that fallacious chronological conception. That is to say that once my prophecy is fulfilled, all intercourse between humans, which at present is based on deceit – think of the charlatans, the mumbo-jumbo of priests, the ignorance of teachers and doctors parading as wisdom, lawyers' super-subtle stratagems, politicians' duplicity, the avaricious sleight of hand of bankers and businessmen in general, not to mention the disingenuous schemes of husbands and wives, all intercourse based on deceit shall be known for what it is when the great day comes when TRUTH WILL TRIUMPH." He raised his voice ot the stentorian level of the Homeric herald.

"But what then" Ishmael inquired, "is the basis for your prophecy?"

"It was Professor Niels Birbaumer at the University of Tubingen who first grasped that it was possible to decipher the workings and the content of the human brain with perfect accuracy. This led to experiments at the University of California incorporating a big brain scanner and the revelation of individuals' thought through TT and KOT: Transparent Thought and the Knowledge of what Others are Thinking. Similar experiments took place with the vast Ferranti Mk 1 Star computer in Britain."

"Yes, but what has been your part in this?"

"I have been in touch with scientists world-wide, and it is only a question of time before, at my instigation, a minute brain scanner, which can be fastened to the underside of a lapel, will become universally available. From that moment there can be no more deceit. Humanity shall live in eternal harmony as the planets and the stars – allowing of course for a few inevitable collisions in the stratosphere."

Michael paused, looking interrogatively at Ishmael. "And can you foresee any disadvantage?"

As Ishmael remained silent Michael proceeded. "There is only one disadvantage. It would mean the loss of freedom. No longer could we choose to tell lies, to betray, to cheat, to flatter, to be faux-naïf. And if we knew how base people really are, dignitaries and celebrities, the great new aristocracy, would no longer be the object of envy, the great driving force of our capitalist society. But the loss of freedom to deceive would be as nothing to the gains of the world revolution that will surpass all previous revolutions in history, and on Earth. Out of chaos will emerge a new order."

Ishmael looked in astonishment at this extraordinary figure, wondering whether he was not insane.

But Michael, sensing the possibility of a disciple, fixed those brilliant blue eyes on Ishmael, continued, "Morality shall be dispensed with, self-righteousness will evaporate, humanity will instead of hatred and strife be enraptured by visions of spiritual beauty. One only has to glance at the domes and minarets of Isfahan to see the truth of my idea."

"Isfahan? Why Isfahan?"

"Because the domes and minarets of Isfahan were the inspiration for the Taj Mahal. That's not open to question, surely?"

Ishmael could not prevent an ironic grimace, that turned against his will into a smile. This seemed to please Michael, so Ishmael persisted.

"Have you been to Isfahan?"

"Indeed I have. It is my physical and spiritual home. I am only absent on account of our poor father's illness. But I hope to enlighten him before his passing from one world to another."

"Could I ask, what do you live on, how do you make your living in Isfahan?"

"I lecture at the university."

"And what do you lecture on?"

"English literature. I have only two students, but they have given me a vast lecture hall. This has the inestimable advantage that I can practise public declamation in readiness for the great day when the universal truth shall be revealed and shall be proclaimed. I get my students to sit at the back of the hall, as far away from my dais as possible so that I have to project my voice at full volume to reach them."

"What works in English literature do you lecture on?"

"Only one. Sheridan's 'The School For Scandal.' It is the only English book I could get two copies of in Isfahan. The students share one, and I, of course, have the other."

"Are they good students?"

"Excellent. By chance they are both diminutive: Mr Salek and Miss Tafazol. Which makes it easier for them to share the book. In one of my last lectures they greeted me in chorus upon my arrival. 'Mister Anderson,' they said, 'we have an announcement to make.'

"And what is that?" I asked them.

Perfectly synchronised, they said, 'Mr Anderson, we think your English is perfect.'

"You must have been very pleased."

"Indeed I was. They very kindly went on to remind me that the English literature examination was the next day, and that it was important for them to do well."

"And did they pass?"

"Oh yes, of course. I always pass all – I should say both – but in fact there are three students. You see I like to help them. The third student is a tall bearded Persian who told me he had so time to waste on 'The School For Scandal.' I believe he is some kind of revolutionary. So naturally I passed him too, although he didn't turn up for the examination. There were only two questions anyway. The first one was 'What characteristics do Sir Benjamin Backbite, Lady Sneerwell and Mrs Candour show?' And the second, 'When Sir Peter Teazle arrives in Joseph's library, who is hiding behind a screen?' We had rehearsed these and similar questions repeatedly."

At that moment the sound of a Land-Rover arriving could be heard, and a moment later the laughter of the girls as they opened the garden gate as well as the cheerful voice of Sheena succouring the tottering shepherd up the path. Not wanting to be involved in this family reunion Ishmael hurriedly said goodbye to Michael, and to Erik, whom he found in the kitchen, and left by the back door.

★

The day after Ishmael's encounter with Erik and Michael the shepherd died. Old Anderson had recently made a visit to Edinburgh with Ishmael and the doctor, the reasons for which he would not divulge, in spite of Sheena's earnest entreaties. He had, he was prepared to say, got very hot in the over-heated train from Inverness and then freezing cold in the biting Edinburgh east wind. A few days later he had insisted, in his very precarious state of health, on going to the sheep market in Dingwall. The two excursions had killed him.

There was a simple burial in the small wild grave yard overlooking Loch Mhor, at which Erik presided in his Jesuit cassock. Only Michael, Sheena and the girls, the doctor and Ishmael were present. Ishmael, who wore his Black Watch kilt, played a lament on his bag-pipes while the west wind blew strongly. Sheep, which had got in through the broken iron railings wandered over the horizontal slab tombstones and between the perpendicular ones, several of which had fallen over at grotesque angles, cropping the grass. Which was the only care that cemetery ever got.

The youngest girl, peeping from behind her mother's skirts asked, "What do we live for?" as the earth drummed on the coffin lid.

★

After the funeral the doctor called at Ishmael's cottage. They drank a dram to the shepherd's soul with great sadness.

The doctor then asked Ishmael what he made of Michael's theory of SOD, society being based on deceit. And his prophecy of the triumph of truth with the advent of universal minute brain scanners.

Ishmael at first laughed but then, looking straight into the doctor's eyes said, "He is obviously a dreamer, but it is perfectly possible that what he prognosticates is true."

"In that case, God help us," laughed the doctor. "He will be the greatest prophet ever. No wonder that when he lifts his pen he cannae write. But I hope I will not be alive if, or when, his prophecy comes true."

ARRIVAL OF THE ARISTOCRATS

Ishmael now had to get ready for the great grouse shoot the following Friday and Saturday. It was to be an aristocratic affair with the famous Englishman Lord Gripon, reputed to be the best shot in Great Britain, as the number one attraction. People in the know from far and wide would flock to see him in action, and Major Tooth himself and his southern cronies from Henley-on-Thames would be there in force.

It was as much a social event as a shoot, and as she normally shunned such things everyone was surprised that Lady Dalry herself was to turn up with a retinue from Dalry Castle. But the Viscount was engaged on 'important' business in London, which might in part explain her proposed presence. But still, people wondered. She had booked rooms at the Ledgowan Hotel at Achnasheen, a nineteenth century shooting lodge, whose spacious hall and staircase was decorated with stags' heads brooding with glass-eyed melancholy from resplendent pitch pine walls. The Hon. Crispin was to accompany her, though he would arrive in his own British racing green Triumph TR4 with his friend and rising parliamentary star Julian Colquhon who was anxious as ever to keep in with the aristocracy to further his career. Lady Dalry would of course be driven by her chauffeur in the white Rolls-Royce convertible in which poor Sheila had been tearfully taken home from the famous 'bash' at the castle.

Meanwhile Ishmael had to supervise the preparations, overseeing McCrone and the ghillies, who were to act as beaters, and some outlandish volunteers. There were a hundred and one other tasks incumbent on him as manager of the estate, bearing in mind that the laird himself was to be of the party. Ruts and holes in the track from the Heights had to be repaired, Land-Rovers serviced and cleaned, al fresco luncheons ordered from the Loch Mhor Hotel, and of course, vast quantities of champagnes and wines had to be laid in to accompany the food hampers, besides a good stock of the best whiskies.

HATRED SIMMERS

When he was close to them, Ishmael could only just restrain the impulse to do violence to McCrone and Gillespie. 'Giving them the strangulation treatment without respite.' But that would have to wait. They eyed one another with black-eyed hatred from some distance, Gillespie muttering to the keeper

"If I haadn't thought he was going for good I'd 'a done for him long ago. Like I did for his collie."

"Hud yer wheesht" growled McCrone, "or the bastard'll hear ye. Bide yer time, maan, bide yer time."

★

THE LAIRD

When the first day of the famous grouse massacre approached Ishmael had got everything in meticulous order. As soon as Major Tooth arrived from the south of England on the eve of this ostentatious event he made a thorough reconnaissance with the factor in tow. Tooth was a bristling little man in his sixties, rotund, bald, moustachioed, and given to making venomous jokes. The factor was the principal butt of his humour when he was in the north, especially now that his timorous wife was left behind. Tooth fancied himself with the ladies. He may not have been very handsome, but he was a multi-millionaire, after all. He was particularly pleased that Lady Dalry was joining the party and had already paid a call at the Ledgowan Hotel. Ostensibly on business. But the major had contrived to meet her in the hotel bar, where she was taking a solitary cocktail as a prelude to dinner at The White Lodge.

"Tooth and tonic, Eliza?" he quipped with a facetious smirk.

Lady Dalry managed a wry smile. While they exchanged banalities Major Tooth was doing a little calculation.

'Twenty-nine from sixty-three' he pondered. 'Only thirty-four years between us. And a woman's finished at forty' he chuckled to himself. Which caused Lady Dalry to look at him sharply. 'Might have a little fun with her while that ass Dalry is out of the way.'

Lady Dalry, however, had not made the journey from the Castle to hob-nob with the likes of Major Tooth, though she had, for reasons of her own, agreed to attend the grand dinner he was giving for local lairds and other big-wigs. And she objected to this parvenu calling her by her Christian name. She regarded him as 'a silly little man' and tired by his self-importance she dispatched a waiter to call Crispin and Julian Colquhon from their rooms upstairs to entertain 'the vulgar bore.' So after a cursory conversation with Tooth she escaped on the pretext of feeling tired after her journey and needing a little rest. For his part, as a self-made man Tooth despised 'those spoilt puppies' and soon left the hotel in rather ill humour.

As a consequence Tooth's inspection of the estate resulted in peculiarly waspish treatment of the bumbling factor. But he found everything better prepared than he had ever known, and having an astute business mind soon realised that the transformation of the hitherto haphazard arrangements was due to his new manager. To whom he took an instant liking.

As many a bully of his kind, the major respected a man who stood up to him. He had no time for forelock-tuggers and mercilessly belittled those he saw were afraid of him. Which included his complaisant wife. Who nevertheless had the inestimable advantage of being the heiress of a biscuit manufacturer from the Midlands. But unfortunately she retained her Manchester accent. Which did not go down well in Henley-on-Thames. And she would have been an embarrassment at the gala dinner.

Tooth even began to think he would retire the factor and install young McCulloch in his place. But he would wait and see how the shoot went and on what terms he could employ his new factor. For in spite of his millions, Major Tooth was careful of his pennies. After a visit to the estate he would always get his chauffeur to stop at the local shop on the way south, although it was half a mile off his route, to collect the deposit on a crate of empty tonic water bottles. Tuppence on each of them.

THE LAIRD'S BANQUET

When all the preparations for the shoot were over, Ishmael went back to his cottage, had a shower and changed his clothes. And then made his way unwillingly towards the great white hunting lodge overlooking Loch Mhor for Major Tooth's dinner party. An obligation he could not get out of if he wanted to keep his job. About which he was not sure. He crossed over the loch in the launch with the half-wit, who was acting as ferryman, with a few early guests.

The dinner was to be at eight o'clock 'sharp,' as Tooth's invitation card stipulated. Finding himself approaching The Lodge half an hour early Ishmael made a detour along the loch shore, having left his puppy with the shepherd for safekeeping. As he emerged onto the narrow roadway by the lodge a ferocious Alsatian bounded aggressively towards him, barking menacingly, got its mouth over the sleeve of his jacket and clamped its jaws closed, biting through the rough tweed and grazing his wrist. Ishmael gave it a swift kick where it would hurt it most, and the dog ran off howling and whimpering to a gawky middle-aged woman with glasses crossing his path.

"Why don't you keep your dog under control?" Ishmael demanded, nursing his tooth-marked wrist.

"He's only playing" shrieked the apparition. "You had no business to hurt him. He's only a puppy."

"Listen, that dog could terrify an elderly or frail person and cause a heart attack. There's an eighty-year-old woman living in that cottage over there. And there are lambs on the estate. So you just do as you're told and keep your dog on that lead until it's trained, and don't let me find it behaving like that again. I'm warning you."

The harridan glared at him through her glasses, but she did put the dog on the lead, stumping off with a stream of shrill vituperation over her shoulder.

By the time he arrived at The White Lodge it was now a little late and the guests, primarily lairds of local estates besides eminent 'sporting' aristocrats, were sitting at a long polished mahogany table, about to begin dinner. Major Tooth, who had placed Lady Dalry on his right at the head of the table, indicated that Ishmael should sit in the middle of one side, introducing him to the assembly with a eulogy as a first-class manager who had made sure that the shoot would get off perfectly tomorrow.

"He's got everything running like clockwork, hasn't he, McKay?" Tooth called out archly to the factor who sat at the bottom end of the table.

"Yes, that may be, but I hold to the traditional ways of doing things," the factor answered peevishly, "I don't like working against the clock."

"Then you don't like life!" the major riposted, raising a ripple of laughter round the table.

When Ishmael sat down he found himself opposite the harridan he had met with the Alsatian less than an hour earlier, who glowered at him in greeting.

Major Tooth may not have been an aristocrat but he was by far the richest man present. Whenever money matters were discussed – the perennial preoccupation of those impecunious lairds – Tooth was dominant and never at a loss for an anecdote. So that when the laird of the Gowan estate was bemoaning the fall of the stock market, Tooth interrupted him and his own chewing, rapid like a rabbit,

"Listen, Gowan, did you hear of the Frenchman who lost his fortune in shares when there was a slump? You didn't? Well, let me tell you. This is a true story. He was so depressed that he decided to kill himself. He went to his local ironmonger's to buy a rope. To hang himself, Gowan! Now being a Frenchman he had already calculated the exact length of rope required. Not a centimetre more, nor a centimetre less. But when the ironmonger told him the price, he threw up his hands and spent the next quarter of an hour haggling over it. Within an hour he was dead! There's a man I admire, eh Gowan!" Tooth declared waggishly, glancing round the mahogany table in search of any dissenters. But all assiduously laughed, nodding their heads. After all, many of them were hoping to sell Tooth part of their estates that they could not afford. And even Lady Dalry chuckled at this apocryphal tale.

Though they all criticised Tooth afterwards as an old skinflint. Having eaten the magnificent dinner he provided and drunk as much of his liquor as they could hold. Some drinking a little more than that.

Ishmael himself, who found the proceedings excruciatingly boring, relieved the tedium with copious quantities of Glenfiddich that he persuaded a jolly waitress to supply him. But he didn't lose his head: even under the sour scrutiny of the spectre opposite.

"Priscilla!" bawled Tooth from the head of the table, keen to provoke the unmarried daughter of the English laird of Achnashellach, who had refused to sell the Major a stretch of salmon river he coveted, "Priscilla, you're up with all these problems of suicides and so on as a social worker. Tell us what you think."

"Social worker indeed!" replied the righteous maiden. "I am a probation officer."

"Oh yes, we're all officers in Britain now, aren't we?" Tooth retorted acidly, "from policemen to civil servants. Just like the old Spanish army."

"A police person, please" interjected the spinster. "That remark of yours is pure sexual discrimination. Whatever are we coming to?"

"The age of the androgyny" Tooth replied, conscious that the elegant Lady Dalry was watching him with amusement; while the poor bespectacled spinster was covered in blushing confusion.

In the awkward silence that followed, Tooth then enquired mischievously whether Ishmael and Priscilla already knew one another.

"I think we've met before" Priscilla assented with a frigid glance at Ishmael.

"I'm afraid we have" said Ishmael.

"Afraid?" she countered, peering acidly through those rather grimy spectacles. "Tell me, Mr McCulloch, are you afraid of dogs?"

Ishmael paused a moment, and answered

"No, only of bitches."

★

'THE PHENOMENON'

The shoot began at eight o'clock sharp, with a great array of Range-Rovers and Land-Rovers at the top of the glen, and a motley crowd of 'sportsmen' and women rigged out in as many garbs as one could imagine. There was a profusion of deer-stalker hats – 'fore and afts' to those in the know – cloth caps, leather jerkins with bandoleers, hideous green parkas with innumerable zips, plus fours and plus twos, shooting-sticks, whisky flasks and, of course, extremely expensive old-fashioned double-barrel twelve-bores of all the best makes, some inlaid with silver and pearl woodwork. Killing, after all, must be done in style. Even if the quarry is only a small fluffy ball of life. A few of the younger set sported American, Italian and German repeaters, but these, in good old British style, were regarded by the true aficionados as infra-dig.

These valiant warriors, well prepared to mete out justice to the unsuspecting grouse, were aided and abetted by a horde of beaters, including the three ghillies and under the nominal control of the game-keeper, but in reality organised by Ishmael, concealed for the moment some hundreds of yards to the east. On the given signal, they set up a horrible shindy, sending countless grouse whizzing over the heads of the noble hunters.

Crispin and Julian, who were still half-drunk from the splendid party at the Ledgowan Hotel last night, were prancing about with their lanky legs in plus twos, none too steady on their feet. They were the first to fire, waving their guns wildly in the air and letting off shots at random, hitting no birds. But a volley of Crispin's from his brand new Fabarm, an Italian nine shot repeater, passed close over the heads of Major Tooth and Lord Gripon, accompanied by Gripon's two loaders.

With furious gesticulations, Tooth waved 'the puppies' aside, just in time for His Lordship to perform what he called his 'tour de force.' He contrived to hit five birds in the air at the same time from his pair of double-barrelled Purdies, with the assiduous assistance of his two loaders, who handed him recharged guns with the speed of the flying birds.

In spite of the fact that two of the grouse were merely winged, fluttering down wounded and in agony, this feat was cheered wildly by spectators who had come from far and wide to see 'the phenomenon,' as this performance was called. The twelve bore genius found time for a quick celebratory draught from a silver flask proffered by his chief loader. A paunchy, bald man with a red face, he then raised an arm in airy acknowledgement of the applause.

"How <u>do</u> you manage it?" simpered the Hon. Hugh McNab from the ranks of the spectators, anxious to ingratiate himself. The Lord Gripon condescendingly let it be known that he always practised until after midnight with his two loaders on the eve of a shoot.

"Kept 'em out of their beds till half past two this morning" the braggart bawled. "That's how we do it, you know, eh! Eh!"

He took another swig from the flask obsequiously held ready by the loader.

"I say, I say!" chirped Crispin, " that was simply splendid!"

"Heah! heah! Twemendous stuff!" extolled the budding parliamentarian Julian Colquhon, never missing an opportunity of keeping on the right side of the aristocracy, or indeed anyone with power and influence. His only regret was that Lord Dalry, detained in London 'on important business' could not be there to hear his 'heah! heahs!'

"Not to worry" confided the Hon. Crispin, "the old man'll be up for stag stalking in a couple of weeks and we can make sure he has your ear, or rather he … as you were … you have his ear, you know, which ever way round it is."

"A splendid wheeze. Spot on! You've said it!" Julian eagerly agreed.

When the first drive had moved forward to get ready for the next, Lady Dalry, wearing a bright yellow blouse over her dark green tartan skirt, her abundant blonde hair ruffled by the wind, was restraining her black labrador on his lead when she saw that Ishmael had come up behind the beaters. He was standing on a knoll with

Black Watch khaki balmoral observing the throng of beaters through field glasses, quite apart now from the general crowd of bird killers.

As it so happened, Charles, Lady Dalry's black labrador, pulled on his lead in that direction and she found herself staggering almost at Ishmael's side. He lifted his binoculars a moment, looking into the bonny face of that twenty-nine year old woman, who was smiling faintly, unsure what welcome to expect. Ishmael then lowered the field glasses and took the small, delicate outstretched hand.

"I don't suppose you've got a moment, Mr McCulloch, with all your responsibilities this morning. Eliza, Lady Dalry."

"Yes, I have" answered Ishmael.

"Now that rabble have gone forward I'm free a while. What can I do for you?"

"Well, I've come on a poaching mission" laughed Lady Dalry, steadying her straining labrador. "I don't quite know how to put it" she said, pushing aside a wisp of blonde hair wind-blown across her face, while Ishmael looked at her intently, wondering what this could mean. He was simultaneously shocked to find that he was powerfully attracted to this woman, his smouldering black eyes riveted on her bonny visage.

"You see, I've had to sack our factor at Dalry Castle. My husband spends most of his time in London, so he delegates the running of the estate to me. Crispin just isn't interested. Irregularities in the accounts. I detest going through the books and always put it off as long as possible, which compounded the problem. At first I could hardly believe what I found. Thought I must have got it wrong. Anyway, I won't bore you with that. I believe you did a course in estate management" she began rather awkwardly, seeming not to be quite sure of herself now, and added pensively as it were, "I wonder whether the factor's post, vacant now, might possibly be of interest to you."

"It might well be, but with your permission, I'd need to think about it."

"Of course. I imagine you'd want to see the estate and the factor's house and so on."

Ishmael nodded.

"Now although I'm booked into the Ledgowan for tonight I'm going to cancel it because frankly I don't much care for being a spectator at this kind of thing. Crispin cajoled me into coming but I intend to go home after lunch today. When does the shoot end?"

"At four o'clock."

"And tomorrow?"

"The same routine. Eight in the morning until four p.m."

"In that case I suppose you wouldn't have time to come back with me and see the estate this evening? My chauffeur would bring you back whenever you like. It's only two hours."

"I don't see why not, if you wouldn't mind about the driver. I must be here at seven o'clock in the morning."

"Whichever you prefer, Mr McCulloch. I could offer you a room for the night at the Castle and send the chauffeur early in the morning. Or he could bring you back tonight, once you've had a good look round. In that case I'd have him take over my room at the hotel."

The guns were firing frenetically now and Ishmael had to get the next drive off after lunch, so it was hastily arranged that he would call at the Ledgowan Hotel as soon as possible after the shoot had finished.

Meanwhile, Lady Dalry joined Major Tooth and his cronies for the cold luncheon of caviar, lobster and crab salad, with an iced champagne aperitif. Followed by the best French and German white wines. Ishmael kept himself apart, making do with a cheese and onion sandwich and a pint of McEwan's export.

TEMPTATION

When Ishmael had parked his Land-Rover in front of the Ledgowan Hotel and entered the spacious lobby, he found Lady Dalry ready and waiting there. She said goodbye to the owner, who came out rubbing his hands and grinning at the lady while the hall porter heaved the luggage into the boot of the Rolls Royce. The chauffeur held the passenger door open for Lady Dalry to take her seat in the back and politely saluting Ishmael, indicated to him that he should sit beside the driver in the front.

The journey south passed without incident and more or less in silence, the chauffeur driving the limousine sedately past mountain, loch and river. Lady Dalry of course knew about Sheila but said nothing. After all, she had been at the Shandon Lodge Ceilidh.

When they arrived at the imposing turreted castle by Bridge of Orchy, Lady Dalry led Ishmael to a small sunken sitting-room three steps down from the main hall with mullioned windows and a polished wood floor. When they had passed through the 100 foot hall Lady Dalry paused a moment to let Ishmael look at its ceiling with painted heraldic crests and the colossal fire-place one could easily walk into. She pointed out the holes in the wall by the great door for letting off arrows or muskets at besieging enemies, and the massive sliding bolt twelve inches square that held the fortified door against attack.

But now they sat in antique upright chairs at a small table in a corner of the adjacent sitting-room, the evening sunlight penetrating the mullioned windows in dusty shafts. Lady Dalry rang a little hand bell and when the butler appeared ordered first a MacAllan for Ishmael and a cocktail for herself, which were duly brought on a silver tray.

When the butler had gone, Lady Dalry looked straight at Ishmael and offered a salary several times greater than the pay at Loch Mhor.

"Twenty-two estate workers" she said quietly, and there was an uneasy silence during which they looked at one another and then looked away. Both knew. Unmistakable lurking passion. And not so lurking. She smiled slowly now, with supreme self-possession, gazing into Ishmael's eyes. If it's not today, then it will be tomorrow, her hazel eyes said. And who knows that she wouldn't be right?

"Well, shall we have a look over the estate?" suggested Lady Dalry brightly once the drinks had been drunk. Their tour in a Range Rover lasted a little over an hour, taking in the magnificent grounds and moorland, river and loch, then stopping at the factor's house, now empty. Ishmael was astonished. It was a four bedroom, white-washed building of two storeys with a periwinkle growing up the front wall. It had, besides two well-furnished sitting-rooms and a dining-room with a french window, two bathrooms and the usual kitchen, scullery amenities. The house was set in half an acre of garden with Scots pines, larch, black poplars and birches. It seemed to be an ideal place: well kept and secluded, about a quarter of a mile from the castle.

"What about a light supper?" asked Eliza suddenly when they had returned to the sunken sitting-room. She had by now succeeded in cajoling Ishmael into first name familiarity, though she could sense by his strained aspect that he was by no means at ease.

"As it's late, I'll rustle up something myself if you'll put up with my cooking" she said, getting up and putting the bottle of Mac Allan on the little table before disappearing through a side door.

She had been right to observe the inner tension Ishmael suffered. The offer of the factor's job, with all the advantages of being his own boss, not to mention the house and the magnificence of the estate itself, was almost overwhelming. And yet….

Ishmael had got no further in these ruminations when the side door was abruptly opened and Lady Dalry entered carrying a small wooden tray.

"Didn't take a moment" she said smiling, "It's so simple."

And she placed plates with succulent asparagus omelettes on the table, besides a cold game pie and a small bottle of Marques del Riscal deep red rioja before them. With a basket of wholemeal bread and exquisitely starched napkins Ishmael felt embarrassed at eating at such close quarters, but the supper was so good that after a quick hefty dram his inhibitions left him. It was now after ten o'clock and twilight.

"Well, which is it to be?" Lady Dalry asked briskly, "will you stay the night or shall I send the chauffeur to Loch Mhor tonight? It won't inconvenience him. As I mentioned, I have cancelled my room at the hotel but I can easily keep the option open so he could stay there. Or he can drive you early in the morning. Whichever you prefer. But come up quickly and I'll show you your room here."

So saying, she was already half way out of the room, and Ishmael felt obliged to follow. She led him upstairs and along rambling passages, stopping suddenly and throwing open the door of a spacious bedroom with a bathroom connecting.

"My own room is at the end of the corridor. Dalry and I no longer share a bedroom. The boys are in the west wing" she added quickly.

Ishmael had already decided he must go.

"It would have to be very early in the morning" he said, "having to be there by seven. We'd need to leave here by four in the morning at the latest. So I will accept your very kind offer for the driver to take me tonight."

Just for a fleeting moment, Lady Dalry seemed to purse her lips. But just for a moment. She immediately smiled, saying

"Please think over the proposition this weekend and let me know on Monday, could you? I won't press you, but I think you would be the ideal man for the position and, if I may say so, the position might be ideal for you."

"I absolutely agree with you about the position being ideal. Everything points to that. I will do as you say and get in touch on Monday, if you'd kindly give me your phone number."

Ishmael didn't know how they would disengage. He could feel intensely that she wanted him to take her in his arms. And he felt a strong temptation to do that. So he rapidly gave her his hand and turned abruptly to go downstairs. But stopped, after taking a step.

"Would you care to say goodnight to the boys while I call James? They're in the card room."

Half relieved and half unwilling to meet 'the puppies,' Ishmael agreed, following Lady Dalry's instructions to that room, from which he could hear a hullabaloo as he got near it. Pushing open the door he was greeted with drunken yells by Crispin, Julian, Giles and the Hon. Hugh McNab. They were grouped round a chemmy board, still dressed in their ludicrous plus twos and now sporting fancy embroidered waistcoats.

"Come and join us, old fruit."

"Oh yeas! Easy money heah, provided you don't mind losing it, heugh! heugh!" crowed Crispin. "Left your shoot. Such a bore, you know. We shan't be back tomorrow, eh, Julian?"

"I say" interrupted Giles, almost knocking over the decanter and port glasses arrayed on the table, "do take a pew and take a swig. Best Cockburn's port.

Ishmael sat on the vacant chair at the table, poured himself a glass out of curiosity and passed the decanter on. Paralytically drunk though the quartet were, one thing did not escape them ….

"I say, chaps. Would you believe!" exclaimed the Hon. Hugh. "He passed the port to the left! To the left, I tell you! By the by, what about that little girl friend of yours? You've lost nothing theah! I heah she's gone back to that nonentity of an accountant. A bit more her style, don't you know!"

"If you weren't so drunk I'd knock your little twit's head off" responded Ishmael, getting up and approaching the Hon. Hugh, who cowered.

But Ishmael had stepped forward for an unexpected reason. He gave the chemmy table a tremendous kick into the air, sending cash stakes, decanter, glasses and all flying, the table top separated from its pedestal.

"Good night, then" said Ishmael from the doorway, "that's what I came to say."

But the only reaction was a chorus of

"I say, that's not on, you know."

"Heah! heah!"

"Not to worry. We'll … we'll … what'll we do chaps … Shall we put him in the pond?"

The quartet staggered to their feet, falling about the room as they did so.

"Get outside" Ishmael ordered, "and we'll see."

Once out, the chemmy players could now hardly stay on their feet, so drunk were they, and had no idea what they were doing, fumbling and shuffling about like blind men.

"Form up in single file" barked Ishmael as they stood by the drive. They had all done National Service except Julian so instinctively they obeyed in an alcoholic haze.

"Right turn! Quick march. Get in step there" hectored Ishmael, prodding the straggling Julian in the back.

It was pitch black and the quartet had no idea where they were but they marched in a parody of a parade until the command

"Patrol halt. Left turn. Stand to attention for inspection."

Ishmael now gave the order "Dress by the right. Get into line," as he walked in front of them and they shuffled to obey.

When he was satisfied that his undisciplined rabble were readily expectant of the next command he gave the order

"Two steps backward, march!"

And moving very rapidly down the line he gave the staggering four in turn a violent push backwards. Which sent them tumbling into the pond that they had neither seen nor apprehended. Amid the spluttering and splashing Ishmael turned to hear the chauffeur say

"Excuse me, sir. The car's ready and waiting whenever you wish. Well done, sir, if I may say so."

INTROSPECTION. RESOLUTION.

The Rolls Royce made good headway northwards in the encroaching darkness, the roads being more or less deserted and the driver, like Ishmael, taciturn by temperament. Which allowed Ishmael to reflect on Lady Dalry's offer. 'The temptation of the devil' he said to himself. 'The ideal work – the work I'm perhaps made for – my own boss, a good house, good pay ...' But he didn't need to think it over for long. He had no intention of becoming Mellors to Lady Chatterley. A book – and Mellors a man – he despised. For that reason – the strong and evident sexual attraction between them – the offer must be turned down.

Yet there was another and more important reason. His encounter with the charming and very beautiful Lady Dalry had acted as a catalyst. He knew now as he hadn't known before that he could not let Sheila go. His meeting with Lady Dalry, and the impertinence of 'the puppy,' had made that certain. Whether 'it would last' or not. No other man was to have Sheila. And he would have no other woman. In spite of all temptation. Sheila was not as beautiful as Lady Dalry. But the fact that Lady Dalry had offered him munificent terms – as had Shandon, after all – eased that sense of financial inferiority that had plagued him with regard to Sheila and her family. Although he had never wanted their damned money. He had been mortified by that ugly shadow that crossed Sheila's face. Something he could barely forgive. He wasn't going to budge on his Loch Mhor job. Sheila would have to put up with that. And why not?

But there remained what was for Ishmael the great question to be resolved. And that of course was to deal with the murderer of his Collie. That would be done without more delay. How he had left it so long was the question that burned into his soul. It must and would be resolved, whatever the consequences.

As the Rolls-Royce cruised through Glen Coe in the eerie

twilight Ishmael thought of Scotland's litany of failure and defeat. And the Scotch propensity to blame it all on the English. But Scottish treachery and disunity were the causes of much of that cherished woe. He didn't hate the English, as so many of his countrymen. On the contrary, he admired them as a last but sinking bastion of civilization in a corrupt Europe. Whose leaders, whether French, German or Italian, had all been involved in evil of one kind or another.

Ishmael was roused from this protracted reverie by the realization that they were approaching Achnasheen. On reaching the Ledgowan Hotel he thanked the chauffeur – though he couldn't thank him for his silence – jumped into the Land-Rover and headed down the 'glen of evil scouring.' As he got near Kinlochewe Ishmael felt the chill of apprehension at what lay before him. His appearance as the Land-Rover passed, half an hour or so later, through Kinloch caused a minor sensation. He was jeered by the crowd outside the hotel bar, at this late hour, among whom he recognized Archie Gillespie, with the proprietress of the Kinloch Inn beside him, her paps flapping in public view. 'Big' Angus was there too, swigging from the usual half-bottle and offering it round. And then Ishmael started. Did he recognize the Inverness poachers he had committed to jail? The ghillies would be celebrating the tips they'd got from Lord Gripon and company. But the Inverness poachers? Maybe it wasn't them.

He called briefly at Succoth Farm, seeing lights shining from the windows, to see if they were all right in the aftermath of the shepherd's death.

"I cannae sleep, Mr McCulloch" said Sheena, "I feel thaat strange wi' John no' being, here. I'm waiting up for Erik. He's in the byre. There's been a couple o' sheep haas taken baad. And Michael's away tae the Edinburgh festival."

"If there's anything I can do, Mrs Anderson, please let me know. Day or night. I'll call in tomorrow evening, after the shoot."

As she accompanied him to the porch Sheena hesitated a moment, and then anxiously

"You won't be staying up there after the shooting party's gone, will you, Mr McCulloch. There's baad folk about these parts, nothing but a lot of rascals. They pick up the dead and wounded birds the dogs hasn't found an' they're not above killing a few an' all if they caan get them. So John's said many a time."

"Don't you worry about that, Mrs Anderson" said Ishmael as he bade her good night.

★

WHERE IS SHEILA?

As soon as he reached his cottage Ishmael poured a large dram, and then telephoned Shandon Lodge.

"Sheila we must meet immediately. I'll come to Glasgow on Sunday. The Kelvin Grove hotel again, in Sauchiehall Street near the park. At 6 o'clock."

That was what he was going to say. The telephone rang and rang. But there was no answer. He dialled again. He could hear the hollow sound of the phone ringing in an empty house. It sounded distant, as though echoing in corridors and passages.

'Will they have gone out?' he wondered. 'Where would they have gone on a Friday night? No one at home? Not even old Tam? Sheila didn't go out in the evenings, she told me. She wouldn't have gone somewhere with John Robson, would she? But why shouldn't she? Nevertheless, the Hon. Hugh's taunt stung.

The more the phone rang fruitlessly, and it seemed lugubriously, the more determined Ishmael was to make contact. He paused a while. What could he do? A telegram would be useless. And he wouldn't get a answer, in all probability. He didn't know any neighbours to ring. But he must make contact with her. If she answered, he'd chuck the shoot in the morning and go to meet her immediately. Even if he had to go in the old Land-Rover. He'd go now, if only there was an answer. He rang again. But still the telephone sounded through an empty house. He could tell there was no one there.

Then a possibility occurred to him. He rang the local Post Office/General Stores at Shandon.

"It's after hours. No telegram can be delivered until tomorrow" answered the hard voice.

"Could you not please take a message to Shandon Lodge? It's very near you."

"That I could not."

"Why is that? It's urgent."

"They never come near me."

Eventually, for it was very late now, he went to bed. But tomorrow morning he'd phone again. She'd be sure to be at home then. And if not, he could speak to Ella … or Shandon. Oh Christ! How would they react?

He slept fitfully, having a strange dream. He was being led as a prisoner by a gentlemanly person who kept hold of his arm. Obviously a functionary of some importance. Ishmael, offended by this performance, gave his escort his word that he would not try to escape. The functionary took his word and let go his hold of him, but accompanied him still.

They came to a shrine in the wild country between Loch Luichart and Achnasheen forming a plain, which Ishmael realized he had constructed in the past but had forgotten about. It was enclosed inside rectangular railings itself inside a lofty vaulted hall without other rooms in a remote part of the plain.

Ishmael's coffin, which he had also forgotten about, could be seen below a fissure in the floor. All of this struck him on account of its beauty, and he wondered at the months he would lie under the snow on the plain every year.

He took up four huge loaves of bread, flat and circular, in his arms and Sheila, who was lying asleep in a corner on the stone floor, woke and asked him the price of the loaves.

"Can we afford them?" she asked.

Ishmael then noticed the inscription on the stone shrine. It said

EVERYTHING CAN BE RESOLVED. EXCEPT DEATH.

Ishmael was awoken in the small hours by a wild unearthly shriek. Leaping out of bed and opening the dormer window he saw the ghostly form of a white-faced screech owl whose wavering flight crossed in front of the window before flitting through the trees. Slamming the window shut with a curse Ishmael vaulted downstairs and telephoned Shandon Lodge again. What did it matter if he woke the whole household. It was now or never. He knew that.

But the result was the same. That damnable echoing, hollow

ring, ring, ringing. Although he telephoned over and over again. He thumped the receiver down into its cradle as though he would break it, smash it to smithereens. And always there was that hollow ringing reverberating through the Lodge.

★

The house was indeed empty. Sheila, Shandon and Ella were staying for the weekend at the Loch Rannock Hotel, which belonged to John Robson's elderly parents. It was only a few miles from Dalry Castle. And they were accompanied by old Tam as chauffeur on account of Shandon's stroke.

As old Tam drove the magnificent Bentley up the drive of the hotel between rhododendrons as high as a house, rounding a bend there was a kilted figure like a scarecrow standing glaring with an eagle's feather in the cap badge of his balmoral and a hawk crouching on the sleeve of a rough tweed jacket.

"That's my father" said John Robson as the car pulled up beside him.

"Who's this then?" the scarecrow demanded in the high-pitched voice of an old man.

"It's your future daughter-in-law" said Robson as his father stepped close to the open car. As he leaned forward to kiss Sheila on the forehead the hawk hopped onto his shoulder. Sheila let out a scream of delight.

"Now, now, dinna faash yerself" said the old man. "You're a bonny wee laasie. I've taken a fancy to ye. But on ye go aand get yerselves comfortable rooms. Morag'll see to thaat."

Sheila was astonished at the contrast between the staid John Robson and his eccentric father. She was lodged that night in a huge curtained four-poster bed at the end of a long dark corridor. Shivering, she could scarcely sleep, torturing herself with memories of the ceilidh on the eve of her 'marriage' to the wild Ishmael and quavering in her resolve to go through with the wedding next day.

Suddenly there was a bloodcurdling yell in the passage:

"Time to change beds!"

After a few moments one or two bedroom doors edged

cautiously open and one or two eyes spied the gaunt figure of the crazy owner, his silhouetted shadow looming menacingly on the corridor wall, balmoral, hawk, and kilt swaying. But the bedroom doors closed as silently as they had opened and there was no apparent movement to comply with the stentorian order. Though some of the foreign tourists, notably a party of Norwegians, declared later that they had full value for their Scottish holiday at Loch Rannoch.

★

A RED SKY IN THE MORNING

It had been a very striking morning. Ishmael felt it was providential. A good omen. For the cloudy sky was a vivid red over the glen, with a blood red reflection on Loch Mhor. He had taken that sunrise as a portent of action too long delayed.

It was early evening now. Ishmael had ignored Sheena's warning not to go back up by Lochan Shuna once the shoot was over, warning him that there might be rascals up there collecting winged birds.

But Ishmael wanted to think out what he was going to do up there in the purity of the mountain air. He went back to his Land Rover, took out his bag-pipes, and walked along the ridge to Lochan Shuna. He stood on a promontory by the Lochan. He would deal with Shiel's killer that very evening. His plan was to call the two suspects, one by one, to his cottage, ostensibly on estate business. After he had got a confession out of Gillespie or McCrone, whichever it was, by holding him in a headlock, he would make him drink the poison administered to his dog. He had poured it into an empty bottle of whisky and he would empty that liquid down the coward's throat. And tomorrow he would meet Sheila, come what may, and life with her would begin anew. How he remembered that transcendental moment by the lochan.

He had decided on this stratagem with a certain uncharacteristic cunning. Storing an agricultural poison in an empty whisky bottle was a not unknown practice. "Where the law won't act the individual must take the law into his own hands," he said out loud.

Hr paused a moment, as an ominous black cloud obscured the sun, and patted his jacket pocket.

'That's strange. It isn't my .38.' He put his hand into his pocket and pulled out the skeandubh that Seonaid had given him as a wedding present.

'But that's another good omen for Sheila' he thought, 'even if I should always have my pistol with me.'

There was something else in the pocket too. He pulled out some dried petals and stalks. The 'primrosees' of the old man in Sauchiehall Street. 'Of course, I changed my jacket for Tooth's dinner and forgot to change back,' he said to himself.

Glancing round at the menacing sky and feeling the first drops of a threatening cloudburst he noticed some curious shapes moving in the heather about forty yards away. He put down his bagpipes on the ground – he had been skirling The Flowers of the Forest, a lament for Flodden – and turned round, facing the phantoms, which suddenly emerged from their crawl revealing two human figures, one much bigger than the other, whose faces were covered by stitched up balaclavas. They ran towards him now, the big one brandishing a 12 bore shotgun, the other a pick-axe. Closing on him rapidly, the big one stumbled in a patch of bog as he yelled

"We'll haave ye now, ye bastard."

But they came on, giving Ishmael time to duck under the gun, whip out his skeandubh and stab the big man in the solar plexus, the gun going off innocuously. The other raised his pick-axe to strike Ishmael, but once again he dived low at him, cutting him in the groin. There were howls of rage and pain as Ishmael forcibly ripped off the balaclavas. McCrone and Gillespie. He hurled Gillespie's pick-axe away, shouting

"You filthy cowards! You've saved me the trouble of looking for you. I know it now. You killed my Shiel. Now I'll kill you."

The two were bleeding profusely from the wounds of the skeandubh but still lurching on their feet, McCrone desperately trying to re-load but fumbling ineffectively and Gillespie pulling out a long, evil-looking knife. With a terrible demonic fury Ishmael lunged again at Sandy Gillespie, knocking his knife out of his hand and ripping through his liver with the skeandubh. At once turning on McCrone, who having failed to re-load was staggering with the gun held high over his head as a club, Ishmael plunged the skeandubh into his heart. As the two fell dead in the heather Ishmael took up his bagpipes and returning to the promontory called out, so that it resounded round the mountain tops,

"Shiel! You are avenged," before skirling 'Highland Laddie' on the bagpipes.

But unknown to Ishmael, two other figures had crept round behind him. The two Inverness deer poachers. The big brute stole up on him and with a leap from behind pinioned Ishmael's arms behind his back, screaming to his accomplice

"Let him haave it, Jimmy."

In a split second Ishmael lifted a knee and gave the beast a tremendous back kick in the testicles that left him reeling with pain. But before the beast's armhold broke, wee Jimmy the weasel stabbed Ishmael to the heart with a commando knife. Ishmael fell dead on the instant without a sound.

Just then there was a terrible flash of lightning and a thunderclap that seemed to shake the very mountains. Lochan Shuna had been whipped into a turbulent sea of angry, white-crested waves by the tempestuous wind. It was as though the heavens were enraged at the evil antics of mortals.

The two deer poachers were now aghast at what they were left with. Three bloody corpses.

"We'll haave to get these outa here" whispered the weasel, now trembling with fright and cold, "or they'll haave us inside for life. We canna leave a single body here or the polis'll get us."

"Right ye are, Jimmy. I'll tell ye what we'll do. We'll leave the maanager's Land-Rover where it is and get our own as close as we caan. Away ye go aand get it now, aand hurry or the ground'll get water-logged wi' this bloody storm."

The sky was now yellow-black and the thunder and lightning incessant. But wee Jimmy the weasel managed to get the Land-Rover 20 yards from the three dead bodies, though the chattering of his teeth could be heard by his accomplice in spite of the storm when he returned.

"We'll haave to lift yon bodies" said the big brute. "You'll tak the legs an' I'll get the arms an' shoulders."

And so they staggered with many a fall and pauses from breathlessness, the weasel terrified by the incandescent storm. Eventually, exhausted and panting wildly they managed to prop the bodies up in the Land-Rover, tying the three of them, grotesque figures that lurched drunkenly as the Land-Rover edged along the mountain ridge to the top of the glen. The big brute stopped the engine now, fishing out a half bottle of whisky and greedily slurping its contents.

"Want a drop, Jimmy?" he asked, when only a drop was left. But wee Jimmy's jaws were clacking so violently that he couldn't hold the bottle to his weasel's lips, and the little left dribbled down his scraggy neck.

The Land-Rover trundled precariously down the glen in the torrential rain, the three corpses continually lurching from side to side, eerily illuminated by the lightning flashes, the crashing of thunder terrifying the weasel, who now began to cry.

"What haave I done? Oh ma! What haas yer wee boy done! Oh! Oh!"

The brute brought him up with a dreadful jab in the ribs with his hefty elbow, sending the Land-Rover careering across the muddy track out of control, only just prevented from plunging over the edge of the track into the ravine by the brute's last minute manoeuvre of the wheel.

"They're speaking, they're speaking to us" shrieked the weasel, "They'll be telling. The devil's after us an' all, he is, I ken he is!"

This time the brute thumped the back of his heavy arm across the weasel's face, cracking a cheekbone and causing him to howl like a beaten dog. Down the glen lumbered that car of death, past Succoth Farm and Shiel's tomb, almost up to its axles in mud in the roaring torrent plunging down to Loch Mhor. The brute drove it on with diabolical will along the loch side, almost facing Ishmael's cottage, and opposite McCrone's house where the 'bubbly-jock' lay cowering in terror at the storm, pulling the sheets over her head at the flashes that lit up her bedroom like daylight and the dreadful reverberations that ensued. Vainly she called for McCrone to come and comfort her.

"Where are we going?" moaned the broken-faced weasel, "where is it we're going?"

"To the witch's pool on the big island" the brute shouted above the roaring elements, "where we hid many a poaching night."

The weasel screamed in terror. "We canna go there. We'll never get across the loch. It's like the sea the night."

But the Land-Rover stopped by two rowing boats moored to a

jetty, heaving wildly up and down, half-full of water. Frantically they hurled water out of the bigger of the two boats with the bailers until the water was only ankle deep.

"Get them down" roared the brute, "go on Jimmy, get movin' maan."

And they dragged the bodies one by one to the shore, throwing them over the jetty into the big boat, the weasel vomiting and the brute cursing, both stumbling, falling, the weasel crying like a woman.

Then they plied across the loch with great waves crashing against the sides, the gunwales two or three inches above the water and all the time lower and lower.

"Bail, Jimmy, bail" the brute ordered, rowing like a demon as the weasel bailed for his life, the boat rolling and heaving towards Eilean Ruairidh Mòr.

With a bump the boat ran aground on the shore of the great island. The two poachers gasped desperately for breath as they staggered ashore.

"Pull, maan, pull now" yelled the brute, and by the hands they dragged the corpses up the shore and then between the great trunks of a stand of Scots pines. Within the circle of the trees was the witch's pool, a sinister bog now simmering like a cauldron in the downpour. It is said that the witch stole a kettle and was chased to the island in a coracle. But she was caught and dropped the kettle into the bog that bears her name.

Laboriously the brute and the weasel now swung the corpses one by one, by feet and hands, one, two, three into the bubbling mire where the bodies rapidly disappeared with a gurgle. Ishmael last vanished beneath a horrible series of bubbles in that seething brown pool.

The weasel now let out hysterical shrieks like some dreadful spectre illuminated by lightning, leaping up and down as though it were a mad dance.

"I'll tell, I'll haave to confess" he screamed, "I canna live wi' this horror. The devil hisself is after us. Let's get outa this hell afore he gets us."

The great brute picked up Jimmy the weasel and hurled him

through the infernal air into the bog as though he was no more than a rag doll, where he quickly sank with ghastly shrieking still. For several minutes greater bubbles broke the dimpled surface in the downpour.

The brute made off in the big boat, pulling the bung as it reached the mainland, racing east in the stolen Land-Rover down the single track road, passing Anancaun, 'Ford of Heads,' up the "Glen of Evil Scouring,' and was back home in Inverness by six in the morning.

★

It was a long time before news of Ishmael's disappearance reached Shandon Lodge. For that was all that was known. He had vanished off the face of the earth. His distraught mother asked everyone in Lentilloch what could have happened. He had not withdrawn money from his bank account and all his belongings, except what he had been wearing, were found in his cottage. His bagpipes and his skeandubh had been thrown out of the sinking boat to the bottom of Loch Mhor.

None of the locals at Loch Mhor could provide any information except that he had organized the grouse shoot that day, and then, simply vanished. Likewise the ghillie and the game-keeper. Seonaid's last memory of Ishmael was that demonic moment in the morning room at Shandon Lodge.

By the time she heard the strange and terrible news Sheila had gone through successive traumas. Her first instinct after the disastrous ceilidh had been to pack her little bag and join Schweitzer in Africa. But she was dissuaded from embarking on an escapade about which she herself was unsure and indecisive by the gentle remonstrances of Ella. And by her abandonment of her medical studies. She remembered also Ishmael's acerbic comments on that wild impulse. 'Would you be going to save your own soul?'

What she did, when the news had arrived, was to make a despairing visit to Loch Mhor where she stayed a night with Jeannie the post woman, who had brought her from Achnasheen. Jeannie sat up with her until the early hours repeating over and over again, between drams, while Sheila sipped lemonade,

228

"I knew things were going to come to a baad end, my dear, from the moment he buried his dog in the lee of thaat aaspen. It's an evil, evil tree, so it is. Crucified Jesus Christ it did, thaat terrible tree. I didn't like to tell Mr McCulloch aat the time, thaat its leaves tremble with shame at its dreadful past.

My husband, Alastair, used to curse them. Took off his bonnet aand cursed them three times he did whenever he passed one on the estate, until the very day he died." Jeannie swallowed a wee dram in her husband's memory.

Deeply dispirited, next morning Sheila went down to Succoth Farm, and getting no reply to her timid knock at the front door betook herself to the offending aspen, which now stood bronze and shimmering in the light breeze. With lowered head Sheila said a little prayer.

Then, hearing sounds from the farmhouse she went back to the front door, as the aspen shed its leaves. On knocking again she was warmly welcomed at Succoth Farm by Sheena and the girls, in spite of the dolorous atmosphere there too, following the death of old Anderson.

With innumerable cups ot tea, Sheena and she went over and over all the possibilities behind Ishmael's disappearance. Taking Ishmael's puppy, Fionn, Sheila then wandered along the track to Ishmael's cottage, where Fionn whimpered piteously, walked up the glen in the rain and even tramped as far as Loch Shuna, which was almost obscured by low cloud. Her memory of their last evening there was unbearable, and she broke down, crying desperately when she remembered how he had said,

"I'd like to die here."

"Why did I ever come back?" she said aloud, drenched by the now heavy rain in that eerie isolation. "A huge police search was made of all the area and they found nothing. What could I hope to find?"

She wended her way miserably back to Succoth Farm where she found Erik and Michael in the sitting room, in silence as usual.

"I have something to tell you" Erik said, "would you please sit down here by the fire. You look cold and wet. Please don't be going out in this terrible weather."

Sheila's clothes were still dripping, so she excused herself and ran upstairs to change before returning to sit obediently in that rickety chair between the brothers, wondering what it could be.

Erik cleared his throat portentously and looking at her fixedly said,

"You know, Sheila, when our father died, the factor came over and told us we would have to vacate the farmhouse as it belonged to the estate. We asked him to give us some time, as the funeral had only just taken place. But he insisted that the house must be vacant in forty-eight hours and not a minute later. He wouldn't give us even one day more. It was about half-past two in the afternoon, and just then Jeannie arrived in her red Land-Rover with the post.

There was only one letter, and it had been sent registered post, marked 'Crofting Commission' in big black letters at the top of the envelope. As soon as I had signed for it, I tore open the envelope with foreboding, for we've not been used to getting good news here. I found the following statement.

"At the instigation of the Manager of the Loch Maree Estate, Mr Ishmael Mc Culloch, the farmhouse designated 'Succoth Farm' and the adjoining twenty-three and a half acres, marked in red outline on the accompanying extract from the Ordnance Survey Map of the area, Section 19, The Crofting Commission, in consultation with the Highland Council, have considered the petition that the said farmhouse and adjacent land as detailed above should be officially designated a Croft in the name of John Anderson Esq. and his descendants, if any. We therefore have to inform you that 'Succoth Farm' and the said twenty-three and a half acres are now officially designated a Croft in perpetuity, and said Croft is in the name of John Anderson and descendants, if any, for their exclusive agricultural use, and henceforth, from the date of this communication, is independent of the loch Mhor Estate."

"You will realize" said Erik, looking over the top of the letter at Sheila, that thanks to Ishmael we are now secure at the farm, although we are still dependent on the estate for grazing ground, which Major Tooth is only too glad to rent as the boggy ground is no use for anything else."

At this point, Sheena and the girls, who must have overheard

Erik's sonorous voice, came running in and embraced Sheila.

"We can't tell you how grateful we are to Mr McCulloch" Sheena said, kissing Sheila tearfully. She was so moved that she couldn't finish what she wanted to say.

All this was too much for poor Sheila, who began sobbing uncontrollably, her shoulders shaking; but after a few moments she managed to smile through her tears and congratulate them all.

"Such a wonderful maan" Sheena insisted, "he haas saved us from destitution. Erik haas now taken over the farm and will live with us here as master of the house."

Michael let out a high-pitched falsetto laugh, which had the merit of breaking the almost unbearable emotional tension, though Erik gave him a glance of searing contempt.

"Aand you can stay here for as long as you like whenever you like, dearie" said Sheena to a chorus of eager assent from the girls. "If you don't mind, you caan share a room with my eldest girl."

Both Sheila and Aileen were delighted, embracing and kissing one another.

So Sheila did stay another ten days at Succoth Farm, taking Fionn for walks when it wasn't raining, which wasn't often, and listening to the extraordinary tales of Michael in the evenings when the girls had gone to bed and Sheena was busy in the kitchen, the autumn gales howling round the house.

Seated by the peat fire, Michael fixed those strange blue eyes on Sheila and narrated countless stories about his adventures in the East, under the stern and disapproving eye of Erik when he came in from the hills after tending to the sheep.

Sheena would come in at about ten in the evening with tea and homemade scones, saying

"Don't you be telling your fantaastic tales to the lassie, Michael, you scallawag. Pay no attention to him, Sheila dear. He's a mad-cap if ever there was one."

When the time came to return to Shandon Lodge, Sheila left with some reluctance, having been made to feel so at home by Sheena and the girls. Although she was quite afraid of Erik, whose dark, sombre moods commanded silence among them all. Those late evenings, on the other hand, before Erik's return, had left her enthralled by Michael's strange tales and by his extraordinary person. He was like a visitor from another world. Sheila fell under the spell of that dreamer, but would come to with a guilty start when the door was flung open in the dark and Erik came in.

Jeannie took her to Achnasheen one stormy morning in the post Land-Rover and after an uneventful if lengthy journey she found herself back at the Lodge.

It soon became clear that Sheila's visit to Loch Mhor had left her more unsettled than before. What Sheila did was to escape from John Robson's Bearsden flat at night and pace the streets of Glasgow. More than once the police had to bring her home. But neither John Robson's gentle reproaches nor Shandon's angry reprimands, nor even Ella's cajolements could prevent the repetition of these incidents.

One night, to the consternation of all, Sheila did not return from these nocturnal excursions. A search was made, involving the police and many of the neighbours of Bearsden and Shandon Lodge. To no avail. Notices were posted in the press and in bus and railway stations, besides airports. Which brought no news. Telegrams were sent to consulates and embassies in Africa requesting envoys to contact the Schweitzer charity hospital and other possible places in the forlorn hope that she might be found there. But answers came back advising that Sheila had not been seen or heard of.

Even John Robson was distraught, though he did his best to comfort the Shandon's, telling them what he believed.

"It'll all turn out right in the end. I'm sure of that. You know Sheila's sometimes ... how can I put it? ... taken by a sudden impulse."

ELOPEMENT

Sheila had indeed been taken by a sudden impulse. She had eloped with Michael. They had boarded the so-called Orient Express – at that time a dirty, decrepit old train – to Istanbul. Where they were to catch the train for Teheran, that tended to take a week on the way, with sometimes a day more, or a day less. Once the train had fallen into Lake Van. But that was unusual.

The Orient Express was packed with hippies on their way to India, who lay in the corridors at night, where hung a heavy aroma of drugs, as they narrated their reasons for leaving the West.

They were tired of crooked politicians and materialism. Nevertheless, when Sheila left that expensive leather handbag on her seat when Michael led her to the filthy restaurant car, by the time they came back it had disappeared. As had her blouses, - embroidered by Ella – and the little silver hand mirror she had hurriedly packed in her holdall.

"They will have needed those things" said Michael, dreamily watching the European countryside receding ever slowly until a station was reached, when all the hippies poured onto the platform to replenish their water bottles and buy a snack from the itinerant vendors' trolleys. At Belgrade the curious natives crowded round, admiringly examining a clasp-top bottle, which was passed from hand to hand.

As they crossed Bulgaria, past innumerable wretched hovels, all painted a sickly uniform green, a stony-faced communist guard sat at the end of each corridor, sub-machine gun at the ready.

Amongst the hippies there were American girls in sarongs with strings of beads pendant, and young men in pig-tails with earrings and bangles, some wearing kaftans, others short skirts. Yet in spite of their youth, their faces were jaded and vacuous as they rumbled towards the promised land.

"Hideous poverty and disease, cities whose ubiquitous slum

streets are infested with dying humans and animals. That is what awaits them," lamented Michael. "No such thing in Persia. Wait till you see the Lotfollah mosque in the Maiden Shah in Isfahan. The most beautiful square in the world. It surpasses anything in Europe or the East."

As the train trundled eastwards, Michael told Sheila endless stories of the wonders of Persia: the silence of the deserts and the salt lakes, the wonderful artistry to be found in the bazaars, and above all the uncanny atmosphere that pervades every part of the country. He told her of adventures with bandits, his fortuitous escape on a motor-bike, his being stoned by a mob of children in Shiraz and escaping only by jumping into the one taxi that was in the great crumbling suburban square. He finally let her know that he had a small harem in a wing of the old Persian palace he rented, and of the lovely mournful cypresses that grew inside the five metre high walls that made his palace perfectly secluded.

Sheila, who had in Scotland been intoxicated by Michael's other-worldliness and by his stories of the East, as though listening to the tales of Scheherazade, began now to wonder. A deep anxiety began to take hold of her as the train finally approached Istanbul. Her thoughts turned to home, and the reliable solidity of John Robson, which she had found endearing but, dared she think it, boring. But most of all she thought of Ishmael, whose intrepid bravery, his absolute individuality, his apartness from society enthralled her.

Uninterested in the material blandishments that society trumpeted, she saw now – though she had never seriously doubted – that her family's fortune had never tempted or influenced him. How she regretted the shadow of suspicion that had momentarily and fatefully, flitted across her face. She was horribly conscious of that moment. She knew it had been crucial for Ishmael. If only … She cried quietly in her corner of the compartment. It had been a tragedy. Ishmael's disappearance could only mean he had been murdered by his numerous enemies. If only …. Sheila had a morbid longing for what was past and irrecoverable. Sepulchral. And idealised what could never be.

But it may be that her heroic vision of Ishmael was not exaggerated.

But what, oh what, had led her to this wild adventure? she asked herself desperately, her thoughts abruptly interrupted by the clanging of the Orient Express as it lurched into Istanbul and the clamour of the hordes of hippies engulfing the corridors.

Michael took her hand and led her trembling through the throng on the platform amidst the yells of touts and porters. He hurried her out to the turnstiles for the great ferries that plied from Hydarpasha to the east of the Bosporous. Telling her to wait there while he went to buy tickets, she was borne along by the surging crowd like a leaf before the wind, and found herself up against an impassable iron barrier, while Michael gesticulated frantically from the other side to pass through the distant turnstile. But there was no way. Suddenly it became clear to her that she could not go, that she would not make that crossing from West to East. Michael was now standing on the heaving gangway of the ferry, calling urgently to her. But Sheila covered her face with her hands and turned back. Irrevocably.

RETURN

All was forgiven on Sheila's return in the tearful reunions at Bearsden and Shandon Lodge. And for a time it seemed that Sheila had recovered her equilibrium. After a while she was reconciled to the modest and selfless attention of John Robson in his flat at Bearsden, after that small, intimate family wedding at Loch Rannoch. And once again, for a time, all seemed to be well.

But then again she began to break out at night and to be found wandering round Glasgow, disconsolate and crying desperately. One night she had even managed to get into the park and was found by the police at midnight lying prostrate beneath that great cedar whose blackened top had been struck by lightning.

Eventually, for her own safety, it was thought expedient to confine her to a 'home' for disturbed persons, one which overlooked the park, where she would spend the days and nights with her face pressed to the window, from which the top of that great cedar was just visible.

★

This was only one of the tribulations of Ella and Shandon, whose shipbuilding yard had descended to a state of absolute anarchy and destruction. Shandon, in the aftermath of the triumphal launching of the Empress of the Clyde, had received an order for a great oil tanker. But it came with very stringent conditions, the principal of which was a tight termination date. And a draconian penalty for non-completion by the stipulated time. Shandon, who was still partly incapacitated as the result of the stroke he suffered at the ceilidh, called a meeting with his colleagues on the board of directors, and, with the indispensable assistance of the level-headed John Robson, a non-strike agreement was drawn up, including the most generous ancillary terms, to be presented to the employees at the yard.

It was rejected out of hand by the shop stewards. Therefore

Shandon took it upon himself, in spite of his dangerously frail physical condition, to confront the men directly in an attempt to make them see reason. To no avail. He was hooted by the assembled mass, who without Ishmael's leadership were now uncontrollably in the hands of the shop stewards.

"We ken fine the noo" shouted Archie Tyas, "whit thaat trick was wi' yon bastard ye put over us. He was in your pocket. We ken all aboot yon car ye gied him, an' the offer tae be a director if he could tame us. We ken a' aboot it, an we're no haein' ony mair o' it. We ken fine this contract ye're tryin' tae maak us sign is just anither con. An' we're no haein' ony o' it."

This speech was backed by uproarious support from the workers, in spite of valiant efforts by Big Billy and Jock Gow to make them see sense.

John Robson quickly led Shandon away from the platform, fearing he should have a further stroke. When he returned to the boardroom Shandon immediately sent a telex to the shipping company saying

"Regret offer rejected. Terminal date terms impossible."

Shandon hoped that more reasonable conditions might then be offered.

But as a consequence, the contract was immediately transferred to a Japanese yard, resulting in the inevitable bankruptcy of Shandons, there being no other work on the horizon. Notices of dismissal were at once sent to all workers. The result was a riot. In a frenzy of retribution, machinery was smashed and the yard was left in an irreparable state by the time the police had arrived, closed the yard and made a few arbitrary arrests. So no buyer could now be found for the yard. It was a ruin.

But there was seething unrest outside the yard gates, exacerbated by whisky and beer supplied by The Highland Fling. The mass of ex-employees had now turned into a murderous mob, bent on further vengeance.

That was to wait until darkness. A small group of the dispossessed and unemployed, not more than ten or twenty, who personally and whose families faced destitution, moved off towards Shandon Lodge soon after midnight. Some of them were by this time so inebriated they hardly knew where they were or what they were doing. But somehow or other they got into the Lodge grounds. Rapidly they unloaded 2-gallon jerricans of petrol from a van, and smashing windows at the back, front and sides of the Lodge, poured petrol through the apertures, throwing in lighted rags soaked in petrol likewise. Instantly a terrible conflagration took hold, and although there was only a light breeze that night the fire spread with terrifying speed through the building, upstairs and downstairs.

Old Tam came coughing and spluttering from a side door, waving his arms wildly at the fleeing arsonists, one of whom, mistaking him for Shandon, stayed behind long enough to bludgeon him with a pick handle, knocking him to the ground, where he lay insensible until the intense heat of the blaze burst blood vessels in his battered head and he took leave of this world.

Meanwhile, Shandon and Ella had awoken in their separate bedrooms, Ella running frantically into Shandon's room, where he was slowly lifting himself up from his bed, badly incapacitated by his stroke. By now the flames had engulfed the whole house, and the curtains of the bedroom were ablaze. With the support of Ella, Shandon tottered towards the stairs, which they could scarcely find, so thick was the smoke. After taking two steps down, the wooden staircase gave way under them and they fell into the stairwell, where their carbonised corpses were found in an embrace by firemen who arrived when the house had been burnt to the ground.

*

John Robson was left without a job at that desperate time of yard closures on the River Clyde under the holocaust of competition from the Far East. He plodded in the rain round the dreary streets of Glasgow, trying everywhere to find employment. Without so much as a vague promise of work in the future. Fortunately, more or less by an act of charity, the directors of the hospice where Sheila was interned gave him work as a porter, besides a small bedroom and three meals a day.

In the north, the doctor, at the instigation of the church elders, and some of the more self-righteous and vindictive among his patients, was stopped by the police driving his Alvis Speed Twenty and quite predictably found to have far over the permitted level of alcohol in his blood. This information was passed to the Medical Council in Edinburgh. And although several of the doctor's patients, including Ishmael and the shepherd, had gallantly made their way to the Council meeting, where their representations as to the outstanding qualities of their doctor were respectfully and sympathetically heard by the members of the Medical Council, a report by the church elders attesting to the doctor's almost invariable inebriation while on duty made his crossing off the Medical Register inevitable.

Unable to take up work, he found lodgings in the high ancient tenements below Edinburgh castle and took to drink in a way that was ungovernable. His long-suffering wife left him, and what with payments from his meagre emoluments, to which she was entitled, it wasn't long before he was penniless and unable to pay for his board and lodging. A small ex-gratia allowance was made by the authorities that permitted him to survive in suburban sheltered accommodation. From where he would take taxis to the pubs in the city centre and whittled away such funds as he had, depending latterly on the generosity of his fellow drinkers for a dram.

At Succoth Farm, in twilight, a dour morose figure had embarked, watched by hundreds of eyes, on the building of a colossal cairn as a monument to human folly. Already the base was inscribed

TO GOD
IF YOU EXIST
10 COMMANDMENTS

Already inscribed were:

I THOU SHALT REVEAL THE MYSTERY
II ALL KNOWING, ALMIGHTY, THOU SHALT NOT PERMIT EVIL
III THOU SHALT NOT MAKE HUMAN PLACES OF LOVE PLACES OF EXCREMENT

Bearing a huge shepherd's crook, he addressed stern sermons to the hundreds of eyes watching to the accompaniment of Gregorian chants echoing round the hills at tremendous volume from the open door of Succoth Farm, assuring them that they would never go to the slaughterhouse but warning them of the imminent self-destruction of the planet.

"Humans, o sheep" he intoned, "have sought utopias, kow-towing to mass murderers as a necessary condition for the realization of Paradise on Earth. Sheeplike, the multitudes in their innocence and gullibility have bowed down to their leaders, who although seminarists and poets have been wolves in sheep's clothing. The Devil has masqueraded as the people's saviour, with ruthless cunning disguising evil as idealism. And so ensnaring the silly human sheep who worshipped evil in never-ending slavery.

While in the so-called Free World, the human sheep have become the slaves of sensuality, the ewes shrieking

"SEX IS THE NEW RELIGION!"

with crucifixes dangling between their udders. And the rams worship the udder, o sheep. Besides engaging in all manner of perversions, surpassing even the ancient in this our new Sodom and Gomorrah.

And now humanity aspires to colonising other planets to procreate such 'civilization' throughout the Universe. But that will never come to pass, for humanity shall destroy itself in hatred.

Hark, o sheep. If God Almighty, All-knowing, presaged such monstrous depravity, then He must deliberately have permitted evil and untold suffering. The Permissive Power and the Glory."

And throwing his arms high above his fiery head, Erik called out in a loud voice

"O God, I have forsaken Thee. I cannot find You, therefore I cannot find myself."

The news of the tragedy eventually reached Ishmael's bewildered mother and sister at their house in Lentilloch, where the spires of the lunatic asylum still tower above those of the three moribund churches.

All that was left to them was the citation of Ishmael's Military Cross, framed above the mantel shelf in the sitting room.

2nd Lt Ishmael McCulloch

At the Battle of the Hook in Korea the Black Watch position was overwhelmed by Chinese hordes who abducted the two South Korean soldiers attached to 2nd Lt. Mc Culloch's platoon.

With no regard for his safety 2nd Lt. McCulloch followed the abductors and with only his .38 pistol killed the five abductors and returned to the Black Watch lines carrying on his back the badly injured Private Lee Suk Ho and accompanied by the walking wounded Private Pak Duk, for which Lt. McCulloch has been awarded the Military Cross, and is simultaneously promoted to Lieutenant.

EPILOGUE

Scotland the Brave began as a short story about the murder of my friend Charlie Armstrong near Inchnadamph in the 1950's when he was Manager of a salmon fishery. Charlie had been a 2nd Lieutenant in the Black Watch in Korea and I could see that his character had been much deepended by his experience in the Far East.

One day his brother-in-law called at our house. He mentioned that he was going north to support Charlie in the dangerous confrontations he was having with salmon poachers.

I also had recently come out of the army as a 2nd Lieutenant and had a BSA .22 rifle, but I didn't attach much importance to the brother-in-law's account, particularly as nothing ever seemed to happen in our sleepy village. But when I heard of Charlie's disappearance I wished I had gone north too. It was just the kind of adventure that would have appealed.

And when his disconsolate mother asked me what could have happened to Charlie, who had disappeared without trace of any kind, I couldn't bring myself to say what I supposed was the terrible truth. Charlie was brave, a "tough guy" and would not have surrendered.

So I began, many years ago, a short story in memory of my friend. Subsequently the story developed to take in the contemporary running down of the Clyde shipbuilding industry and the question of Scotland's independence.